"If I said I'd be your lover, no strings, the entire time we were in Stockholm, you'd do it?" asked Joss.

The situation was rapidly slipping out of Bax's control. "Look," he said, backpedaling, "it's not that simple to retrieve stolen property from a serious criminal—even if it is your property."

Something predatory entered Joss's eyes. "Sure it is."

Before he could react, she'd risen, pushing his shoulders back against the office chair.

"What are you doing?"

"A feasibility study," she told him, and placed one knee on either side of his thighs, straddling him. And when her mouth touched his, all he could feel was the hot, slicing arousal.

He had no business doing this, Bax told himself even as he closed his eyes. She was a client, or a potential client, they were in his office, at his desk and oh hell, she was all he could feel with only her lips on his and the warmth of her thighs bracketing his own.

"What kind of game are you playing?" he asked hoarsely.

"Just making sure we have chemistry." She sat back. "After all, the best detectives and their sidekicks always have it."

Blaze™

Dear Reader,

The stories I write are often influenced by my surroundings. When I found out I was going to go to Stockholm last fall, I immediately began working on a way to bring that experience to my characters. The result was *U.S. Male,* the sequel to *Certified Male.* I had great fun prowling Stockholm, searching out locations. Who knew they had a postal museum? And what a surprise to find in their collection a pair of post office Mauritius stamps, the very stamps featured in *Certified Male.* Best of all, I got to meet the editors at Harlequin's Stockholm offices and have a brainstorming lunch figuring out character names and locations for a variety of scenes. Ewa Högberg and her colleagues helped me bring this book to life.

I hope you'll drop me a line at Kristin@kristinhardy.com and tell me how you liked reading a Harlequin Blaze novel with an international location. And don't worry, we haven't forgotten about SEX & THE SUPPER CLUB—look for the stories of Paige, Thea and Delaney to come in 2006. To keep track, sign up for my newsletter at www.kristinhardy.com for contests, recipes and updates on my recent and upcoming releases.

Have fun,

Kristin Hardy

Books by Kristin Hardy

HARLEQUIN BLAZE

*Under the Covers
**Sex & the Supper Club
***Sealed with a Kiss

U.S. MALE

Kristin Hardy

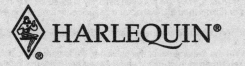

TORONTO • NEW YORK • LONDON
AMSTERDAM • PARIS • SYDNEY • HAMBURG
STOCKHOLM • ATHENS • TOKYO • MILAN • MADRID
PRAGUE • WARSAW • BUDAPEST • AUCKLAND

ISBN 0-373-79203-4

U.S. MALE

This edition published by arrangement with Harlequin Books S.A.

® and TM are trademarks of the publisher. Trademarks indicated with
® are registered in the United States Patent and Trademark Office, the
Canadian Trade Marks Office and in other countries.

www.eHarlequin.com

Printed in U.S.A.

To Ewa and Anna,
tack så mycket for all the help
and to Stephen kärlek

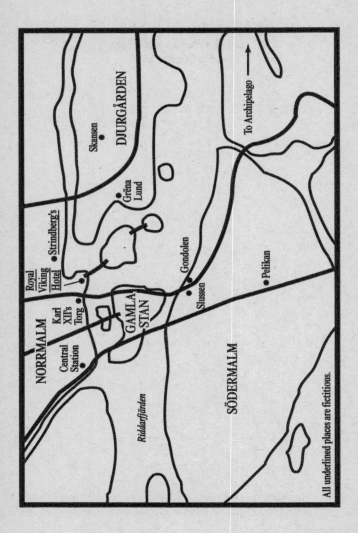

All underlined places are fictitious.

Prologue

"WHAT DO YOU THINK of this one, Brandon, sweetie?" The woman looked at her towheaded young son, who sat like a spoiled prince in his tall chair. "It's got an airplane."

Maybe seven or eight, he thumped down his Game Boy and poked bad-temperedly at the stamps she showed him.

"Please don't touch them with your fingers," Joss Chastain said sharply. "They're easily damaged."

"Oh, Brandon doesn't mean anything by it, do you, sweetie?"

Brandon scowled. "I wanna play my Game Boy."

"In a minute, sweetie. This is something special you can do with Grandpop."

It gave Joss a twinge. She'd never collected stamps with her grandfather. Instead, while he'd been on vacation recently, she'd let a collection of the most valuable of his many rare stamps be stolen.

Giving her head a brisk shake, she laid a stamp collector's kit on the counter. "This has all the basics he'll need for collecting: an album, tongs, a perforation gauge, a magnifying glass and some nice starter stamps."

"Oh, this is perfect. He's got to join a club at school," she explained to Joss. "We thought stamp collecting would be good for him."

Meanwhile, Brandon's sister sat quietly on a chair nearer Joss. She was maybe three or four, quiet and big-eyed in a way that reminded Joss of her own sister. Joss smiled to herself and used sleight of hand to make the pen she held disappear.

The little girl's eyes widened. Her mother and brother bent over the merchandise, oblivious.

Joss winked at her. Enjoying herself, Joss made the pen reappear, then seemingly put it up her nose. She held her nose and blew, and brought the pen out of her ear and held it up.

The girl giggled.

"Don't bother the nice lady, now, Sarah," the mother said and the girl subsided obediently. Joss guessed she was often the quiet one in the background while darling Brandon got what he wanted.

Finally, the woman made her selection and Joss rang it all up. "That will be forty-three sixty-five," she said, making a mental bet that the purchase went in the back of the closet for good as soon as Brandon got home.

The woman handed her three twenties and Joss made change. "Here you are, that's ten, fifteen, sixteen ten and…hmmm, I seem to have lost the quarter somewhere. Do you see it on the ground?" Joss leaned over the counter and looked on the burgundy carpet. Sarah looked down, shaking her head.

"Nope," Joss said, "it's not here and it's not on the counter." She leaned toward Sarah. "I know, maybe it's here." Joss reached out and pulled a quarter from behind the ear of the little girl, who giggled delightedly. "Yep, that's it," Joss said, dropping it in the palm of the aston-ished Sarah.

She was still alternately staring at the quarter and look-ing at Joss over her shoulder as they walked out the door.

When the phone rang a moment later, Joss picked it up, still smiling. "Chastain Philatelic Investments."

"It's me," said a leaden voice.

The pleasure over entertaining children vanished in a sharp wave of concern as she recognized her sister's voice. "Gwen. My God, what's happened? You sound like hell." Gwen, who had spent the last three weeks in Las Vegas, as she tracked down the thief who'd stolen the rare stamps valued at four and a half million, and which represented their grandfather's retirement.

"It's done." Gwen let out an audible breath.

"You've found them? What happened? Did Jerry have them hidden in his room where you thought?" Jerry was the slick little hustler they'd hired to help Joss at the store while Gwen had traveled to some stamp auctions. It still made Joss burn in impotent anger to remember the way he'd conned her and broken into the safe to steal the stamps while her back had been turned.

"Brace yourself. Jerry wasn't working on his own. He was hired by Stewart."

"Stewart Oakes?" Joss repeated in shock. "How can that be? He worked for Grampa. He was Grampa's friend."

"He's not anyone's friend," Gwen said flatly. "Joss, he shot Jerry. I saw him do it. He was going to shoot me, too."

Joss groped for the chair behind her and sat. She swallowed. "Let me get this straight. Stewart pulled a gun on you?" On her little sister? She was going to hurt him, Joss vowed grimly. She was going to find him and wring his neck. He'd been like a big brother. No wonder Gwen sounded so shattered. "What was he thinking?" Joss demanded.

"I don't think he *was* thinking at that point. They said he owed money to some leg breakers and thought he'd pay them off with the commission fee he got from a collector who wanted some of Grampa's stamps. Only Grampa said no sale, and Stewart had already spent the money."

"He couldn't explain and pay the guy back over time?"

"I don't know. He won't say who the collector is but he sounds scared spitless."

Joss shook her head. "God, Gwennie, I just can't believe...I'm so sorry you had to go through this." She dragged a hand through her hair. "And I'm just sitting here being a lump. You could have been killed."

"I wasn't, though."

"As long as you're safe, that's what's important. And you got the stamps back."

"I didn't get them all. Stewart already sent one of the stamps to the collector."

"Not the Blue Mauritius?" Joss whispered, her hand tightening on the phone. The Blue Mauritius, their grandfather's prize. It was one of the most valuable stamps in the world, worth some one million dollars at auction.

"I got the Blue Mauritius back okay."

Joss closed her eyes in trepidation. "I hear a really big 'but' coming."

"The stamp that's missing is its companion, the one-penny Mauritius." Gwen hesitated. "If anything, it's worth even more."

1

San Francisco, two weeks later

"HEY, GWEN, I'm going to have wild sex on a jetliner today." Joss announced. She was sprawled on one of the chairs in the back office of the store, coffee in one hand and the newspaper in the other.

Gwen, blond and poised behind her desk, merely raised an eyebrow as she sat on hold. "And here I didn't even know you were going on a trip."

"It says so, right here," Joss said, pointing to her horoscope. "'Love and romance are in the air. Travel likely. Big dreams will come true if you leap for the stars.' And yours says, let's see, oh, yeah, 'Hunky, adoring sportswriter will sweep you out for dinner and wild sex in his marina condo afterward.'"

"You don't say." Gwen's tone was dry. "Horoscopes have gotten a lot more interesting, lately."

"So has your life," Joss observed, pointing to the photo of Gwen's new boyfriend smiling out at them from the sports page of the newspaper.

Gwen grinned, then snapped to attention as someone apparently came on the line. She cleared her throat. "Yes, this is Gwen Chastain of Chastain Philatelic Investments. I'm calling to check on the progress of the investigation of my grandfather's stamps."

Joss listened for a few minutes, then abandoned the effort. Better to wait until all was said and done and Gwen could fill her in. In the meantime, she took a sip of coffee and stared at the print on the paper.

Big dreams will come true if you leap for the stars.

Or maybe not. After seven years of leaping for the stars in pursuit of a career in music, she'd finally fallen to earth with a resounding thud. Four bands, four breakups, a résumé dotted with gigs at bars and small clubs around the Pacific Northwest. Along with doing street theatre magic shows, it had paid the bills, but not much more than that. At twenty-six, she wasn't a single step closer than she'd been as a nineteen-year-old with big dreams. She had nothing, no career, no money, not even a car. Maybe it was time to admit that she wasn't going to find the lucky confluence of circumstances that was going to let her perform for a living.

At twenty-six, maybe it was time to look for something else.

All things considered, she was probably fortunate that the most recent band implosion had taken place in San Francisco, home of her sister and her grandparents. After all, it had been a place to stay and a place to work while her grandparents went on their three-month tour of the South Pacific. For a few weeks, she'd pitched in without complaint, trying for once to fight off the inevitable restlessness and get on her feet.

And then everything had gone to hell in a handbasket.

"Dammit!"

Joss jumped at the sound of Gwen slamming down the receiver in the cradle. "You've gotten louder since you came back from Vegas, that's for sure. What's up?"

"Interpol," Gwen said, investing the word with an immense amount of disgust. "They're dropping the investigation of the one-penny Mauritius." Her voice vibrated with frustration. "A million dollar stamp, one of the rarest in the world, and they're just giving up."

"How can they drop the case? I thought you knew who had the stamp."

"I have a theory, even a name, but apparently that's not enough."

"They're investigators, aren't they?" Joss set down her coffee. "Can't they figure it out?"

Gwen pushed back from the desk in annoyance. "They can't find any leads. They say there's nothing to follow up on."

"I suppose Jerry could have just cooked up the story to make Stewart look bad," Joss speculated.

Gwen shook her head. "It doesn't make sense to me, not the way they were talking that night in the hotel room. I mean, Jerry says he stole the stamps for Stewart because the collector wanted them. It makes sense that Stewart might have slipped and said too much to him. They were buddies."

"Is that why they're testifying against one another?" Joss asked wryly.

"I think Jerry took it kind of personally that Stewart shot him."

"Sensitive. So Interpol doesn't believe that Jerry's Swedish collector is the same guy who tried to buy the two Mauritius stamps from Grampa?"

Gwen shrugged. "I don't know if they don't necessarily believe it, but they can't find anything to substantiate it." She rose and stalked over to rip a photograph of the smiling Stewart off a bulletin board and toss it in the trash can. "The stamps Stewart had stolen from Grampa's collection were for Karl Silverhielm, I'd bet money on it," she said, crossing back to her seat. "He's got a reputation for being obsessive and he's been after the Post Office Mauritius pair for the past five years."

It mystified Joss that anyone could be that hung up on little squares of colored paper. "What's the big deal about the Mauritius, anyway?"

"There are two of them—the one-penny and the two-penny. You know the two-penny stamp, it's the indigo one."

"The Blue Mauritius."

Gwen nodded. "The one-penny is a kind of red-orange."

"The Orange Mauritius?" Joss guessed.

"No one calls it that. They just say the one-penny Mauritius."

"Does anything about stamp collecting make sense? I mean, how can a measly stamp be worth over a million dollars? Why does anyone care?"

Gwen smiled. "They're over a hundred and sixty years old, for one thing, and they've got a story. It was all a big mistake, see? That's where the most valuable stamps usually come from."

"Like the upside down airplanes?"

"Sort of, only whole sheets of the Inverted Jennies are out there. Only a handful of Post Office Mauritius stamps exist."

"So what's the big deal? What was the error?"

"They were made by an island printer when the local post office ran out of stamps. The postmaster told him to print 'Post Paid' on them but he screwed up and put 'Post Office' on them, instead."

"The wrong words? That's what a million dollars of fuss is all about?" Joss shook her head in amazement. "You collector types."

"Silverhielm wants a Post Office Mauritius pair, badly."

"So why didn't Grampa sell? He's ready to retire, why not take the money?"

"I don't think he liked Silverhielm," Gwen said slowly. "There's something a little off about him and I think Grampa sensed it. Besides, his offer was only a million for each."

"I thought that was what they were worth."

"Separately. Together, they've gone at auction for as much as three million."

It paralyzed Joss to think about that kind of money. It paralyzed her that she'd been the one responsible for losing at least part of it. "Did Grampa have any idea they'd be worth that much?"

"He got them from his grandfather and they probably weren't cheap when he got them. Like investing in gold bars. Expensive, but worth it."

"Except that it's not so easy to stick gold bars in your pocket and walk away with them the way Jerry did with the stamps." Joss stared moodily into her coffee cup. "It kills me to think about telling Grampa about this."

"It's not as bad as it was," Gwen said softly. "We got most of them back."

"You got most of them back, and you almost got shot doing it." Joss picked a quarter up off the desk and began rolling it in her fingers. "So why is Interpol dropping the case? Didn't they look into Silverhielm?"

Gwen nodded. "They say they've done some investigation but their hands are tied at this point. They can't just walk in and search his house or his safe-deposit boxes."

"I suppose not, but have they interviewed Stewart?"

"He doesn't know anything."

"Or won't say." He was a thug and a liar. As far as Joss was concerned, there was no reason he might not be a coward. Still… "Why don't you try talking to him?" she asked suddenly. "He might tell you."

"I'm not sure I could do it," Gwen said, resting her chin against her hands. "It's too hard, knowing what he did and seeing him again. He was practically family."

Fresh anger coursed through Joss. Stewart had worked at the store when Gwen had been a gawky fourteen-year-old, looking up to him. She'd trusted him. They'd all trusted him and gotten only betrayal for their troubles.

Gwen shook her head. "Anyway, even if he confirmed that it was Silverhielm, what am I going to do, fly to Stockholm and camp out on the guy's front porch?"

"Stockholm?" Joss blinked and sat up. "Wait a minute, isn't the International Stamp Expo in Stockholm next week?"

"Yes, but I've got too much going on here. I can't go."

"No, but I could," Joss said, her eyes flashing. "Remember? *Travel is likely.*"

"Don't be ridiculous."

"Why is that ridiculous? You did it." A chance, she thought, a chance to make things right.

"I went to Las Vegas. This is Stockholm. You don't even speak the language," Gwen said in exasperation.

"I'll find someone who does. Hell, I'll hire a translator. Look, Gwen, all of this was my fault."

"It was both of our faults."

Joss shook her head. "If I hadn't left Jerry in the store with access to the safe, he'd never have had the chance to steal everything."

"He would have gotten to them sooner or later," Gwen countered. "I should never have hired him."

"Which you did because of me. I'm going." In an instant, it had gone from a passing thought to something Joss wanted passionately. Needed passionately.

"There are other ways."

"How?" Joss jumped to her feet and began pacing.

"You've done all the work here. I've just sat around doing nothing." And it had rankled her, every minute. "I want my chance to make it right. You already had yours."

"And I almost got a bullet in my brain, remember?" Gwen said hotly. "It's too risky. Silverhielm isn't just some rich guy. He had Stewart hurt, Joss. He scared him to death. It's not a job for us. It's a job for the police."

"The police aren't doing anything," Joss flared. "Do you want to just write off a million dollars of Grampa's retirement? I don't. I can't, Gwen. I couldn't live with it."

"You may not live if you try to get it back."

"So I'll get some help."

"Like who?"

"I don't know," she snapped. "I'll call my friend Tom, the promoter at Avalon."

"A music promoter's going to be able to go with you to Stockholm and get stolen property back from a criminal?"

"Why not? A sportswriter helped you. Look, Tom knows this town inside and out. He might be able to point me to someone who could help." Joss sank back down in her chair and looked at Gwen pleadingly. "I want to do this, Gwen. I need to."

Gwen sighed. "Well, we've still got most of my poker winnings as a war chest. We've got the money to do it, but only if you find someone who can really help you," she warned. "Not the music promoter. Someone who'll know what to do when you hit Stockholm."

"Okay." Joss reached out for her coffee and took a sip. "Can he be cute?"

"Wait a minute. You didn't cook all this up just so you could have sex on an airplane, did you?" Gwen asked skeptically.

Joss laughed. "Who, me?"

2

JOHN BAXTER leaned back in his chair and stared at the check in his hands. Smack in the upper end of the five figure range. Not bad for three months' work, he thought in satisfaction. For the first time since he'd started his executive security business two years before, he'd banished the wolf from his door. Not just banished it, kicked its ass from here till Sunday.

It was about time for a vacation.

The corner of his mouth curved a bit at the thought. It was an uncompromising mouth, some might have said hard, as they might have called the planes of his face hard with the high cheekbones, straight nose and taut jaw. Lines of care had been etched into his forehead and bracketed his mouth, but those who looked closely enough would see lines of humor as well.

Always, it was a face that was impossible to read. He'd cultivated the look in the seven years he'd spent working for the FBI and then Interpol. Even now, two years later, his eyes could still flatten into cop eyes that gave away nothing.

He hadn't left because he couldn't handle the work, he'd left because he'd been sick to death of politics and the endless levels of supervision and interference. Then again, he'd always done his best work alone.

He tore the check along the perforation and endorsed

it, laying it on top of the deposit slip he'd filled out so he could hit the bank on the way home. His office was spare, the mahogany desk clear of nearly everything but a blotter, the check and the phone that now burbled at him.

He picked up the receiver. "Baxter."

"Bax, Simon Fleming."

"Hey, Si." Simon Fleming, his contact at Mayfield, Cross and Associates. The young attorney was quick, a little cocky and hellaciously good at one-on-one basketball, as Bax regularly found out the hard way. Bax was under retainer to do occasional investigations for the law firm and they, in turn, sometimes steered clients his way. Like the client who'd written the hefty check Bax was currently admiring. "I didn't think you lawyers worked this late."

"Are you kidding? I'm trying to make partner. This is lunchtime."

Bax grinned and leaned back in his chair. "So what's up?"

"I'm sending someone over to see you. She's a friend of one of our clients, needs some work done."

"She?"

"Damsel in distress. Isn't that what you P.I. types live for?"

"I'm not a P.I., I'm an executive security specialist."

"So that's why your rates are so high."

"My rates are high because I'm good." Bax scrubbed at his wavy brown hair, kept cropped short for convenience. "So what's her problem?"

"Like I would know? I'm just trying to help out a client. It's your job to make me look good."

Bax grinned. "Is that covered by the retainer?"

"Making me look good? You know it, buddy."

"Then I want a bigger retainer." A light flashed on the

phone. Bax frowned. "Wait a minute, she's not coming over here now, is she?"

"Dunno. Depends on how desperate she is. I talked with her a little while ago."

"Hell, Si, it's the end of the day. I'm surprised the receptionist is even still out there to page me."

"Maybe you'd better go check it out."

"Whatever she wants, it's going to have to wait," he warned Simon. "I just finished the last job you threw my way. I'm taking a couple of weeks off." His first vacation in over three years, a trip to Copenhagen to see his cousins, maybe, or a jaunt to Prague.

"It's no big deal. A slick guy like you can probably figure it out while you're still booking your flight." He cleared his throat. "You make my client happy, you'll make me happy."

Bax snorted. "Next time we go back to contract, I'm upping my rate."

"Whatever you say, buddy, whatever you say."

Bax hung up the phone and stepped out into the hallway that led to the reception area of the communal office suites. So maybe having space here cost a couple hundred more in rent than a one-room office somewhere, but it gave him access to a receptionist, mail room and a slick conference room. More important, it gave his business an established air that reassured the kinds of clients he sought. Just because he worked without a staff didn't mean he had to look like a one-man show.

As long as he *was* a one-man show.

"MR. BAXTER will be with you in just a moment," the blond receptionist told Joss, punching the button on her console with one red-lacquered nail before she pulled off the telephone headset and prepared to go home.

Joss turned to the deep, pewter-colored couches that lined the walls. A receptionist? Who'd ever heard of a private eye with a receptionist? Then again, who'd ever heard of a private eye having a lobby with ice-blue carpet so thick you could snag a heel in it? And five-foot-tall ficus plants? Weren't P.I.s supposed to work out of tiny offices with venetian blinds and half-glassed doors, in tired old buildings on the wrong side of town?

Tom's lawyer was going to have a lot of explaining to do. She should have known better than to trust his referral. Simon Fleming had told her his investigator might be able to help her out. He'd neglected to tell her the guy was going to be some corporate clown.

An expensive corporate clown.

Scowling, Joss stalked over to the wall of windows that overlooked Montgomery Street, now pooled with shadow in the late afternoon. She didn't like the idea of telling her problems to some pretentious twit who'd look down on her. She knew the type—if you didn't have a brokerage account and an MBA, they wouldn't take you seriously. She could just imagine the kind of private eye who'd have an office here. He'd probably be short, for starters, pasty and soft. And balding, with a comb-over that didn't hide anything.

"Are you here for Executive Security Consulting?"

Joss jumped and whirled.

He didn't look soft at all, was her first thought. He'd come up behind her so quietly on the plush carpet that she hadn't heard a thing. Then again, he looked like he always moved silently. There was something about him that reminded her of a panther, dark, sleek and dangerous.

Then he smiled and the impression evaporated. He looked, if not entirely friendly, at least approachable.

"I'm John Baxter."

Tall, she thought, tall enough that she had to raise her chin to meet his eyes as he came closer. Not lanky, though. Self-possessed and lean, solid without being bulky. He looked like the kind of guy who could snatch flies out of midair or explode into violence if the need arose. Confident, capable and eat-him-with-a-spoon sexy.

She squared her shoulders and held out her hand. "Joss Chastain."

BAX WASN'T sure what he'd expected, but it wasn't her. She looked like nothing so much as a gypsy in her long flowered skirt and cropped T-shirt, her dark hair sweeping loose and wild down her back. It had red highlights, he noticed, then frowned at himself.

"Simon Fleming sent me over." Her hand was softer than he'd expected, and stronger. When she tugged it away from him, he realized he'd been holding it for far too long.

"I know. He called me. Come on back to my office."

He led the way down the winding hallway with its crown molding and subdued lighting.

"Pretty fancy digs for a private eye," she commented.

"I'm not a private eye. I'm a security consultant."

"Which means?"

"I check out security setups and do some investigative work—legal, industrial espionage, that sort of thing. My kind of clients expect to see this kind of office."

"Are you saying that I'm not your kind of client?"

Prickly, he thought. Nerves, maybe. Sometimes people got that way before they had to spill their story. Or maybe she was just feisty. She had that look. "I usually deal with corporate personnel. They're more comfortable with this sort of look."

"But you're not a cop?"

He opened his office door. "No. Strictly private sector."

"Exactly. Private eye." She walked past him, leaving a whisper of scent in her wake that had every one of his hormones sitting up and panting.

Now he was the one feeling prickly. Bax crossed to his desk. Taking his time, he studied her. She had the kind of bone structure that you saw in old Italian paintings, the mysterious arch above the eyes, the haunting hollows in the cheeks. Something in the set of her shoulders told him that she was very used to having her way. Her mouth was wide, the upper lip just a bit more full than the lower. When he'd first seen her, it had given her the look of a mistreated child, but now it made him think of stolen kisses in the darkness. He wondered suddenly what she looked like when she laughed.

"Let me know when you're finished," she told him, shifting to get more comfortable in his client chair, draping an elbow over the back. The trouble was, she didn't look like any client he'd ever had before and she was playing hell with his concentration.

Bax leaned his elbows on the desk and tried to ignore the taut belly exposed by her T-shirt. "So why are you so dead set on getting a private detective?"

"I need someone who's good at finding things. Are you?"

"When I decide to be. What do you need to find?"

She studied him in her turn. Finally, she nodded to herself, apparently deciding he passed muster. "A stamp."

"I've got a whole roll of them here in my drawer."

"Cute. This particular stamp is worth a bundle. It was stolen from my grandfather and I want to get it back."

"Why isn't he the one here?"

"He's on an extended vacation with my grandmother. My sister and I have been taking care of his business and the theft happened on our watch." She pushed the tumble of dark hair back over her shoulder. "I want to get the stamp back before he comes home."

Just for a second, that anxious kid expression came back. The urge to wipe it away flickered through him. "Do you know who stole it or where it is?"

"I have an idea. A colleague of my grandfather's, Stewart Oakes, was approached by a Swedish collector who wanted my grandfather's prize pair, the Blue Mauritius and the one-penny red-orange Mauritius."

"I've heard of the Blue Mauritius," Bax said slowly. One of the most valuable stamps in the world, as he recalled. "It's extremely rare, isn't it?"

"And worth a bundle. About three million for the two of them together."

Bax whistled. "I can see why you want them back."

"It. We got back the Blue Mauritius. It's only the one-penny Mauritius that's still missing."

"What happened?"

"The Swede made an offer, my grandfather said no. So Stewart hired a thief to get a job in the store and steal the stamps."

"Some colleague."

"Ex-colleague." Anger tightened her voice. "My sister was able to get most of the stamps back, and Stewart and Jerry—the thief," Joss elaborated, "are in jail."

"Sounds like something for the cops." The twinge of regret he felt surprised him. "It should be pretty easy to track since you know who the collector is."

"Well, that's just it. Stewart claims he doesn't know, just that maybe the guy is Swedish. He only met a go-between. As far as the police are concerned, the trail has dried up." Again, that look of desperation flickered across her face.

Bax shook himself irritably. No matter how vulnerable—and touchable—she looked, she was not for him. "You still have to leave it to someone like Interpol."

"They've given up on it. My sister is pretty sure she knows the identity of the collector, but Interpol said they'd investigated him and can't find any evidence to substantiate a theft or to allow them to search. They're on to more important things, I guess," she finished bitterly.

"Or maybe you don't have the right collector," Bax commented. Joss fixed him with a look that would freeze water. Definitely feisty. Amused, he leaned back in his chair. "All right, so, what do you want me to do?"

"Investigate, if you think you're up to it." She gave him an appraising look. "Simon said you'd worked in Europe and spoke a bunch of languages. I want to go over to Stockholm and check out the collector, see what we can find out. There's a stamp expo over there next week and we can—"

"Whoa." He held both hands up. "Hold on there just a minute. One, I haven't agreed to take on your case yet. Two, if you hire me, you have to let me do the job. There is no 'we.' I work alone."

"Well, maybe you're going to have to change the way you work. I can be a good partner." The corner of her mouth curved and for a fraction of a second he found himself putting a whole different translation on that phrase. "Besides, Simon said you'd help me."

"Simon's wrong." And he was way out of line sitting here getting hot for a possible client.

"He says you have a contract with him."

Simon had been saying entirely too much, Bax thought with annoyance, shaking himself loose. "But it doesn't guarantee referrals. All it says is that I'll talk to you." He pushed his chair back a little, preparatory to getting up. "It's an interesting case but I just finished a big job and

I've got some time off coming. And even if I did decide
to take you on as a favor to Simon, I don't let clients work
as assistants. It's not a game." The hurt kid look was back
on her face, he noticed with discomfort.

His comments didn't dent her determination, though.
"You want time off, come to Stockholm. Once we get the
stamp back, you can jet off to anywhere you like. Who
knows, we might have fun."

Then she smiled and the punch of sexuality blasted
through him. Her smile was generous, radiant and filled
with naughty promises. He found himself almost ready to
say yes without thinking, just for the chance to see what
came next. Still... "This isn't audience participation. If
there's a crime, there's danger. I can't babysit and investigate at the same time. I can't have you involved."

"You have to," she blurted, then took a breath. "Look,
you need me for your cover."

"What cover?"

"I've got it all figured out. We go over there together,
as lovers. I'm Jerry's girlfriend—or ex-girlfriend, actually,
only I've still got the Blue Mauritius that he's stolen and
I'm trying to fence it." She rose and began to pace around
the office intently, creating a picture with her hands as she
walked. "I dangle it in front of the collector and tell him
that for a small fee, he can have his property." Like her
face when she smiled, her body in motion was a fasci-
nation that made it impossible for him to look away.

"*His* property?"

"You know that's how those people think."

He nodded as he folded his arms across his chest. "Oh,
of course. And what happens after that?"

Her hands dropped. "I haven't figured that part out
yet. But I'm working on it," she added hastily as he shook
his head.

"No way."

"It'll work," Joss insisted. She leaned a hip on the corner of his desk, entirely too close for his comfort. "It'll at least let us confirm that he has the one-penny Mauritius and get a dialog going. You know how these criminal types work, Simon said you used to do undercover work. We can play like we're a couple, get a room together, all that." She gave him that smile of temptation again, like Eve holding out the apple. "Jerry's a hustler, through and through. I figure the type of girlfriend he'd pick would glom onto whatever guy could help her. Jerry's in the slammer? She'll find someone else useful."

He didn't want to want her. It had no place here. He groped for reason as her scent spread around him in an invisible net. "So why do I feel like *I'm* getting glommed onto as someone useful?"

"Of course you are. I'm trying to hire you, although you're making it difficult. What's it going to take with you?" Impatience filled her words. "I have to get that stamp back and I need your help to do it. Why not go over there and play pretend?" She leaned forward until she was just inches from his face. "Or do I have to make it for real? Would you do it then?"

It would take so little to close the distance between them. "Maybe." He regretted the response the minute it was out of his mouth. What the hell was he thinking?

He wasn't thinking, that was the problem.

A smile slid slowly across Joss's face. "Really?" she said, stretching the word out like it was hot taffy. "If I said I'd be your lover, no strings, the entire time we were in Stockholm, you'd do it?"

The situation was rapidly slipping out of his control. "Look," he backpedaled, "It's not that simple."

Something predatory entered her eyes. "Sure it is."

Before he could react, she'd risen to step in front of him, pushing his shoulders back against the chair.

"What are you doing?"

"A feasibility study," she told him and placed one knee on either side of his thighs, straddling him. Her eyes were deep and dark enough to dive into. Her scent wound around his thoughts. He watched without moving as she leaned in.

And when her mouth touched his, all he could feel was a hot, slicing arousal.

He had no business doing this, Bax told himself even as he closed his eyes. She was a client, or a potential client, they were in his office, at his desk and oh hell, he thought and gave himself up to it.

He'd kissed women before, even thought he'd loved one once, but he'd never felt anything like this. She was all he could touch. She was all he could feel even though she tempted him only with her lips on his, with the warmth of her thighs bracketing his own.

Her mouth was warm and mobile, her lips parted and ready to go deeper. With one impetuous move, she dragged him into want, into need. He wasn't used to needing anyone, but even as he struggled against it, she beckoned to him with her mouth, her hands and her body.

And he followed willingly.

SHE'D NEVER been able to resist a dare, Joss thought hazily as she let the taste of him flow over her. She'd planned to kiss him until his head spun, until the little head began to overrule the big head and he gave in and agreed. Maybe she'd been a little curious, too. After all, if she could give them what they both wanted physically and get him to Stockholm at the same time, what was the harm in that? She'd expected kissing him to be good and sexy.

She'd never in a million years expected the taste of him to rock her back. She'd never expected the feel of his hard shoulders under her fingers to set up a drumming demand in her head for the rest of him, naked. She'd never expected desire to take control. All too quickly, the kiss stopped being about persuasion. It existed for itself, for the tempting brush of his tongue, the soft slide of his mouth, the touch of his hands sliding up her back.

More. She wanted more. She wanted to toss aside caution and dive into this heady sensation, dive into him. And somewhere in there, she might lose control. Trembling, she pulled back.

"Well." She resisted the urge to press her fingers to her lips.

Bax stared at her as she walked back to the client chair. "What kind of a game are you playing?" he asked hoarsely.

"Just making sure we had chemistry." She sat because her knees wouldn't hold her. "So, do we have a deal?"

BAD IDEA, he told himself as his system refused to level. She was trying to play him and he was walking right into it. And yet, looked at a certain way, it made sense. Why not? Why not take the case? Solve her problem, make a little money and get a free trip to Stockholm and a warm and willing woman in his bed in the bargain. "Maybe," he found himself saying. "I'll think about it."

She ran her tongue over her lower lip. "You'll think about it?"

What could it hurt, he thought. "All right."

"Great. And you'll let me be part of the investigation?"

Not on his life. "Only if you can demonstrate to me that you know what you're doing," he hedged.

Joss rose and leaned over the desk to brush her lips against his. "Oh, I know what I'm doing, all right, Bax. Just wait and see."

3

"YOU'RE KIDDING." Gwen stared at Joss across the table at Rose Pistola that night, while the waiters bustled back and forth behind them. "You've promised to go to Stockholm and sleep with some guy you don't know from Adam?"

Gwen didn't sound nearly as horrified as she once would have, Joss reflected. Vegas had certainly changed her. "It's no worse than a one-night stand, which you've had recently yourself. Besides, I sort of know him from Adam. He comes with references anyway."

"How about blood tests? This is pretty out there even for you, Joss."

Joss forked up a bite of salad. "Why? The guy is sexy as hell. Why shouldn't I have a fling with him? You and Del just did out in Vegas."

"That was different."

"How? You might be serious about each other now, but it wasn't that way at the beginning. Look, we'll get the job done and have a good time while we're at it. Besides, you know the saying—if you've got 'em by the 'nads, their hearts and minds will follow."

"Ah. So, you're going to sexually enslave him and have your way with him, is that the plan?"

Joss considered. "It has its advantages." She leaned forward and the humor vanished. "The guy's good, Gwen, and we need someone good for this job."

Gwen looked at her, lips twitching. "Just don't bonk his brains out so much that he can't do any detecting."

"I sincerely doubt that'll happen, although you never know." Joss thought of the hard swell of his shoulders under her fingers. "If he was that good with his tongue when he was kissing, who knows what else he'll be good at."

Now Gwen did grin. "You're so bad."

"Oh, come on. Tell me the thought hasn't gone through your head when you've first kissed a guy."

"So, what's he like?" Gwen asked, ignoring her.

Joss considered. "Confident," she said finally. "Maybe a little bit of a control freak. Hot, though, really hot. He's serious but he's got this wonderful, strong face and you just know if he'd let loose, he'd be…" She thought of the way he'd looked after they kissed. "I got to him at the end, I could see it in his eyes."

"Watch out that you're not the one who becomes enslaved." Gwen pulled some bread out of the basket on the table.

"He's a guy. They're pretty easy to manage," Joss said carelessly, giving the busboy such a brilliant smile he accidentally overfilled her glass, slopping water on the tablecloth. "I'm not worried about it."

"So you fly to Stockholm together and then what? I mean, you can't just wander around asking everyone you meet questions."

"You said you knew this Silverhielm guy has the stamps."

"I said I *thought* he had the stamps. Not the same thing as knowing."

"Well, I hope you're pretty certain, because I've got a plan for getting in good with Silverhielm. It means taking a risk, though."

"How do you mean?"

Joss hesitated. "I need to take the Blue Mauritius."

"You're out of your mind." Gwen's reply was immediate. "That stamp is in the bank vault where it belongs, and that is where it's going to stay."

"We've got to have it to smoke out Silverhielm," Joss argued and outlined the plan, leaving out the fact that Bax had had doubts.

"It's too risky," Gwen almost wailed. "Do you know what it would do to the value of that stamp if it got so much as creased? Let alone wet or torn. It wouldn't even be worth the price of a replica. We can't take that chance."

"We have to," Joss told her. "It's the only angle I can think of. Don't you want the one-penny Mauritius back?" she coaxed.

Gwen pressed her face into her hands. "I can't believe I'm even considering this. You swear you'll be incredibly careful with it?" she demanded, raising her head.

"I swear."

"And you'll put it in a bank vault over there until you need it?"

"Don't worry about it, Gwen."

"Oh, like that makes me feel better. You need to take this seriously, Joss."

"I *do* take it seriously. Haven't I been different since I came back this time? Haven't I?" she demanded.

Gwen nodded grudgingly. "You've done a good job at the store. Frankly, I expected you to be gone a long time ago."

"I've changed, Gwen, I really have. Letting Jerry steal the stamps was a screwup by the old me. I need to make it better. Anyway, we've got Bax on the case, remember? He knows what he's doing."

"And what is he doing so far to earn his exorbitant fee?"

Joss shrugged. "He doesn't go on the clock until we leave, and that's got to wait for me to get my passport. Right now, he's looking into Silverhielm's background. I figure I'll see what I can find out, too."

"How are you going to do that?"

"Get a briefing from you, for starters. I need everything you know about the stamps Silverhielm has, who he deals with, where he lives, anything. If you've got it electronically and can send it to Bax, so much the better."

"That's not going to help you find him, though," Gwen pointed out.

"I know." Joss paused. "I need to go see Stewart."

Gwen sat absolutely still for a long moment. "Why do you need to go see Stewart?" she asked finally. "I told you before, he says he doesn't know anything."

"I don't believe that. Maybe nothing obvious, but I bet he knows some little nugget that will help us."

"He's in Las Vegas. It'll mean driving or flying."

"I know."

"It's not free, Joss," Gwen said with an edge to her voice.

"I *know*. You said we could use your winnings from the poker tournament to pay for Stockholm and Bax. I found a ticket that's twenty-nine bucks each way. I'll fly down in the morning and back in the afternoon. You won't even have to pay for a hotel."

Gwen drummed her fingers restlessly on the table. "What makes you think he'll talk to you?" she demanded. "He'll barely remember you."

"That might make it easier. He's probably so stir-crazy in the slammer that he'll see anyone just for something different. Besides, he's already pleaded guilty. At this point, he's just negotiating with the Vegas and San Francisco D.A.s, so it's not like anything he tells me will make a difference. What's he got to lose?"

Gwen mulled it over as the waiter set her grilled trout in front of her. "I feel like I should be the one doing it, but I just can't." She swallowed. "Do you understand?"

Gwen had always been so self-sufficient that she sometimes seemed more the grown-up than Joss. Seeing her vulnerability now, Joss felt fury at Stewart Oakes anew. "Of course. Don't worry about it. I've got it handled." She stared at her sister. "I'm going to bring back the one-penny Mauritius, Gwen, I swear it."

"Well, you'd better be quick about it. Grandma and Grampa are due back in a month."

Joss grinned. "Hey, with me and Superhunk on the case, it's a done deal."

Joss SAT in the visitation room at the Clark County jail, waiting for Stewart. Even though she was on the outside, there was a heaviness in the air that made her shiver a little as she sat in front of the Plexiglas window at her assigned booth. She was here voluntarily. She could leave at any time. What must it be like to be inside, to be without a choice?

Except that an inmate like Stewart Oakes had made his choice long since.

Around her, the faces of the other visitors largely mirrored her unease. The expressions were sober, mostly, and distracted. It wasn't a happy room. People came here because there was trouble. Only the children seemed blithely unaware of the tension in the air.

For a while, nothing happened. Then she heard the faint sound of a door opening and the prisoners began to file into the visiting area on the other side of the Plexiglas, under the watchful eyes of the guards.

She wasn't sure what to expect. She'd had no recent connection with Stewart as Gwen had had. Then again, knowing him hadn't protected Gwen from nearly being shot, so Joss wasn't sure it really mattered. He'd either show or he wouldn't, he'd talk or he wouldn't. Either way, she'd at least know she'd tried.

The man who sat down, wearing tired-looking orange coveralls, looked nothing like she remembered. Joss had seen a photo of Stewart pinned to the office bulletin board. In it, he'd been laughing, his arms around Gwen and their grandfather. Despite the streaks of gray at his temples, he'd looked young, lighthearted.

He didn't look lighthearted now. Jail had not been kind to him. Age sat heavy on his shoulders. Dark smudges underlay his eyes and his skin looked grainy, his expression defeated. Some of her anger morphed to pity. She picked up the phone on her side of the transparent barrier.

Stewart blinked at her and scowled, picking up his phone in turn. "What do you want?"

"I'm Gwen's sister Joss. I was hoping we could talk."

He studied her. "Is Gwen here?"

Joss shook her head. The disappointment that flickered over his face erased her pity and aroused her anger all over again. "Are you surprised? Stewart, you held a gun on her."

He closed his eyes for a moment and then shook his head. "I wrote her a letter. Did she get it?"

"I don't know." She wasn't going to give him an inch, not here. After the damage he'd wrought, a letter of apology was laughable. "You put her through the wringer. She's still getting over it." Joss watched him rub his temples. "It looks like you're doing the same."

He gave a humorless grimace that might have been a smile. "That's all right. I've got lots of time to work on it. But then, you're probably not here to talk about me." He frowned. "Exactly why are you here?"

Joss studied him. "Trying to undo some of the damage. I'm hoping you might be able to help."

Before she even finished the words, he was shaking his head. "No. No way. Not without a lawyer."

"Stewart, you're already pleading guilty. It's all over but the shouting."

"Yeah, well, that shouting you're talking about could mean the difference between doing a year or rotting in here for five to ten. Besides, like I already told the detectives and inspectors, I don't know anything."

"Maybe you know more than you think, something that could help us."

"You got no business coming here." His voice rose and he started to get up.

"I've got no business coming here?" Joss snapped like the crack of a whip. "You threatened to kill my sister, you stole millions from my grandfather, you betrayed us all and *I've* got no business coming here?" She clenched the phone receiver, fury making her dizzy. "I don't give a damn what kind of a sentence they hand down to you. That's not why I'm asking. I'm trying to undo the damage that you've done. I'm trying to get back the one-penny Mauritius and you're the only one who can help me."

"How do I know you're not taping this?" he demanded.

"How could I be?" She gestured at the phone. "Anyway, what would be the point? It wouldn't affect your case, except to help you. You think they're not going to look a little more kindly on you if my grandfather has back all his property? Come on, use your brain."

"My lawyer would kill me."

"Your lawyer's not here now and neither is the D.A. It's just you and me, Stewart," she said persuasively. "You can't erase what you did to Gwen but you can help make things better. Don't you want to? Don't you want to try to fix it?"

She waited in silence, hoping that she'd read him right.

Finally, Stewart sat back down and rubbed his eyes wearily. "You don't understand. I couldn't help if I wanted to. I dealt with an intermediary the whole time. I never even found out the client's name."

"Don't sit there and tell me you didn't at least have an idea. Gwen thinks it might be Karl Silverhielm."

Stewart's gaze skated off to one side. "I told you, I don't know. I only dealt with my contact."

"What did he look like?"

"It's all in the police report."

"Save me some work. What did he look like?" she repeated.

Stewart shrugged. "Light hair, tall, blue eyes. One of those Nordic faces."

"What was his name?"

Stewart snorted. "Do you think for a minute he gave me his real name? You can bet it was a fake."

"What was it?"

"Michael Houseman." When she rolled her eyes, he shrugged. "I told you, there's nothing I can give to help you."

"Was there anything else about him, anything that would let us identify him?" Joss persisted. "Think about how he moved."

"He didn't look like a thug. He was smooth, classy, even. And he moved like he was trained, like a boxer or something."

"Can you remember anything about him that couldn't be changed, his ears, maybe, or the shape of his fingers?"

"Nothing that stands out. His features were normal, nothing unusual about them. His hands were—" He stopped.

"What?"

"Well, it might not be important."

"Let me decide that. What?"

"His right hand. There was a scar on it, between the thumb and the forefinger. I noticed it when we were shaking hands."

"What was it shaped like?"

"A jagged line, like a knife had slipped or something."

"Nice company you keep," she said dryly.

He bristled. "Look, you wanted me to help, I'm helping."

"I'm sorry. You're right. Look, you've given me something that might be useful."

"And my lawyer would knock me in the head if he knew I was talking to you."

"You did the right thing, if it helps."

He gave a brooding stare. "Little enough of that lately."

"Stewart." Joss hesitated. "This'll mean something to Gwen."

"Tell her…" The tone signaling the end of the visiting period rang. He waited until it was silent. "I'd give anything to have done things differently," he said finally. "Tell her that, would you?"

4

BAX SAT in his chair with his feet up on his desk, rubbing the back of his neck. He'd spent too much time on the phone that day, trying to clear up business so he could leave for Stockholm. And wondering if he were nuts. Now, as the afternoon bled away, he was trying to decide whether to write up his notes or just call it a night. He hadn't slept well the night before, waking in the darkness from dreams of unfulfilled cravings and dangerous pursuit.

And Joss Chastain.

The bargain they'd struck the previous day had been absurd, he knew that. He'd given her his word that he'd take on the case and he'd hold to it, but there'd be no charades of being lovers, no charades of being partners. His better judgment might have been overruled at the time but it had reappeared and he needed to do the responsible thing.

With a thump, Bax dropped his feet to the floor just as Joss swept through the door, all color and light in a pleated royal blue miniskirt and a stretchy blue and silver striped shirt that wound around her body.

"I've found something," she announced.

She was something, something he'd fought all day not to dwell on. Now, with her standing in his office practically vibrating with energy, their agreement seemed just a way to make a formality of the chemistry that flowed between them. The wide ebullience of her grin tempted him to taste. The curve of her waist begged him to touch. In a whirlwind second, she filled the room with her presence and completely destroyed his concentration.

And it pissed him off. "Now what?"

"I just got back from Las Vegas and I've got a clue."

"Let me guess. You figured out that we'll all be better off if you leave me alone to do my job?"

"Not that kind of clue." She gave him a withering stare and sat in his client chair, taking her time getting comfortable. The getting comfortable involved lots of shifting and stretching that made him only more aware of her body. "Now, if you're nice, I'll share with you. If not, I'll just keep quiet and let you tell me what you found out today."

Irritating, he thought. "Let's get something straight—"

"As your client, I've got a right to a report on anything you've found out," she reminded him serenely.

What she didn't have was a right to blow in here smelling of summer and seduction and completely fracturing his ability to think. "As my client, you pay me to do the investigating. That means if anyone was going to Vegas, it should have been me."

She didn't rise to his tone. Instead, she gave him a smile that made his pulse bump. "Some things need a woman's touch. Anyway, in two days we'll be flying all the way to Stockholm. Vegas is small change, by comparison."

"You still should have told me before you went. I've already got the police report." He held up a thick bundle of paper and slapped it back down on his empty desktop. "You wasted your time."

"Not at all. I went to the Las Vegas jail to visit Stewart Oakes."

"Who told you to take a flying leap, I hope." Bax frowned. "His case is still in progress. You shouldn't be talking to him."

"His case is a formality at this point. He's copping a plea on both sets of charges. Talking to me won't change that. Besides, I can be persuasive when I want to be."

Didn't he know it, Bax thought, tearing his gaze away from her mouth. "All right, Nancy Drew, what did he tell you?"

Amusement crossed her face. She obviously knew where he'd been looking. "Well, I tried to get him to say something about the Swedish collector, but he played dumb."

"Now there's a surprise."

"Not dumb enough. I mentioned Silverhielm's name and his eyes shifted. Even if he doesn't know for sure it was Silverhielm, he believes it is."

"You flew to Vegas for that?"

Joss bristled. Good, he thought. Keep her at a distance. Don't let her get close with that gypsy hair and those eyes that promised everything. "No. I've got information about the intermediary."

"Right. Houseman or whatever his name was."

"Stewart said the guy looked Nordic, moved like an athlete."

Bax gave a dismissive shrug. "That's all in the police report."

"And just exactly how did you get your hands on the police report, anyway?"

"A friend or two in the right places." And his good fortune that San Francisco had jurisdiction over the larceny portion of the case.

"Did the report also mention the scar on his hand? Ooooh, I guess it didn't," Joss singsonged with enjoyment and walked over to lean against the edge of his desk, facing him.

Bax looked at her. "There's a perfectly good chair over there." And he'd be much more comfortable with her at a distance.

"I'd rather talk face-to-face." Mischief lurked in her eyes.

"You're on my desk."

"Good." She leaned on one hand. "Something ought to be. There's something slightly disturbed about a person having such a clean desk."

"I like things uncluttered." Which meant not sleeping with clients, he reminded himself, but he couldn't stop staring at the long, lean lines of her body.

"Sometimes clutter is a lot more fun," she purred and touched the tip of her tongue to her upper lip.

Bax cleared his throat. "What about the scar?"

"Well, obviously it's an identifier. If we find Silverhielm, we look at his soldiers and try to find the guy with the mark."

"It's a long shot."

"It's something concrete. Anyway, what did you come up with today, Phillip Marlowe?"

"My Interpol contact didn't know a whole lot but he promised to ask around. He was able to pass on a few interesting tidbits, though."

"Such as?"

"Our boy has his fingers in a lot of pies. Officially, he does import/export. Jewelry, mostly. He seems to consider himself a connoisseur of the finer things. Lives on a private island in the archipelago to the east of Stockholm."

"Nice. Has he been in trouble with the law?"

"Nothing that showed up on any of the systems my contact could access. He's rumored to be responsible for several ugly murders. Word on the street is that he's not to be crossed."

Joss nodded thoughtfully. "Interesting."

"Interesting? How about disturbing?"

"Are you scared?"

"No, but you should be. If Silverhielm is involved, you have no business coming to Stockholm with me."

"But how else are we going to be lovers?" Joss sank down to lie across his empty desk, propping her head on one hand. "Why Bax, a person would think that you've forgotten all about our agreement."

He swallowed, his mouth suddenly dry. "I've changed my mind."

"But how can that be?" She slid her hand over her hip. "Oh, I know, I forgot about your retainer."

IF HE THOUGHT he was backing out of their deal, he was dreaming, pure and simple. She was going to Stockholm with him and she was going to be part of getting the one-penny Mauritius back. And if it took sex to make him putty in her hands, well, then sex it would be.

Small sacrifice for the cause.

Joss moistened her lips. "Something about an office has always given me the urge to misbehave," she murmured, trailing her fingers down her neck, into the deep vee of skin exposed by her blouse and over the soft swells of her breasts until she saw Bax's eyes darken.

Fluidly, she rose and crossed to the door. "Perhaps I'll just lock this." She flicked the bolt with a metallic *snick,* then turned to face him. "Well, now that we're not likely to be disturbed, how much of a down payment do you require?" she asked. "Enough to need one of these?" She rummaged in her purse to pull out a condom.

Without asking, she walked over to Bax's side of the

desk and sat across his lap. Then she laughed, a low, husky sound of delight as she felt the unmistakable shape of a hard-on beneath her.

"That's enough, Joss," he ground out.

"Oh no, Bax, surely your services don't come so cheaply." She slid her hands around to the back of his neck and into the springy waves of his hair. "And if you'd wanted it to be over, you'd have stopped me long before."

Joss leaned in to nibble his neck, tasting the taut skin, roving to the hard line of his jaw and cheek. His chest rose and fell unevenly, as though he'd been running. His hands sat still and loose at his sides. With the tip of her tongue, she traced the line of his mouth, absorbing his flavor, teasing him.

"Poor Bax. You try so hard to be good." She pressed her forehead against his. "But you want this as much as I do. Why don't you just admit it?" Her lips were a hairbreadth from his, her breath blending with his. "Why don't you just give in?"

And in that instant his control snapped and he claimed her mouth with his own.

The kiss was hard and deep and heedless. Her head fell back, inviting him to devour. She might have done the tempting but it was he who laid claim to her. He didn't ask permission, he just took. Hard and proprietary, his hands roved over her back, along her side and hip, then up under her blouse to curve over her breast. He touched her as though she were already known, already owned and he could amuse himself at will.

Joss gasped at his touch and pressed against him. "Mmm, more," she whispered. She felt his mouth curve against hers, then felt the trail of his fingertips up the inside of her calf, the inside of her thigh. She shivered as the light touch traveled up under her skirt and higher still, searching for that place at the apex of her thighs, that place where she was already slick and hot and craving his touch.

And then his fingers dipped in under the satin barrier and Joss jolted against him, moaning into his mouth.

Outside, in the hallway, voices sounded, footsteps thudded as people walked home for the night. Within the room there was only the two of them, touch and taste, sound and scent.

Bax's fingers slid against her, teasing, tormenting her with each stroke. When they slipped inside her, his tongue dipped into her mouth and a coil of tension began to build, tightening with each stroke. "Oh my God," she whispered.

And she heard the low rumble of his chuckle. "I'm not nearly done," he murmured, then gathered himself and rose, still holding her. Taking a step, he laid her back on the desk.

She felt the wood, smooth and cool beneath her shoulder blades. When he reached up and stripped the satiny fabric of her thong down her thighs, it was another kind of cool and another surge of excitement. Both were overshadowed by the warm stroke of his hands up her calves, over her knees as he knelt before her, dragging her thighs over his shoulders. Joss caught a breath of anticipation. He folded back her skirt, blowing on the sensitive folds of skin. And then the heat of his mouth was on her.

He didn't waste time teasing her and she didn't want it. His mouth was relentless, driving her, taking her up until all she could do was feel. She wanted it hard and urgent, she wanted the orgasm that curled in her, still half-formed. As he brought her close, though, he slowed down to leave her balanced on the edge, half gasping with pleasure, half delirious with want. And a fraction before the point of inevitability, he stopped and stood.

"No!" Joss cried out.

"Oh yes," he said softly. She heard the clink of his belt, the growl of his zipper, the crackle of plastic and his slow exhale as he sheathed himself.

The tip of his cock brushed against her, making her jolt. She stared at him, at his face drawn in taut lines of concentration as he positioned himself. And then he pistoned his hips to slide into her, fast and deep, and she gave a strangled cry.

Hard and urgent. She wrapped her legs around his waist. It was what she'd craved, this rush of sensation. His hands were unwrapping her blouse, pulling up her bra to find her bare breasts. The feel of his cock possessed her, the fullness, the slick rub against her tender inner flesh as each move teased her clitoris, tormented, inching her closer and closer to orgasm.

Bax caught at her ankles, straightening her legs, pulling them apart to watch as he buried his cock deep in her tight, warm wetness. Stroke after stroke, he got thicker and harder, thicker and harder as the orgasm gathered. He gritted his teeth, holding on, promising himself one more stroke, and one more until she began to shudder and shake and cry out as orgasm burst through her. And when it was done, he let himself follow.

"I DON'T KNOW about you, but I'm thinking we'll be able to do a pretty believable job of pretending we're lovers," Joss said lazily as she pulled her clothing back on.

With her hair loose and wild and that light of satisfaction in her eyes, she looked more enticing than ever. If there had been a bed in the room, Bax would have been giving serious thought to tumbling her back into it.

"Too bad you don't have a couch in here," Joss commented, as though she'd overheard his thoughts. "Just think about Sweden." She leaned over for a quick kiss, and topped it off with a bawdy wink.

Bax tucked in his shirt. "I don't like the idea of you going over there," he said. "Silverhielm and his guys are too dangerous. Do you really understand what you're getting into?"

"It's not your decision. I'm going over there, whether you want me to or not," she told him. "Now, if you want to be involved and work with me, that's great, but I'm doing it no matter what."

The desperate kid look was back again and it tugged at him. Mentally, he cursed. He didn't get the sense she was doing it for show. She was telling him the truth as she saw it. Stubborn, contrary, unpredictable and somehow very good at getting over on his blind side.

He'd be better off stopping right now, but there was something about her that he couldn't walk away from. If it meant going to Stockholm with her to keep her safe, he'd do it, he realized.

And if it meant giving in to both of their desires against his better judgment, he'd do that, too.

5

AT FIRST GLANCE, Stockholm seemed to be as much water as land, vivid bands of blue weaving their way among the confusion of islands that formed the city. Whereas most metropolitan areas boasted a single river winding through, in Stockholm water charmed the visitor at every turn, from broad passes to narrow inlets between the steep rock, or tree-lined edges of the islands. Bridges vaulted from shore to shore and boats and ferries sailed in between, seeming more a part of the city than the streets and cars.

As the taxi brought Bax and Joss into the heart of Stockholm, the modern utilitarian structures that had dominated the landscape at the fringes gave way to the aged, graceful buildings of the old city. They sat shoulder to shoulder on the waterfronts, their ornate and gabled facades tinted ocher and blush, tan and pale yellow. The old city was a pastel fantasy, reflected in the rippling waters of lake and sea.

"It's lovely," Joss murmured. "So much blue and so many trees. I had no idea."

"You should see it farther east, in the archipelago," Bax said. "It's something else, just islands and water. That's where our friend lives, on his own private island."

"His own private fortress, more like." Joss stared out the windows of the cab, eagerly taking in the sights of the city. "So you've been to Stockholm before, I take it?"

"Passed through a few times."

"Often enough to know anyone useful?"

He gave her a pitying look. "Isn't that why you hired me? As a matter of fact, I've already arranged a meeting."

"I apologize for underestimating you," Joss said, looking over to see him relaxed on the seat in his travel clothes. She should have known he'd be organized. There was nothing for getting to know another person like taking a long and complicated international flight together. Bax always had ticket and passport in hand, chose the right line, knew where their seats were. That wasn't too much of a surprise to her. What had been a surprise was how quickly the hours together had gone, lightened up by his flashing humor and odd bits of knowledge.

She'd expected the trip to be illuminating on the subject of John Baxter. She hadn't expected it to be fun.

The taxi swung around a U-turn and pulled to a stop in front of a rococo fantasy of a hotel. "The Royal Viking," the cab driver announced. Windows topped with stylized lintels marched across the high, sheer front of the hotel. On the first floor, elaborate carvings decorated the rosy stone facade. Flags flew from the green copper roof, snapping in the breeze. Behind them, script letters spelled out Royal Viking against the sky.

At the foot of the hotel lay the waterfront, lined with the white tour boats and ferries.

The building had the same sort of presence as an aging prima ballerina, stylish and graceful, but mellowed. There were small signs, perhaps, of the passage of time, but the bones and muscles remained disciplined.

"The Royal Viking, huh? You've got expensive taste," Bax commented as they got out.

"I figure if we want to get our friend's attention, we've got to walk the walk, as well as talk the talk," Joss said with a little smile, watching the blue-uniformed bellhop bring a wheeled luggage rack out to collect their bags. "If I've inherited some of Jerry's stolen swag, I should already be living well off the more easily fenced items, right? Besides, if they think I'm not too smart, they're likely to drop their guard."

"To their peril."

She smiled at him. "Exactly. By the way, the room's under your name," she said over her shoulder and walked through the doors into the hotel.

"What?" Bax stopped her, brows lowering.

"Well, we don't want our friend to somehow find out that a Chastain is staying here, do we?" She didn't see the point in mentioning the fact that she didn't have a credit card to her name. That was the old, feckless Joss. The new Joss was getting her act in gear. Bax didn't look convinced, though. She tried again. "Look, if we're lovers, we'd be registered under your name, wouldn't we? It makes sense. Breathe," she patted his cheek. "We'll pay you back at the end."

"I'll make sure of it. Any more surprises?"

"Only of the most enjoyable kind," she murmured and continued through the doors.

Like the city outside, the lobby was a fantasy of gold and blue. Marble pillars with gold-leafed crowns soared to fifteen-foot ceilings ringed with crenellated moldings. Crystal chandeliers glimmered overhead. Underfoot, herringbone-patterned hardwood floors gleamed at the edges of royal blue carpet woven with twisting gold vines.

"Good evening," said the smiling woman behind the polished mahogany counter.

"Hej," Bax said, using the Swedish word for hello. He then astounded Joss by producing a stream of what sounded like Swedish. Once or twice, he searched for a word or the desk clerk frowned, but mostly they chattered

along like magpies. Finally, he signed the registration card and received the key.

"Was that what I thought it was?" Joss asked as the bell-hop collected their luggage and they headed toward the elevator. "Are you fluent in Swedish?"

"Not exactly. I'm fluent in Danish. I can get by in Swedish. Not all the words are the same, but the two are close enough that we can generally understand one another. I'm sure nearly everyone here speaks English—but I wanted to get the rust off."

"Didn't sound like there was any rust on it to begin with," Joss said, thinking of the lilting conversation she'd listened to.

Bax shrugged and punched the call button for the elevator. "My mother was Danish. I lived in Copenhagen until I was about six."

"No kidding. Was your father Danish, too?"

Bax shook his head. "American. He was a marine, an embassy guard. We lived all over Europe until I was about sixteen."

"Wow. You must be one cultured guy."

"I have my moments." The elevator appeared.

"So do you wish you lived over here?"

He shrugged and opened the door to let her walk into the car ahead of him. "I'm not sure I know. I don't exactly feel like an American, but I don't really feel like a European anymore. I'm somewhere in the middle."

"I know what you mean," Joss said as they got into the tiny car. "I grew up in Africa." An experience she wouldn't have traded for anything, but one that had left her homeless in a way, and always searching for more.

"Really?" He looked at her with interest. "How did that happen?"

"My parents are doctors," she explained. "We lived all

over. Zimbabwe, Botswana, Tanzania, mostly out in the bush."

"What was it like?"

"It was amazing, the animals and the landscape and the people. I loved it. There was always something new. I was free there, you know? No rules." And it had been so hard to get used to life in the real world.

"Ah. Now it all makes sense." The car stopped on their floor and they got out.

Joss gave Bax a quick smile as they stopped at the door to the room. "Are you saying that I'm not good with rules?"

"I'm saying that you like to make your own."

He stood there in his jeans and denim shirt, his jaw darkened with stubble from the long flight, looking just about good enough to eat. Joss took a step toward him and flowed into his arms. "Let me tell you about my rules," she began.

"Good afternoon," someone said cheerfully from behind them. They turned to see the bellhop walking toward them with their suitcases on the shiny brass birdcage luggage cart. "Welcome to the Royal Viking Hotel."

Joss gave Bax a rueful grin as the bellhop opened up their door.

It was like walking into a room in some eighteenth-century palace. Glossy white paneling with gilt moldings spread across the walls. White and gold swags of fabric framed the wide windows that overlooked the waterfront. Rich aquamarine damask covered the reproduction antique chairs—surely they were reproductions, she thought feverishly—as well as the coverlet of the half-tester bed. And what a bed, high and wide and piled with pillows, just made for all manner of aristocratic decadence.

She looked over at Bax and their eyes met. And desire throbbed through her.

The bellhop came through the door with their last bag and set it down. "Let me just get your suitcases," he began reaching for the luggage rack.

Bax took it from him and set it aside. "I don't think that will be necessary," he said smoothly.

"Well, then, I can show you—"

"Nope, won't be necessary," Bax told him, turning him around and ushering him toward the door. "In fact, I think we're all set." Bax slipped a twenty-five kroner tip in his hand and closed the door in front of his startled face.

"Now." Bax walked back toward Joss and tumbled her onto the bed with him. "What was that you were saying about rules?"

WHEN JOSS opened her eyes the following morning, it took her a moment to remember where she was. The big bed was empty but for her, the room silent. Yawning, she found her way to the bathroom, with its aqua and white tile walls and gleaming chrome. By the time she'd brushed her teeth and washed her face, she was feeling almost human.

Wrapping herself in one of the hotel's thick terry robes, she wandered over to the window to look out over the water. Beyond, in a pastel fantasy, lay the island of Gamla Stan, the oldest part of Stockholm. It beckoned to her from across the water. Forget about the room, however gorgeous it was. She wanted to be out there, exploring.

In time with her thoughts, there was a rattling at the door and Bax came in.

"Good morning."

"Good morning." She jammed her hands deep in the pockets of her robe. "I thought maybe you'd headed out for the day."

For a moment, he looked taken aback. "I was downstairs having coffee. I didn't want to wake you. Sorry, I should have left a note."

It was awkward, she thought. They'd become lovers without warning. Now, they were essentially living together as intimate strangers. She knew how to make Bax shudder with arousal but couldn't name his favorite color. They still hadn't found their rhythm with one another, they didn't know what to expect.

At least not out of bed.

"Well, I'm up and around now," she told him, sitting down on the bed. "Hey, is anything important going on today? The guide book mentioned a postal museum on Gamla Stan. I thought it might have some useful information for us. You know, stamps and stuff."

"Sure." He walked restlessly over to the windows to peer out. "By the way, I saw something in the paper about a stamp auction later on this week. The preauction viewing and reception are tomorrow night."

"So?"

"So Silverhielm will very likely be there. It might be a good opportunity to make his acquaintance."

"Wouldn't that be convenient?" Joss said, watching Bax. He was tense enough that he was making her tense. Too many more days like this and they'd be crawling the walls. It was definitely time to do something about it.

She reached for the sash of her robe. "Well, if we're going to be meeting Silverhielm, we should probably get prepared."

"I think I told you, we're going to get a briefing."

"I mean you and I should get prepared," she said, sliding her robe off her shoulders.

"Get prepared how?" Bax turned away from the window to look at her.

Joss gave him a wicked smile. "If you'll just come into the shower with me, I'd be happy to explain."

THE NARROW cobblestone streets of Gamla Stan wound between the high gabled buildings, the air still echoing with the past. Tourists and Stockholmers sat at the sidewalk cafés drinking coffee in the warm afternoon. The whole scene held the feeling of a gentler age.

Inside the postal museum, history permeated the air. All around them were displays with stamps from other eras, other places. They walked past the prize holdings of the stamp world. At least, that was Joss's assumption. Given that all the signs and labels were in Swedish, and her current vocabulary consisted of "hello," "goodbye," "please" and "thank you," it was hard to be sure.

Context was everything, Joss thought with a sigh. Otherwise, the stamps were just colored squares of paper. "I don't suppose I could translate for me, could you?" she asked Bax.

He gave her a calculating look. "I suppose, but it'll cost you."

Joss frowned. "Wait a minute, I thought you were supposed to be my devoted lover. Wasn't that what we were just talking about?"

"Well, I'm not sure that includes translation services beyond *la langue d'amour.*" He stuck his tongue in his cheek.

Joss raised her eyebrows. *"La langue d'amour?"*

"I was raised in Europe," he said blandly.

"I see." This was a new Bax. She'd never seen him be playful before. It was something she could get used to. "Well, if I could talk you into translating, I'd be happy to discuss some sort of compensation for your efforts."

"What do you have in mind?" He looked at her speculatively.

"Perhaps we could take it out in trade."

"I can work with that. Let's see," he squinted at the label. "Well, what you're looking at here is a stamp on a letter."

Joss crossed her arms and leaned against the doorway to the display case. "You don't say."

"It's true. If you want to hear more, I'll need a deposit."

It took her away, the taste of his mouth, the feel of his arms around her. It didn't matter that they'd just spent a couple of hours making love. She wanted more, and more wouldn't be enough.

Sounds echoed into the exhibits area from the next room, the voices of children in a school tour. Hurriedly, they broke apart.

"I trust you found that sufficient?" Joss pressed her lips together.

Bax grinned. "Well, we do have a minimum deposit, but I suppose under the circumstances I can waive it."

"You're so kind."

They worked their way slowly through the museum, past rare stamps and printing presses, past relics of ages gone by. In the next room, Bax drifted past her to look at a perforating machine with its pointy-toothed wheels. Just inside the doorway sat a small safe on a pedestal, its thick, black door swung wide. Inside, on even tinier pedestals stood a pair of stamps.

Joss took a look and blinked.

One blue, one reddish orange. A white profile of a queen wearing a circlet around upswept hair showed on each; the words Post Office ran along the left-hand margin in white block letters and Mauritius on the right. The indigo stamp was twin to the one they'd installed in a bank vault earlier that day.

"Bax," Joss said softly.

He was on the other side of the room.

"Bax," she said again.

"What?" He walked over to stand at her side.

She pointed to the safe. "It's them. The Post Office Mauritius pair."

He studied them. "The queen doesn't look the same on the orange one. Her hair's different. They look more like sisters than the same person. Look, the one on the Blue Mauritius almost looks like she's smiling."

"So, what are the chances that we'd stumble across them here?" Joss commented.

"Not necessarily that surprising, when you think about it. Maybe seeing them here is what whetted Silverhielm's appetite to have his own."

"Maybe." She continued to stare at the little squares of color, still vivid after all these years. So small, so fragile to have caused such grief. "I thought it would be a different color. More yellow, from what Gwen described."

"Didn't you ever see your grandfather's copy?"

She shook her head. "It was always in the vault. The only reason I've seen the Blue Mauritius is because we brought it here."

The two stamps sat on their little pedestals under the lights, the plump-jowled images of the monarch looking serenely off to the left.

"Hard to believe that people are willing to pay so much money for something like this, isn't it?" Bax said.

"Oh, I don't know. It's a bit like owning a piece of history, isn't it? A little bit of immortality. I think that's what my grandfather finds so magical about them." She stroked her finger down the glass protecting the contents of the safe.

"We'll get it back," Bax whispered. "One way or another, we'll get it back." He kissed her forehead.

First playful, now nice. Joss blinked back the sudden stinging in her eyes and blew out a breath. "Well, I think we've seen everything we need to here. You want to stop and get something to drink somewhere? Maybe that café we passed?"

He tangled his fingers in hers. "I've got a better idea."

SLUSSEN, just across from Gamla Stan on the island of Södermalm, was a whirlwind of motion. Cars and buses converged on the transportation hub from a dozen directions. Ferries lined the waterfront, poised for journeys to the archipelago and beyond. After the charm of old town, Slussen seemed garishly modern, but even here there was the beauty of the water, the green of trees, the aged loveliness of historic buildings.

Joss and Bax sat in the broad public square in front of the Swedish state museum, watching pigeons search for crumbs among the cracks of the cobblestone-striped concrete. To their right, the bluffs of Södermalm rose sheer and high. On their left, bridges vaulted to Gamla Stan. Directly ahead of them, propped up at the far end by a fragile-looking tracery of iron, a slender finger of blue projected out from the building that climbed up the face of the bluff.

"What is that?" Joss asked.

"Gondolen. It's a restaurant bar, very fashionable. The strutwork at the far end is the Katarinahissen, an elevator that takes you up to the public walkway on top. It's a pretty amazing view." Propped up on one side by the office building and across the street by the Katarinahissen, the restaurant hovered high in the air over one of the streets that fed into Slussen.

"It's almost cocktail hour," Joss said. "Why don't we go on up and have a drink and you can show me?"

"In a bit. We're here for a reason. Our friend Silverhielm has his city offices in the building attached to the restaurant." Bax glanced at his watch. "I'm told he comes out between four and five every afternoon." He rose and held out a hand to her. "Would you like a closer look at the Katarinahissen?"

Joss grinned. "Lead the way."

Crossing the various streams of traffic between the square and the Katarinahissen took longer than she expected, but eventually they stood by the doors to the elevator, across from the office building. Bax led her a few steps along the sidewalk, staring out at the water. Without warning, he swept her into his arms, his mouth hard on hers.

It should have been different. They knew one another's bodies now, they'd kissed plenty of times. It should have been pedestrian. It shouldn't have sent her blood fizzing through her veins.

It shouldn't have left her stunned with wanting.

"There, coming out of the doors," Bax murmured against her lips and lifted her off her feet to spin her a little, as though he were a lover overcome with the moment. "Take a good look so you'll know him later."

Face pressed into his neck, Joss opened her eyes and looked across the street.

There was no doubt which one was Silverhielm. Bodyguards flanked him but he walked as though he were alone, head raised arrogantly as he approached the gleaming black sedan that sat idling at the curb. He wore an impeccably tailored suit, slate-blue with a chalk stripe. His hair was thick, wavy and entirely gray; his eyes were pale. About him, there hovered an indefinable air of implacability and menace.

It was a well-choreographed scene, like the footage

she'd seen of presidents and prime ministers walking to vehicles. In seconds, he was safely ensconced in the car and his entourage was inside.

The sound of the car door slamming behind him echoed across the street. Joss shivered as the car drove away. "So that's him."

Bax nodded and released her.

It shouldn't have shaken her. There was no good reason why it did. Joss walked away from the lift building to lean on the railing and look across the water to Gamla Stan. "He looked...ruthless."

"He hasn't gotten to where he is by being kind. So are you ready to step back from this and let me take care of things?"

"No." She turned to him, shoulders squared. "I know who we're up against now, which is going to make me that much better against him."

"Stubborn," Bax commented, bouncing his loosely curled fist lightly off her chin.

"Determined," she countered.

"Not to mention sexy as hell. I seem to remember something about a payment due, by the way."

"Payment?" she echoed innocently.

"If I don't get it, I'm going to have to send you to collections," he warned.

Joss smiled. "Well, then, I guess I'd better pay up."

6

THE CHERUBS SMILED at her, golden-haired and rosy-cheeked, their bellies coquettishly round. Hanging on the wall over her head, their lively faces stared out, not at Joss, but at the sailing ship behind her, the enormous relic of a bygone age, the ornately carved king's folly that hadn't even made it out of the harbor before capsizing centuries before.

It was hard to say what was more extraordinary, Joss thought, the fact that for over two centuries people had forgotten where the *Vasa* warship lay, just a few hundred yards from the bustling waterfront, or the fact that the ship had been rediscovered and brought up to the surface nearly intact.

When she'd capsized, the sailors on the *Vasa* must have prayed to God for salvation. Now, the vessel was ensconced in a temple of its own, a soaring building of soft light designed to protect and display the ripe and luscious lines of a sailing ship that barely sailed.

"It's incredible," Joss murmured turning to stare at the stern rising high above them as she and Bax stood on one of the observation floors of the multilevel museum. "How can anything be this big?" As they walked toward the front of the ship, the height of the ship's side dropped in a slow, graceful curve until they were looking down at the deck by the time they'd reached the midway point. "How could anything be so beautiful and yet so useless?"

"Makes you wonder if there wasn't some sort of collective memory behind the drive to Swedish functionalism."

"The *Vasa* begat Ikea?"

"It's a theory."

"As amazing as it is, though, I feel guilty playing tourist. Shouldn't we be doing something to get the one-penny Mauritius back?"

"We're not playing tourist. We're going to meet my contact here, see what he can tell us about Silverhielm."

"Mysterious meetings in public museums. And you told me being a detective wasn't glamorous."

"Most of it's not," he said frankly. "It's a lot of legwork, most of which winds up being pointless. But eventually if you get enough information, you'll find something you can use, just like we will with Silverhielm. We'll get to him and take the stamps." He considered. "Unless he keeps his goodies in a vault somewhere, in which case we're out of luck."

"He won't keep them in a vault," Joss said positively.

"How do you know that?"

"You could see it in the way he moves. Stamps aren't just a business for him. There are too many other ironclad ways to make money." She followed the mizzenmast of the *Vasa* with her eyes as it rose overhead. "There's something about the stamps that he wants and needs, and that means having them handy. Besides, with all his goons around, he's got to feel smug, like no one can get to him. That's how we'll take him down, his pride."

"She's right, you know," said a lightly accented voice. Next to them stood a stocky, round-faced man with an incongruously tip-tilted nose. More than anything, he looked like a middle-aged elf.

A smile broke out on Bax's face, though he merely looked at the gun ports of the ship. "Rolf."

"Bax."

"Rolf Johansson, meet Joss Chastain."

Following Bax's lead, Joss simply nodded. "It's a pleasure to meet you. Are you one of Bax's Interpol friends?"

"No, I'm with Stockholm's organized crime division. We met when Bax was working in Stockholm. Perhaps Interpol is where you learned this sort of rendezvous spot, Bax. Certainly, the Swedish police would not think of it."

Bax shrugged. "They should. Less likely that someone would follow you here than to a restaurant or bar."

Rolf considered. "Perhaps you have a point. So what brings you to Stockholm?"

"Work, of course."

"Ah. Our friend who lives in the archipelago."

"So you are watching him."

"Of course." Rolf leaned on the rail of the observation deck. "He is my favorite waste of time. What do you know about him?"

"Officially that he's an import/export man for jewelry." Rolf nodded.

"Organized crime?" Bax asked.

"Not in the classic way. In fact, he and the mob do not get on. Our friend is what you might call a freelancer, a very successful one. The mob disapproves."

"I can imagine. So how would you characterize him, a businessman pushing the edge of legal?"

"A criminal with a legal front," Rolf said flatly. "His jewelry business has been amazingly successful, from the very beginning."

"Isn't that interesting."

"Suspiciously so. We know he uses it to launder money but we can't prove anything."

"Where does he get the dirty money from?" Joss asked.

"Smuggling. Drugs, currency, rare goods, so the rumor

goes. And he's not shy about hurting anyone who gets in his way. We've had more than a few dead bodies attributed to his organization."

"Have you infiltrated?"

Rolf shook his head. "The one time we tried, the agent was killed in a convenient accident."

"Murder?"

"I honestly could not say. If he were not involved in Silverhielm's organization, I'd have no doubts it was just bad luck. Because he was…" Rolf shrugged.

"Can't you turn someone?"

"No one wants to talk." He smiled faintly. "It is not healthy. We occasionally get anonymous information. Always, we follow up but the leads come to nothing. Two years ago, we came close to putting him in jail and perhaps getting more. His wife of the time filed battery charges against him."

"Battery?"

"He beat her quite badly. She promised to testify to all she knew about his business."

"And?"

"What do you think? A few days passed, she had visitors, and she withdrew the charges. We could do nothing. She has since left Sweden. He sits out there on his island like the king of the archipelago and laughs at us and gets richer every day."

"Frustrating."

Rolf's eyes hardened. "He will make a mistake one day and when he does, we will be there."

"How would you like to have something to truly hang on him?"

Rolf casually walked a few steps past them toward the bow of the boat and leaned again on the rail, using small binoculars to examine the upper reaches of the mast. "Bax, my friend, nothing would make me happier. What's on your mind?"

"We have reason to suspect that he may have arranged to have a very valuable rare stamp stolen from Joss's family."

"That is work for Interpol."

"Interpol tried to run it down and came up with nothing."

Rolf put down his glasses. "He is very slippery, our friend. So you come to visit us, instead?"

"I figured I'd be more effective on site."

"We are watching him, Interpol has already pursued him. What makes you think that you can do what we can't?" Rolf's voice hardened a little.

"I'm not trying to run down mobsters, pedophiles and prostitution rings. I can afford to just focus on him. Besides, I'm not even trying to lock him down. I'm just trying to get back Joss's family's property."

For the first time, Rolf turned to look directly at him, eyes cool. "We don't think well of vigilantism in Sweden."

"Don't think of it as vigilantism," Bax returned. "Think of it as help."

"Help?"

"I'm having to poke around in Silverhielm's life to do this job. If I happen to come across evidence of a crime, I would pass that to the proper authorities."

The corner of Rolf's mouth twitched. "I am sure the proper authorities would be happy to pursue it. They are always glad of help."

"Help goes both directions, of course. Depending on what happens, I may need the help in a hurry."

"Perhaps now is a good time for us to trade mobile telephone numbers."

"It might be quicker than leaving a message on your voice mail," Bax allowed.

"You Americans," Rolf tsked, "always so impatient."

"We get that way when we face master criminals."

Rolf smiled briefly. "Don't we all."

THE SKY WAS still light as Bax and Joss walked across the cobbled expanse of Berzelii Park toward Strindberg's auction house. Trees hung over the broad stone benches and the reflecting pond glimmered. To the other side lay the sea that seemed to be at every turn in Stockholm, this time a narrow inlet that gleamed in the afternoon sun.

In such a beautiful city, it was easy to forget that their business was serious, indeed. He could imagine that Joss was just his lover, walking next to him in the slanting afternoon sunshine. She wore a splashy black and white patterned halter dress, her hair a loose mass of curls, big white hoop earrings dangling at her ears. Her spike heels were fire-engine red.

It had been a long time since a woman had captured his imagination so fully. Since Stephanie. Since his biggest mistake.

Bax stopped and drew Joss down to sit. "We need to talk," he said abruptly.

"Shouldn't we be getting inside?" she asked.

"Sure, but not together."

She frowned. "Why not? They'll find out we're a pair eventually. It's part of our cover."

"I want to get the lay of the land first. Information is power. If they know everything up front, we lose any advantage we have." And in a situation like this, they needed every advantage they could get.

"So how do you want to do it?"

Alone, was his first thought. Alone, he'd be efficient. Alone, he'd be free to do the most practical thing without worrying about her safety. Alone, he wouldn't have to worry about his own. "I'll go in first, just to check it out. I'll ring you on your cell phone when it's clear to come in." It was against his better judgment. Why in God's name had he agreed to this ridiculous situation?

Then he looked at the dapple of sun and shade on her bare shoulders and he knew why.

"So you'll stay back and I'll hook up with Silverhielm."

"Be casual. Don't tell him everything all at once. You've got time. Remember, you're the one who has something he wants, so ultimately you're in control."

"Have some faith, will you? I've stalked music promoters for years. I know how to meet someone accidentally on purpose. Don't worry, I'll find a way to start a conversation with him. Why do you think I wore this dress?" She glanced down at the swells of her cleavage.

To drive him nuts, Bax thought, remembering the feel of her naked body against his.

"I figure Jerry would be dating someone a little cheap, a little flashy," Joss continued, oblivious. "It fits with the profile."

"It fits a few other things, as well," he observed dryly.

Joss flashed him a quick grin. "Thank you. It'll get Silverhielm's attention, I think. And if it helps distract him a little while I'm talking with him, so much the better."

Bax couldn't say about Silverhielm, but seeing the way the dress molded itself around her body distracted him, and at a time he could ill afford it. "I'm sure it'll do the job."

"Thank you." She gave him an amused look, reminding him that not much got past her. "So once I get talking with him, how far do I go? Do I mention Jerry and the Blue Mauritius?"

"Play it by ear. Remember, we just want to catch his attention at this point. Keep him a little off balance. That gives us the advantage."

"Okay." Joss took a deep breath.

"You sure you're up to this?"

She blew the breath out. "Of course I am. So we meet at the hotel afterward?"

Bax nodded. Without thinking about it, he reached out to take her hand. "One important thing to remember. Don't trust Silverhielm and don't, under any circumstances, leave with him. No matter how good an opportunity it seems, we can't afford the risk."

"Even if he offers me a ride in his way cool limo?" Joss said, widening her eyes.

"Especially then."

"Relax." She gave a quick grin. "I get my adrenaline rushes other ways than hanging out with murderers."

Bax knew it wasn't smart, but he couldn't resist leaning in to kiss her, just for a moment. He wouldn't think about what a familiar pleasure the taste of her was becoming. For a few moments, he just let himself savor her mouth, warm and mobile against his. Finally, he straightened. She would be okay, he told himself. And so would he. "I'll beep your mobile when the coast is clear." He rose. "Be good."

Joss gave him a reckless smile of promise. "I'll be great."

7

STRINDBERG'S CATERED to the wealthy and it showed in every aspect of the auction house, from the tony address to the rich decor. The furnishings whispered of discreet luxury—thick carpets, softly lustrous silk wall coverings, fresh flowers everywhere. A sweeping marble staircase led to the second floor showroom, with a richly patterned Aubusson runner held in place at each step with brass rails. The carpet was worn slightly in the center from the footsteps of decades worth of Scandinavia's affluent collectors.

In the showroom on this particular evening, the sleekly designed mounting pedestals displayed a selection of rare stamps and coins from around the world. The Strindberg management had probably planned the event to coincide with the stamp expo, but it was the type of auction that dealers would fly in to attend—at least the kind of dealers who, like Gwen and her grandfather, bought issues for millionaire clients.

Joss wandered around the room, holding a martini and inspecting the lots to be auctioned off the following evening. A glance at the auction catalog showed her that there were no stamps of the caliber of the Post Office Mauritius set going on the block, but a number of them were valued in the mid- to high-hundreds of thousands of dollars. The auction would make a tidy profit for Strindberg's, no doubt, not to mention the owners of the objects.

She did another circuit of the room, glancing around casually for Bax. He stood near an alcove by some plants, holding himself in a way that rendered him innocuous and unmemorable, though he was neither. It made her feel better to see him there, to know that he was around if she needed him.

In the center of the room, a small knot of people chattered animatedly around a Lucite display case. In an art museum, it might contain a sculpture; here, it held the two most valuable lots in the auction.

And in front of it stood Karl Silverhielm.

Up close, his eyes were a pale gray, the same shade as his hair. He wore another elegant suit, this one the color of steel. His tie was a pattern of small, interlocking black and cobalt diamonds, tied in a Windsor knot. A matching blue display handkerchief showed in his breast pocket.

The force of his personality came across even more strongly at this distance than it had from across the street. This time, though, the sense of menace was banked back. He looked refined, courteous, even affable.

She mistrusted him immediately.

Unobtrusively, Joss made her way to the central display case as the couple talking with Silverhielm wandered away. She stared at the stamps, throwing all of her concentration into what she could see with her peripheral vision. He glanced over at her, looked away and then turned her way.

Score one for the dress.

"Can I answer any questions for you about these issues? I'm the current owner." His voice was deep and expansive, filled with confidence.

Joss favored him with a smile. "Josie Astin." She gave him the alias she'd agreed to with Bax.

"Karl Silverhielm." He spoke English with a faint hint

of an accent. When she held out her hand to shake, he raised it smoothly to his lips. "You don't look like the typical philatelist. To what do we owe the pleasure, Ms. Astin?"

"Oh, I've heard people invest millions of dollars in these stamps. I figured I'd come see some of them myself."

"And what do you think, now that you're here?"

She shrugged and took a drink of her martini. "They look just like anything you can buy in the post office, only older."

"Well, that's where the value comes in. When you own a stamp that's over a hundred years old, you buy a slice of history. That's power, in its own way."

"And you want to buy power?"

"I don't need to."

She opened up her catalog and looked up the stamps in it. "But these are yours. If stamps are power, then why are you selling them?" Across the room, Bax moved to another spot by the wall, seemingly staring at the exhibits though she knew he was watching her.

"A collection changes all the time. You update it, consolidate, the same way a smart man consolidates financial holdings."

Joss considered him. "Are you a smart man?"

"I'll let my deeds speak for themselves."

"And what do you do?"

"I broker goods. Import/export."

"What do you import?"

"Whatever sells." He looked over her shoulder. "Hello, Markus."

Joss hadn't seen the tall, blond man materialize at her elbow and she started just a little.

"I apologize if I startled you." His English was entirely without accent. He had the high cheekbones and the sharp jaw line of the classically Nordic face.

Silverhielm nodded at him. "Ms. Astin, meet my associate, Markus Holm."

Joss found herself staring into a pair of entirely emotionless blue eyes. He looked at her the same way he probably looked at the potted plant behind her, and she had a feeling he'd cut her down with no more emotion.

Unnerved, Joss glanced down at the hand that clasped hers.

And saw a thin, uneven white line running between the thumb and forefinger.

A stir of excitement went through her. If Markus was the intermediary that Stewart had dealt with, that meant that Silverhielm was her man. Joss blinked and gave Markus her most brilliant smile.

"So very nice to meet you."

"The pleasure is mine," he said and released her hand.

"So what do you do for Karl?"

"I assist him with his various projects." Markus smiled so faintly she couldn't be sure she'd seen it.

"He is indispensable to me," Silverhielm assured her. "Excuse me a moment." Markus leaned close to him to murmur something in his ear. Silverhielm shook his head. "Take care of it," he told him. "I'll let you know when I'm ready." Markus nodded and left and Silverhielm turned his attention back to Joss. "So where are you from, Ms. Astin? You do not look like the usual collector."

"I'm from Las Vegas." Was it her imagination, or did he come to attention when she said it? "My boyfriend— actually, my ex-boyfriend—has acquired a few stamps. I was in town and thought I'd come here and see if I could make any contacts that would help me unload them." She drifted toward the floor-to-ceiling windows that overlooked Berzelii Park and Silverhielm drifted with her.

"Alas, I am not in the market for stamps at present. In

fact, as we were just discussing, I am reducing the size of my collection."

"Really? Does that mean you've just made a nice acquisition?" She stopped to study another exhibit.

He gave her a bland look. "I buy and sell stamps all the time, Ms. Astin. A collection that does not change becomes stagnant and loses its luster."

"Perhaps you should get something new. I was just at the Postal Museum earlier today and saw the Post Office Mauritius pair. The most valuable stamps in the world, or so they say." She reached the windows.

"Many collectors prize the Post Office Mauritius set," he agreed, looking at her carefully.

"So I hear. I understand you've been in the market for a Post Office Mauritius pair for some time."

That got his attention. "And who do you understand this from?"

"I also understand that you've managed to accomplish half of that goal," she continued softly, ignoring his question.

Had she thought that he was affable? The stare that he aimed at her was nearly toxic in its intensity. This was a man who'd killed more than once, she reminded herself. The hairs on the back of her neck prickled up one by one.

"I do not understand you, Ms. Astin." Silverhielm's voice remained calm but now icy cold, the control almost more alarming than anger would have been. She looked for Bax in her peripheral vision.

Brazen it out, she told herself. "Transactions don't always go as anticipated, Karl," she said, gesturing carelessly with her nearly empty glass. "I should know. My ex-boyfriend, Jerry, is an…associate of Stewart Oakes." She finished off her martini and turned toward the bar.

He caught her wrist in an iron grip. "You will explain yourself."

She refused to wince. Instead, Joss aimed an icy look at Silverhielm. "You will let me loose and I will go get a drink," she enunciated. "After that, I may choose to continue this conversation or I may not." She saw Bax come to attention and shook her head infinitesimally at him.

"No." Silverhielm signaled Markus, who appeared at her elbow. "Another martini for Ms. Astin."

"Ketel One, with two olives," Joss told Markus. She trembled down inside but her hand remained steady as she pulled the skewered olive from the remains of her current glass.

"So, Ms. Astin." Silverhielm stared at her as Markus walked away. "Pray continue."

Joss looked right back at him, refusing to be intimidated. Then she turned to look out at the moonlit cobblestones of Berzelii Park. "I can make it very simple," she said calmly. "I have something you want. You have something I want. We ought to be able to come to an agreement."

"What do I have that you want, Ms. Astin?"

She raised her martini glass. "Money," she said and took the final swallow.

SILVERHIELM ESCORTED her down the marble stairs that led to the front door of the auction house, Markus trailing behind them.

"I am sorry that the other potential bidders interrupted our very interesting conversation, Ms. Astin," Silverhielm said. "There is a very fine bar nearby. We can go for a drink and talk further."

"I must be getting back to my hotel." She slipped the strap of her small black evening bag over her wrist.

Silverhielm suppressed a flare of irritation. He was a man used to being obeyed. "Where are you staying?" he persisted. "Perhaps I could offer you a ride home." He opened the door and gestured for her to pass through.

"That won't be necessary. I can get a cab, thanks."

"Oh no, I insist." He waved and his gleaming black car pulled smoothly up to the curb.

"Thank you, but no." She turned to shake hands. "I will be in Stockholm for several more days. I am sure we'll have an opportunity to talk." She smiled and turned to head across the square toward the lights of the boulevard and a taxi.

A wave of fury washed through Silverhielm. People did not treat him this way. People did as he told them. He watched her go and Markus stepped up beside him. "A lone woman playing a dangerous game," Silverhielm said softly. "She has the Blue Mauritius, she hints."

Markus looked at Silverhielm impassively. "Is she here to deliver?"

"For a fee." The gleaming black car idled gently in front of them. "I refuse to pay twice for something I should already possess." His voice hardened, the polished sophisticate erased by the ruthless thug. "You will take care of it."

8

BAX STOOD INSIDE the doorway to Strindberg's and watched Silverhielm's soldier close the door to the sleek black limo, shutting Silverhielm inside. Then the car pulled away, leaving the blond man at the curb. For a moment, he just stared after Joss. Then he tucked his hands into his pockets and set off through the gloaming, across Berzelii Park.

After Joss.

Bax stepped swiftly out the door. She'd stood her ground with Silverhielm and refused to get in the car, he reminded himself as he followed them, suppressing a little twist of concern. If she was taking a risk now by crossing the park alone in the evening, at least there were people around. Anyway, it was only until she'd reached the broad boulevard where she could get a taxi to the hotel.

He quickened his pace a bit to get closer to Silverhielm's man. Once she got into a cab, her tail would be stymied, unless he wanted to try a "follow that cab" routine. Bax had a pretty good feeling that the guy was a little too smart for that one.

And then he cursed. It looked like Joss was going to save the guy the trouble. She didn't even bother to stop on the corner but just made the turn down the street that led toward Gamla Stan and the Royal Viking.

It was why he didn't like working with a partner, Bax

thought in irritation. When he worked alone, he didn't have to worry about someone deviating from plan, he didn't have to worry about them taking foolish chances and putting the whole operation at risk. Even on a busy street, especially on a busy street, a professional would have no problem pulling someone like Joss aside and threatening her until she told him what was really going on. She didn't have the skills to fight off a professional thug or to withstand an interrogation, even a short one.

And Bax couldn't stand the risk.

He worked his way closer to Silverhielm's man. It wasn't easy to follow someone solo, but Bax was operating at an advantage this particular night. The Swede appeared convinced that Joss was alone and wasn't worried about being shadowed himself. He seemed to be focused entirely on her.

Bax was good enough at reading lips and body language to be pretty confident that Joss had brought up the stamps to Silverhielm, who hadn't been happy about it. It was a good guess that Silverhielm had put his guy onto her when they chatted outside of Strindberg's.

The question was what were his orders? Was he following her to see where she went, following her to get her alone somewhere and scare information out of her, following her with an intent to do harm? Bax had been trained over his years on the job to suppress any emotion while he concentrated on the task at hand. Somehow, it was more difficult this time around. He couldn't quite get rid of his concern for Joss.

He cursed again. It was what he got for working with an amateur.

Instinct warned him to drop back further on the tail so that the Swede wouldn't make him, but he didn't dare. He couldn't take a chance of being too far away to react if Silverhielm's man made a move.

Joss crossed the boulevard and the Swede followed as the light turned yellow. Bax broke into a slow jog but the light had already gone red and a steady stream of cross traffic was whizzing by when he hit the corner. A bus stopped in front of him to let off passengers.

Bax moved impatiently through the bus riders, skirting the front bumper of the bus when the light changed and sprinting across the crosswalk.

Joss and the Swede were nowhere in sight.

His pulse began hammering in alarm. The boulevard he was on led straight to the waterfront and the street of the Royal Viking. It was the quickest way to get there. There was nowhere else they'd logically be. Unless the Swede had pulled Joss aside and was now interrogating her.

Or worse.

Keep the feelings out of it, Bax reminded himself. When you felt too much, you started acting on emotion and not reason. There was no place for the Swede to pull Joss aside on the brightly lit main boulevard. He slowed his steps and looked around before leaving the corner. Half a block away, he saw the opening to a narrower street that paralleled the boulevard to the waterfront.

Bingo.

He knew the street, a narrow lane of exclusive shops that would be thinly populated at this time of night. He jogged over to it, wishing that he had a weapon on him besides his hands, his feet and his wits. Holding his breath, he stepped around the corner.

And saw Joss a block and a half away, ambling slowly past the storefronts, glancing at the window displays. Well away from her, the Swede hung in the shadows of a doorway on the other side of the street for several seconds before following.

Bax let out a breath he hadn't been conscious of holding. When Joss made the turn onto the waterfront, Bax watched the Swede stay back and follow her in his turn. Finally, Bax himself reached the end of the street to observe Silverhielm's man watch Joss walk into the hotel.

She was safe. For a split second, it was all he could think.

The Swede wandered over to the waterfront to stand by the ferries, looking back at the hotel facade. He lit a cigarette and stood for a few more minutes, watching. Finally, he walked briskly away.

Bax strode hurriedly from his shadowed corner to the hotel, his concern morphing into irritation, an irritation that intensified moment by moment as he made his way up to the room.

"It's him." Joss jumped off the couch to meet him as he walked through the door.

Bax glowered at her. "Which 'him,'? The one you talked with at the reception or the one who just followed you home?"

"Oh, did he follow me?" she asked happily, ignoring him. "I was hoping he would but I couldn't quite see him in the shop windows."

"What?"

"Well how else are they going to know where to find me?" she asked reasonably. "I didn't just skip the cab for the heck of it, you know."

"Are you out of your mind?" he demanded.

"To walk half a mile in these shoes? I'd have to be," she told him as she sank down on the couch and pulled off her stilettos with an expression of bliss.

"Joss, it's not a goddamn game," he snapped.

Her effervescence evaporated, making him feel like a bully. He was only trying to get her to understand the risks she was taking, he told himself, fighting off the guilt.

"Bax, I didn't just do it to be foolish. I did it because I thought it was important. He's Silverhielm's guy and Silverhielm's our man."

"You think."

She raised her chin. "I know. I saw the scar on the hand of the blond guy. His name is—"

"Markus Holm," Bax said flatly.

Joss blinked. "Yes. How did you know?"

"I know him. We ran into each other during an undercover assignment I did for Interpol in Amsterdam."

"He's Interpol?" she asked incredulously.

"No, he's a genuinely bad guy. I was Interpol, posing as the shooter for a Dutch heavy while I looked into Markus's boss."

"Silverhielm?"

"Someone else. Markus is an equal opportunity employee," he said sardonically. "If the fee's right, so is the job."

Joss gave a little shiver. "He kind of gave me the creeps."

"He should." Bax stalked over to the minibar to pull out a scotch. "He's dangerous. Stable, which is more than you can say for a lot of people in that line of work, but capable of doing just about anything if he considers it the most expedient means to an end."

"I could see it in his eyes. It was like he didn't even register me as a human being."

"He's very smart and very, very good at what he does. It ups the stakes considerably." And if it was an advantage to have an enemy whose moves he knew well, Markus would have just as much of an advantage on him.

"So what's our play now?"

"Stop taking foolish chances, for one. Go slow, for another. Having Markus involved changes things. The longer we can go without him knowing I'm involved, the better."

"Did Markus know you were with Interpol?"

Bax shook his head. "I was pulled from the assignment long before they took action. As far as he knows I'm a Danish-American shooter named Johan Bruhn, just another freelancer like him. Brothers in arms." He smiled faintly.

Joss shivered a little. "You and he are worlds apart."

"Not so far as you'd think. I got to know him well during the time I was on assignment. He has a code of honor of a sort, it's just not the kind that you or I recognize."

She frowned. "You sound like you like him."

"I don't know that like is the right word, though he can be intelligent company. Respect, maybe. By our lights, he's totally amoral, but he seems to have a set of standards that he lives by. And I saved his life once."

Joss raised her eyebrows in disbelief. "Now this I have to hear."

"In a minute. First, I want to go get some ice." He took the bucket and a key and went out the door.

JOSS LAY BACK on the bed and stared at the ceiling, trying to imagine Bax working with Markus, saving his life. It seemed incomprehensible. Then again, she didn't know Bax very well. She had to remember that.

The phone rang. Joss reached out to grab it from the bedside table. "Hello?"

"Ms. Astin." Unaccented English. Markus.

She sat up, the hair on the back of her neck prickling. "Yes."

"It is Markus Holm."

Attitude, she reminded herself and took a deep breath. "Well, when I said I hoped to hear from you soon, I had no idea it would be this soon."

"Your discussion with Mr. Silverhielm generated many

questions. More questions than answers. Of course we need more information, much more information, before proceeding."

Hook, line and sinker, she thought. "What did you have in mind?"

"We should meet with you to continue the discussion. Tomorrow morning, perhaps?"

"I'd have to think about it." She looked at the door, waiting for Bax to return. How far did a person have to go in this hotel for ice, anyway?

"What is there to think about? It is just a discussion. Mr. Silverhielm wishes to know more about your proposal. If you are interested in progress, we must talk."

"I guess, but…"

"So a meeting is good, yes? It is a simple thing to do."

In concept, delaying was a good strategy, but somehow it wasn't working. "All right."

"Good. Look out your window."

She felt a little twinge of consternation. She wasn't surprised that he knew her hotel, but her room location? The hairs on the back of her neck prickled as she picked up the phone and carried it with her to the glass.

"There is a small park ahead of you, just off the water. It is called Karl XII's *torg,* in front of the Kungsträdgarden, the King's Garden."

Cobblestone walks separated tidy flowerbeds in the moonlight. "I see it."

"Meet me there tomorrow morning at seven."

"Why so early?"

"Mr. Silverhielm does not care for enigmas. He wishes more information as soon as possible."

The words sounded vaguely ominous. At first she was alarmed, and then it just got her back up. "Then perhaps he should show up for the meeting instead of you."

"Mr. Silverhielm will attend when it is time. For now, you and I can discuss what needs to be discussed. It is enough. Until tomorrow morning, Ms. Astin."

"Okay."

At first, she was merely irritated at being outmaneuvered. Quickly, though, excitement began to bubble up. It was progress, real progress. She wasn't sure where it would take them, but going forward beat standing still.

Behind her, the door opened and Bax walked in.

"How good am I," Joss crowed. "See, my little walk home paid off. I just got a phone call from your friend Markus."

Bax set down the ice and stared at her. "And what did my friend Markus have to say?"

"They want more information. I'm meeting him tomorrow morning." She began to speculate, thinking aloud. "We'll have to work out what I should say. Do you want to be there? I wonder if—"

"What are you, nuts?" Bax's brows drew together. "Meeting with Markus? Haven't you heard a word I've said?"

"Of course I have. He wanted an answer. They want more information. What was I supposed to do?"

"Stall." He bit the word off.

"I tried to. He wouldn't fall for it."

"You didn't push hard enough. He would have caved eventually. You've got what they want, or at least they think you might. They'd do whatever was necessary to find out more. And we'd tell them more, on *our* timeline." He paced across the room. "Joss, listen to me, you can't run around doing whatever you feel like whenever you feel like it. You hired me to do a job. Stand back and let me do it."

"I'm trying," she flared. "Look, I was supposed to drop the bait tonight. I did just what we'd agreed."

"And then turned around and went totally off plan."

"Off plan? We hadn't worked out a plan yet. I was winging it."

"You don't know enough to wing it."

"Thanks very much." She rose and paced across to him. "What would you have liked me to have done?"

"Make him wait. Give me some time to check with my contacts on what Markus has done lately." He dumped his scotch into a glass and added some ice.

"Stall, wait, that's all you want to do. I thought this was about getting the stamp back, not collecting a nice per diem in a cushy hotel."

"Trust me," he said through gritted teeth, "right now I'd be thrilled to have that stamp in my hand so that I could end this case before I wring your neck."

"Oh, nice, Baxter."

"You didn't hire me to be nice. Now, you are not going to that meeting tomorrow. We don't know enough yet. It's an unacceptable risk."

"It's an unacceptable risk not to show."

"Cancel."

"I don't know how to reach him."

"You didn't even get a number?" he asked incredulously.

"You think the bad guys give out their cell numbers?" she retorted.

"Okay, so you just don't show. Leave them wondering. They'll call."

"Will they? What if they think it's all a fabrication?"

"They can't afford to. Look, you're not going tomorrow and that is final."

Mutinously, she rose. "I'm going to take a bath," she muttered and walked into the bathroom. If he thought he was going to push her around and make all the decisions, Mr. John Baxter, P.I. was going to have another think coming.

9

MORNING SUNLIGHT slanted across the bathroom floor as Joss stepped out of the shower. She yawned, drying herself with a blissfully warm towel hot off the rack. Bax might have effortlessly transitioned to Stockholm time, but she hadn't found it so easy. Let him have his early morning ritual of going downstairs for coffee. She'd stay in bed until she was good and ready.

Except for this morning. This morning, she had a different plan.

She dressed quickly, throwing on a scarlet studio jacket over jeans to ward off the morning chill. Then she slipped out the door and looked for the emergency exit. It would bring her to a back stairwell, she figured. Once she'd exited the hotel unobtrusively, she could work her way around to the waterfront and from there to the park.

The fire stairway dumped her out on the lane that she'd come down the night before. Hurriedly, she backtracked toward the boulevard and cut across the back of the hotel before heading to the waterfront and on to Karl XII's *torg*.

Bax might be furious with her for sneaking out, but he had only himself to blame. He'd refused to discuss the matter further the night before, seeming to think that his veto was enough. Well, it wasn't. He was wrong, wanting to skip the meeting. They couldn't take a chance on losing contact with Silverhielm and they couldn't lose another day, not with her grandfather's stamp at risk. Markus was expecting to see her. She had to be there.

Karl XII's *torg* was a smallish formal garden right on the waterfront. Tree, shrub and flower, everything was exactly in its place. Decorative black metal railings edged the tidy beds of plantings. Painted wooden benches dotted the flagstone walks. In the little café next door, a ragged queue of Stockholmers lined up for coffee. The occasional cyclist whizzed down the bike lane on the opposite side, but at this hour on a weekday, the park itself was nearly empty.

Joss glanced around the park, looking for Markus. He materialized behind her shoulder.

"Good morning, Ms. Astin."

Silent as a cat, she thought, trying not to jump. In the warm morning sun, he looked icily Nordic as ever, with his pale hair and pitiless eyes. Bax's voice echoed in her head. *He's a genuinely bad guy.*

Well, maybe he was, but it was broad daylight in a public park and she refused to be intimidated. As far as he and Silverhielm were concerned, she had what they wanted. She had the upper hand, that was the important thing to remember.

"Good morning." Figuring that shaking hands was bad form, Joss moved, toward a bench.

"Perhaps we should walk, instead," Markus suggested.

"Certainly." They began to stroll slowly down one of the pathways toward the water where the white tour boats bobbled, waiting for their first customers.

"You made some surprising allegations to my employer, last night," he said without preamble.

"Not at all."

"Karl Silverhielm may have made inquiries about a Post Office Mauritius pair in the past, but so have many collectors in similarly fortunate positions. There is, after all, no crime in inquiries. Or in legitimate purchases, for that matter."

Joss admired a row of nodding pink blossoms. "True enough. It's theft that the authorities frown on."

"Certainly, if any transpired," he said blandly. "Mr. Silverhielm would of course find such activities reprehensible."

"Of course."

"But you accused him of such last night."

Joss shot him a quick look. "I find it interesting that that was his interpretation. I merely told him I'd heard from a reputable source that he'd obtained one half of a Post Office Mauritius pair, and attempted to gauge his interest in obtaining the other half. Hypothetically," she added.

"Of course. I believe the subject of money came up, as well."

"I'm a businesswoman, Mr. Holm."

"Call me Markus, please."

"It's a simple business proposition, Markus. I've found something of value that I have reason to think Mr. Silverhielm prizes highly. It seems reasonable to think that he would be willing to negotiate appropriate compensation for my trouble."

"My employer is a thrifty man," he told her. "He does not see why he should pay again for an object that should already be his."

"I wouldn't call it paying again," Joss said.

"What would you call it?"

"A delivery fee."

"Nonetheless, all fees and commissions have already been paid to Mr. Oakes. You are acting on behalf of Mr. Oakes and your boyfriend, I assume."

"Ex-boyfriend," she corrected him. "Actually, neither.

I'm acting on my own behalf. And Mr. Silverhielm's. I could just hand it over to the authorities. That's probably what I should do," she said thoughtfully and stopped to look at him. "Unless you have an alternate proposal."

"I believe I do, Ms. Astin," he said, unbuttoning his coat.

"Josie, please."

He smiled thinly. "Josie." He moved his arm a bit and his coat fell open enough for her to see the gleam of steel from the gun holster at his side. In a flash, it was in his hand and against her side. "Perhaps, we should go back into the hotel."

He caught at her wrist and pain shot up her arm. She tried to twist away, but it only hurt worse. Adrenaline vaulted through her. Stay calm, she reminded herself. He had nothing to gain by killing her and he wouldn't do it in public. It was all a game.

Joss took a breath through her nose, trying to ignore the pain. "If you're thinking that I'm foolish enough to have the Blue Mauritius in my room, you are going to be disappointed."

"I am sure once we chat in private, you will happily tell me where it is."

"It's a little early for threats, isn't it, Markus?" She stopped.

He twisted her wrist a bit and pressed the gun more firmly into her side. "It is not a threat, it is a promise. Now, you will begin walking."

"I don't think so," a voice said from behind then, followed by a metallic snick.

Both Joss and Markus froze. Slowly, they turned around.

And saw Bax standing there. He gave a not entirely pleasant grin. "Hello, Markus."

BAX DIDN'T LIKE surprises, not even a little. One minute, he'd been sitting in the front window of the Royal Viking's café area wondering how it was that European coffee tasted so amazing, the next he'd caught a glimpse of Joss's red jacket out of the corner of his eye. He'd watched as she slipped out of the side street and hurried along the waterfront, headed toward the park.

In an instant, he'd tossed down a few bills and headed out without a backward glance, even as he was overwhelmed with anger. For surely it was anger that crouched hard and cold in the pit of his stomach, not fear. How could she be so foolish as to put herself at risk yet again? After what he'd told her the night before, he couldn't believe that she'd been obtuse enough to barge out and meet Markus.

Then again, he thought grimly now as he took one hell of a chance and pulled a gun on Markus in the open to save Joss's stubborn neck, maybe he could.

Markus stared calmly back at him. "Ah, Johan, you know how much I hate surprises."

"It shouldn't be a surprise at all. I'm predictable. You threaten one of my people, I'll take steps."

"I didn't know she was one of yours," Markus said, slipping his gun back into the holster.

"Now you do," Bax told him curtly, easing off the hammer of his own gun and stowing it out of sight.

Markus looked him up and down. "You are no longer with van den Berg?"

"On to new things. You're no longer with Stuyvvens?"

Markus shrugged. "You know how it goes. A smart man follows the market."

"I do indeed." Bax stepped closer to Joss.

Markus studied the two of them together. "So you are working out of the U.S. now?"

"When the right opportunity comes up. Right now, it appears I'm working out of Stockholm."

"That makes us a pair yet again." Faint crinkles of humor appeared by Markus's eyes. "I have an employer who could use a man with your talents."

"I'm surprised at you, Markus, recruiting me in front of my current employer."

"I see your current position as temporary. My employer would have steady work for you."

Bax shrugged a little. "So let's resolve our current matter and after that we'll talk."

"So we will."

"Now, what were you discussing with my client before you tried to strong arm her into the hotel?"

Markus buttoned his jacket again. "That is an unfriendly way to put it."

"Pulling guns on people is an unfriendly business."

"She is asking my employer to pay again for a product he has already paid for."

"That's one way to think about it. Another is that it is a finder's fee for Josie, who did not turn in the stamp and has instead brought it to Silverhielm. He could easily pay her and still get his goods for a bargain price."

"But my employer is a proud man."

"Pride is a luxury."

"Ah, and Mr. Silverhielm is a man accustomed to luxury."

"Then he must also be accustomed to paying for it."

"Perhaps you are right."

And in that moment, Bax knew they would get what they sought. "So let us be clear what we're talking about. It'll save time."

"Ah, Johan. Always impatient. It is reassuring to know you haven't changed. So what's on your mind?"

"Some rules, first."

"Such as?"

"No more private meetings with my client. You want to talk with her, I'm present. Always." Even if he couldn't get it through Joss's thick skull, he might be able to get it through Markus's.

Markus inclined his head. "Of course. And?"

"A discussion with your boss, the four of us. We don't negotiate with you, we negotiate with him. No offense."

"None taken, but Mr. Silverhielm is a very busy man."

"I'm sure we can find a client who's not so busy." Bax began to turn away. "Excuse us—"

"Johan, please rein in that impatience for a moment."

"Yes."

"Allow me to consult with my employer."

Bax's teeth gleamed. "I thought you might."

"I will find out what will suit him."

"Soon, Markus."

"Always, with you. Very well, then. You will hear from us." He nodded sharply and walked away.

JOSS WATCHED Markus climb into the passenger seat of a polished gray sedan. In seconds, the car had disappeared into the flow of traffic into Gamla Stan and she was left trying to absorb the surreal—she'd just had a gun pulled on her in broad daylight. Trembling started in the long muscles of her thighs.

Bax turned to her with a face like thunder. "What the hell were you thinking?" he snapped. "You could have gotten yourself killed." Then his eyes narrowed and he took her arm.

She pulled away from him. "Don't grab me."

"Sit," he ordered, "now. You look like you're going to keel over."

She stood, face mutinous. "I'm fine."

"You almost weren't."

"He wouldn't have hurt me," she retorted with more confidence than she felt.

"He had a gun on you, Joss." He took a few steps away and swung back to her.

"He was trying to scare me."

"And you're a fool if he didn't succeed. He doesn't mess around."

"He wouldn't have done anything here in public," she insisted, clinging to it. "Too many people could have seen him."

Bax gave her an incredulous look. "You have no idea who you're dealing with. I once saw him shoot a man in a crowd of people and just walk away."

Her jaw dropped and she closed it with a snap. "I don't believe you." But in her gut, she knew it was true.

"Joss, accept it," Bax said wearily. "You're out of your league trying to deal with him. You don't know what he's capable of. I do."

"But you said you saved his life. How could you save the life of a killer?"

"Because it wasn't my place to say he should die."

"That sounds like a line from a bad TV show."

"It's anything but TV, which you have got to realize if you're going to go any further with this. And you have got to start listening to me or this little game is over," he said, coldly furious. "I thought we'd agreed that you weren't coming out here."

And now they were getting to the heart of it all. "We never agreed to anything. You just gave the orders and assumed I'd go along. Well, it doesn't work that way, Bax." She stood nose to nose with him, glaring. "This isn't about just you. I'm a part of this too, remember? We're a team."

"Then act like it. You can't just go off and do things on your own without telling me."

"And you can't just arbitrarily run the show and order me around," she retorted.

"You hired me because of what I know."

"I hired you to help, not to wade in and be John Wayne. I told you from the beginning I was going to work on this project, too." Her voice rose.

"This isn't a game, Joss. You're not some character in a novel."

"I know that, but I've got to be a part of this."

"Why?" he demanded in frustration.

"Because it was my fault," she burst out.

On the bridge leading to Gamla Stan, horns rang out. Bax stood staring at her.

Joss swallowed. "The one-penny Mauritius isn't just a valuable stamp, it's a big part of my grandfather's retirement. And it was my screwup that let it get stolen." She turned and sank down on the bench behind her, putting her face in her hands. Bax sat beside her.

"You had a lot of very driven people after those stamps. One way or another, they were going to get them."

"It doesn't matter. Reality was, I was the one who made it easy for them."

"And how, exactly, was that? Did you hand them over?"

"No."

"Did you insist the stamps be kept in the safe instead of a bank vault where they belonged?"

"No, but I just as good as handed Jerry the key. He'd come to work for us because I didn't want to work alone. He and I were the only ones in the store when he stole them. Gwen was out of town—she'd given me the key and combination to the safe. I locked them in the desk and went out for lunch." Joss turned to look out at the water. "That was all it took."

Let her deal with it, Bax told himself, but he found himself reaching out to rub his hand comfortingly over her back. "If he was a pro, he'd have found a way."

Joss turned back to him. "He didn't have to because I made it easy for him. That's why I've got to be a part of this."

Her face was pinched and pale with misery. It was the face of the hurt kid, again, looking back at him, and all he wanted to do was fix things. "We'll get it back," he said helplessly, knowing there couldn't be any other outcome.

"It has to be we, Bax. It can't be just you. Gwen already did more than her part. Now I have to do mine. I need to know that I was a part of it."

"You will be," he assured her with a sinking heart and folded her against him. "We'll do it together."

10

CLOUDS DRIFTED IN as they sat in the *torg,* watching the tour boats come and go from the dock.

"So how are you doing now?" Bax asked and kissed the top of her head. "You okay?"

"What, with the gun thing?" Joss stirred and grinned at him. "I'm tougher than you think, Bax. I've played some truly scary dives, slept on the street, even gotten mugged once. There's not a whole lot that gets to me."

At their feet, a pigeon trundled along, searching for crumbs on the pavement.

"So what's with the whole music thing? You mentioned it last night, too."

"My brilliant career, or at least that was the plan." It was increasingly embarrassing to talk about, increasingly discouraging to realize that she'd devoted seven years of her life to music with almost no success. How clueless did that make her?

And where did it leave her now?

"So what were you, a singer? A musician? Both?"

"A singer. Or maybe just wanted to be. I was going to be the next big thing, a huge star." She sat up and leaned forward, elbows on her knees. "It didn't quite work out that way."

"Band broke up?"

"Bands," she corrected. "I've played with one group or another all over the Pacific Northwest."

"How long?"

"Seven years." Her smile held no humor. "I'm a slow study sometimes." How she'd loved performing, the feeling when everything clicked, the band in a groove, the audience feeding into it. It had been because of those magical nights that she'd had such a hard time finally giving it up. "I just really loved doing it," she said wistfully.

"Then why quit?"

"Because sooner or later you've got to admit that it's not going to work, you know?"

"Couldn't you work a day job and still perform nights?"

She reached down to pick a small stone up off the cobbles, rolling it between her hands. "I suppose. The problem is the day job. I don't really know how to do anything."

"College?"

"A year. I dropped out of the drama program to go on the road with the first band. We were going to do a spring and summer tour of small clubs. I never went back. Used to do street theatre for food money."

"Street theatre?"

"Merlinda the Magnificent." She held up the stone between her thumb and forefinger and passed her other hand across it. "Voila!" The stone was gone.

"Nice."

"Oh, I was a big hit on the pedestrian mall circuit. I probably made more money at that than singing."

"So what comes next?"

It was the question that kept scaring the hell out of her. "TBD. The last band went kaput the week before I came back to San Francisco and went to work for my grandfather's store. It was supposed to be a temporary gig while I got my act together, only I managed to screw everything up."

"We're going to fix that."

"And then all I have to do is decide what to do with my life," she said wryly.

"Sooner or later, we all do."

Joss tossed her hair back and rose, catching his hand in hers. It wasn't in her nature to be gloomy for long. "This is not a crisis. I'll work it out. Sorry to bend your ear."

"You weren't bending my ear. It was educational."

"Educational?"

"Joss Chastain 101."

"You've been doing very well in the course so far." They began walking toward the waterfront.

"Thanks. I've been studying."

"That's good. There's a practicum coming up, you know." She leaned in for a quick, teasing kiss. "It might be very involved," she murmured against his lips. "Maybe we should go back to the room."

He ran his hands down her back. "Maybe we should." They turned toward the hotel. "Of course, now that I know you're hell-bent on doing risky things no matter my advice, I'm thinking that there's a better course to take."

"A better course than making love until we're both cross-eyed?"

He cleared his throat. "Different, anyway. How about Defense 101?"

She gave him an amused look. "You're going to teach me how to kick ass?"

"That might take a little more time than we've got. What I can do is teach you a few nasty tricks that might help you discourage the bad guys long enough to get away, though. Come on." He picked up the pace. "Let's get to the hotel."

"I like the sound of that," she said.

INSIDE THE Royal Viking, they walked across the elegant lobby and into the elevator. Bax didn't punch the number for their floor, though. He hit the button for the top floor.

"Wait a minute. I thought we were going to the room."

"There's not enough space there to do what I have in mind."

"There's enough space in our room to do what I have in mind." She pressed him against the elevator wall and traced his lips with the tip of her tongue. "In fact, there's enough space here." She felt the stir of his cock against her, and that quickly, all she could feel was need.

The chime sounded and the doors opened on the top floor. Joss hit the button for their floor. "Back down."

Bax put his hand in the door. "Let's do this first."

"Can't it wait?"

"Look, waiting for you to get yourself in trouble is already making me old before my time. Let me at least teach you a few things so I can let you out of my sight."

It gave her a little pulse of pleasure. "Why, Bax, you're worried about me."

"Don't let it go to your head," he muttered, a little flush creeping up the back of his neck as he walked down the hallway ahead of her.

Inside the emergency exit stairwell, they climbed upward the last few flights until they reached the top landing and the door that barred their way.

"You know," Joss said conversationally, "I can't read a lick of Swedish but there is an English translation there that says if you push that crash bar you're going to make an unholy amount of noise and have every security guard in the hotel down on us. Maybe we'd better go back to the room and try it there."

Bax gave her an amused look. "Who said anything

about a crash bar?" he asked as he pressed one palm against the door and pushed it open.

"Well," she said.

"It's one of those security tricks. Makes life easier on the maintenance guys and the warning signs scare off all the amateurs."

"Are you saying I'm an amateur?"

"You've got potential."

"I might surprise you. I might just decide to become an investigator. What would you say to that?"

"I'd be scared."

"Damned right."

The roof was broad and open, covered with some sort of grayish white pebbly tar paper. At intervals stood boxy heating and air-conditioning units and other structures too mysterious for her to identify. Near the edge of the roof, where the hip-high wall met the verdigris-covered facing that surrounded the outside roof, stood the Royal Viking sign. It towered over them in slanting cursive letters. By night, it was outlined in neon; by day, it was black sheet metal, with a line of metal rungs climbing up the slanting sides of the letters, just about where a stepladder would end.

"Their name in lights, huh?" Joss asked, slipping off her jacket and tossing it down at the foot of the *R*.

"Something like that," Bax said.

"Okay, sensei, tell me what to do."

The top she wore was white and stretchy and left absolutely nothing to the imagination. He watched her breasts rise and fall with each breath and shook his head. Business first, pleasure later, he reminded himself.

"I can't teach you martial arts in an afternoon. What I can do is teach you ways to hurt an attacker. You want to think about things like jabbing the eyes, chopping at the throat, hitting the nose with the heel of your hand. Sudden, surprising pain. It makes the eyes water and triggers an involuntary protection response. If someone's behind you, jab them with an elbow, stomp their foot with your heel."

"I stomped the mugger back in Portland," she said helpfully. "He let go of me real quick. I think I broke something in his foot. I don't know, I didn't stay around to find out."

"If you're dealing with someone trained, like Markus, this kind of stuff will only take you so far, but it's good to know."

"What about someone trained like Markus? How do I deal with what happened in the park today?"

"There's only so much you can do about a gun. He had you in a come-along hold, though, and we can talk about that."

"That was something else. Hurt like hell every time I tried to get loose."

"It's supposed to."

She grinned. "So how do you get out of it? I finally just stopped moving."

"That's the first part. You need to relax your arm, above all. A wristlock is designed to make you work against yourself. The more you do, the more you hurt. If you fight it, you can break your wrist." He wrapped his hand around her arm in a light wristlock, feeling the surprisingly fragile bones of her arm under his fingers. He liked her when she was spitting and fighting. He didn't like noticing her fragility. It unnerved him. "So if the bad guy has you in a wristlock, you want to rotate your arm like this and yank your hand against the thumb. The thumb is weaker than the rest of your hand, so you've got a chance to break the grip. Here, try it." At first, he had to shepherd her through the move, but surprisingly quickly she was able to break his grip with a quick motion.

"Looks like I've got it. Do I get a reward?"

"What do you want? I'm all out of chocolate treats."

"I'll settle for something noncaloric," she murmured, leaning in to press a kiss on him.

It was always new, the way she tasted, the way she felt, the way her avid mouth moved under his. He'd been with other women before, but somehow Joss stood out. Somehow, Joss erased all the others, as though there were only her, ever before and ever after.

"So how do you break this hold?" Joss whispered, licking his earlobe.

By keeping the end point in sight. Bax raised his head. "Let's move to the next topic. What if someone's trying to throttle you?"

"This isn't some deep-seated urge of yours, I hope."

"You're safe for now," he said dryly. "So come on, what do you do?"

"Apply pain," she said promptly. "Poke the attacker in the eye or stomp their foot."

"Good idea. The down side is that you might miss or the assailant might be out of range. Breaking loose before applying pain is better. Think, now. You want leverage. Move one of your feet back behind you. That's called Hidden Foot in martial arts. Look, let's do it. I'll put my hands around your neck." The slender column of her throat was soft beneath his fingers. Her pulse beat against his palms. The slanting letters behind them threw shadows over the gray tar paper of the roof. "Okay, now slide your left foot back. See how you pivot a little so your right shoulder comes toward me? If I'm a bad guy and I'm shaking you, I won't notice. Now here's the payoff. Take your right arm around and over my hands, scything, like you're trying to touch your left hip. Do it fast and all in one motion."

She whipped her arm up and over, knocking his hands down and away, taking him by surprise.

"It worked!" she said delightedly.

"It did. You're a fast learner."

"I'm a woman of many talents," she said, giving him a bold gaze.

"The thing to remember is to do it fast and hard."

"I always thought slow and hard was the ticket," she said with an entirely naughty look in her eyes. Her hands strayed to his belt buckle. "Shall I demonstrate?"

"You're a bad influence," he told her and pulled her to him for a long, deep kiss. When he felt her soften, he turned her in his arms to cradle her from behind, kissing her neck until her head fell back against him helplessly. "You should watch out," he murmured in her ear. "Kissing can be dangerous." He slid his arm up around her neck. "Now let's talk about choke holds."

Joss's hands flew up to his arm. "Dirty trick, Baxter."

"There's no one to make your opponents play fair," he reminded her. But she wasn't playing fair, either. Her hair was against his mouth, fragrant and sweet. He glanced down to see the tempting curves of her breasts. Desire tugged at him.

"Any time, sensei," Joss said and he shook it off.

"All right. I've got you in a choke hold." He wrapped his free arm across her taut body.

"It feels like a hold, all right." She slid her right arm down his side and over his butt. "Is this a kinky sex thing?"

"Pay attention," he said, as much to himself as to her. "You might need this some day."

"Kinky sex?" She slid her hand over his thigh and into his crotch. "Or maximum persuasion?" Quick as a snake, her hand surrounded his cock and balls. And she waited.

Bax stood absolutely still. "Careful."

"Mmm. So, what was that you were saying about playing fair?"

"It's bad form to emasculate your instructor," he said in a strained voice.

"Is that what's happening? It feels like something else," she murmured.

Indeed, under the heat of her hand, his cock was beginning to twitch and lengthen. She rubbed her fingers over the denim and the slight friction had him taking a breath. The second time she did it, he stiffened and tried not to think about her touch and what he could do with the woman in his arms. The third time she did it, he gave up.

Bax let his hands slide down over her body, feeling the lush curves of her breasts. It was ironic that he was teaching her self-defense. He was the one who needed defense, because when he got around her, his better sense went out the window and all he could do was want. Focus on the job, he thought, edging his fingertips under the hem of her tank. He managed pretty well most of the time, but when she was unzipping his jeans and sliding his cock into her mouth it just made him dizzy and work was the last thing on his mind. Instead, his world was wet heat and slippery friction that stood his hair on end as he looked down to see himself disappearing into her mouth, looked down to see her beautiful eyes, a glimpse of her breasts, the wonder of this gorgeous, sexy, amazing woman at his feet.

When he feared he was the one who was truly helpless.

He reached a hand out to brace himself on the slanting side of the *R* and touched her head, caressing her hair before stilling her motion. "Wait," he said hoarsely. "I want to be in you." He dragged out his wallet, fishing out the condom he'd tucked there even as Joss eeled out of her jeans and thong.

"A condom? Bax, you must have been a Boy Scout," she purred, taking it from him. She took him in her fist, stroking her hand over him from root to tip until he stiffened. "Well, you're hard enough to put it on, but maybe not slippery enough." Then she knelt on her jeans and slid him into her mouth, alternately licking him and rolling on the latex until he was sweating and grinding his teeth to keep from coming.

Then she stood and leaned back against the side of the *R.* "Now," she whispered, and wrapped one leg around his waist as he pressed against her.

Bax held his cock in one hand, his fingers sliding into her slick folds, rubbing her sweet juices down over himself. He traced the tip of his cock over her clitoris, running across it, down it, circling, over and over.

Joss moaned. Reaching up over her head, she touched the lowest of the steel rungs that climbed up the side of the letter. Her hand gripped the bar, pulling herself up so she could wrap her other leg around Bax's waist. "Put your cock in me. I want to feel it," she panted.

And in one swift push of his hips, he was inside her.

It was better than any buzz he'd ever had, the feel of having her wrapped around him, tight and hot and wet, so wet. Knowing how aroused she was, knowing that he had aroused her intensified the feel of every stroke. He looked down and watched his cock slide in and out of her. He could never get tired of this, seeing it, feeling it, hearing the cries she couldn't keep from making. When the sensory onslaught dragged him toward the edge, he resisted, changing his motion to prolong the experience. He pressed his finger against her mouth and slipped it between her lips, feeling her suck on him. Then he pulled it out and slipped it between her other lips, feeling her clitoris standing out in a hard, slick nub. He stroked it in time with the stroke of his cock, feeling her shudder, hearing her stifled moan.

And when she flushed and began the gulping, gasping cries that he knew heralded her orgasm, he abandoned control, surging against her hard and fast and deep until it launched him into climax with her.

THE TOUR BOAT dock was a stone's throw from the Royal Viking. Joss had watched the low, white, glassed-in boats navigate in and out of the little inlet by the hotel, alternately taking in and disgorging their crowds of passengers. Now, she and Bax stood in line at the kiosk to buy tickets of their own.

"First the museum, now a tour boat?" Joss asked. "This isn't just an excuse for sightseeing with you, is it?"

"Our friend is out in the archipelago, so we ought to get oriented. And you never know what you might learn on a tour like this. It's worth doing," Bax said, picking up the tickets that the counter clerk passed over. "We might learn something."

They wandered over to stand at the gate to the dock. The clouds that had blown in earlier had brought a light drizzle with them that had the happy effect of discouraging sightseers. Instead of the normal crowd, she and Bax stood among a small handful of tourists lined up waiting for the flat, white boat to arrive.

It chugged merrily toward them, churning up a froth of whitewater with its blunt bow. As the boat neared the dock, gradually slowing, a young deckhand appeared on the prow with a line. He gathered himself as the landing neared and leaped across several feet of open water to gain the dock and make the ropes fast.

Even though it was just a quick water tour of Stockholm, Joss couldn't suppress a little charge of excitement.

She ought to be above it, she told herself as they lined up to board. After all, she was in Stockholm for serious business. Hadn't that just been graphically demonstrated to her?

But it was the first time she'd been somewhere foreign, other than Africa, somewhere historic. Surely it was understandable for her to want to enjoy herself just a little bit, wasn't it? After all, they were going on the boat whether she liked it or not. Having fun would be the best use of time and money.

The little tour boat sat low in the water. A narrow central aisle threaded through the ranks of padded crosswise benches that bracketed narrow tables, like a series of restaurant booths. Headsets hanging on hooks on the tables played the tour narration in a dozen languages. Bax chose a seat up front and the boat was thinly populated enough that they had their entire booth to themselves.

Joss put on her headset and looked around. The whole top of the boat seemed to be made of Plexiglas. The windows rose from beside them and curved over to form the top of the boat, allowing them an unimpeded view on nearly all sides as the vessel backed out and began to chug away from Gamla Stan.

They headed east past the island Djurgården with its amusement park and open-air museum. The swells were larger here, sweeping in from the outer margins of the archipelago.

"If we keep going this direction, we'll find ourselves out by Silverholmen," Bax murmured to her.

"We'll have to go out there eventually, won't we?" she asked as the boat came around and headed for the pass between Gamla Stan and Södermalm, the SoHo of Stockholm.

"Probably. First, we've got to find a boat."

"Do you know how to pilot a boat?"

"It's been a little while, but yeah. I can navigate too, if I need to, but most boats come with GPS units these days. Takes away some of the guesswork."

The boat slowed as it went under a bridge and in between the high stone walls. Joss frowned and put on her headset.

"And now," announced the recorded narration, "we will proceed into the locks that will allow us to enter Lake Mälaren, at a different level than the Baltic."

The tour boat moved slowly into the lock, stopping and idling by the high stone walls. The pilot looked forward and back to check his position. The mate stepped lithely out of the forward hatch of the boat and up onto the transparent roof over their heads. Guide rope in hand, he vaulted onto the stone sidewall of the lock, walking nonchalantly along, directing the boat.

There was a careless efficiency to his movements that belied his skill as he guided the tour boat to the proper position and tied it down as the water level changed. Slowly, a hair-thin crack of daylight appeared at the center of the massive gates of the lock, widening as they parted, moving smoothly and ponderously backward. Finally, they had moved completely out of the way, leaving the path clear. The deckhand unwound the rope from its cleat to let the boat move forward, leaping lightly onto the foredeck at the last minute.

As they moved onto Lake Mälaren, the mate came back into the main cabin. He collapsed onto the seat opposite Joss and Bax and grinned. "All the work is done for a while." He was in his early twenties, with disordered spiky dark blond hair and a charcoal sweater that had probably seen better days.

"Hard work?" Joss asked.

"I'm outside all the time and on the water," he said with a shrug. "It is not so difficult a life."

"It's so beautiful, here." Joss gestured to the tree-covered slopes of Södermalm and the smaller island of Langholmen. "Stockholm is gorgeous."

"Ah, if you want to see true beauty, go out to the archipelago," he said. "No buildings, just islands and sea."

Joss felt Bax come to attention, though he looked as outwardly relaxed as ever. "How would you suggest we get there?"

"You would have to get a ferry in the Nybroplan or perhaps Slussen. It depends where you wish to go."

"The central archipelago, probably. A small island between Nämdö and Bullerö."

The mate tipped his head and looked at them consideringly. "Sightseeing?"

"Could be," Bax answered. "What if we wanted to pilot ourselves? Is it difficult to navigate the archipelago?"

"In places, of course. There are shallows or narrow passes between islands. Charts help. Do you have experience boating?"

"With launches and speedboats, not with sailboats."

"Motorboats are best, here."

"I will need help finding a place to rent one."

"Maybe I can help you out." The kid grinned and stuck out his hand. "I am Oskar. My friend and I have a boat. We do some deliveries to the archipelago. Perhaps we can do business."

"I'm Johan and this is Josie."

"A pleasure to meet you both." He put his hand out to shake.

Behind them, the pilot turned and barked something in Swedish. Oskar answered in the same and turned to them. "He tells me not to socialize with the passengers, that I am boring you, perhaps."

"Not at all. I think it's been a very interesting conversation, indeed," Bax said. "I'd like to continue it."

"As would I. Alas, we are approaching the lock to return to the Baltic. I must attend to my job."

"We all have to, sooner or later. Say I wanted to reach you about a boat. How would I contact you?"

Oskar considered. The pilot barked at him again and he took a quick glance behind him. "There is a restaurant called Pelikan on Södermalm. You can find me there most nights after work."

Bax nodded. "I might need information, also."

"I know much about the archipelago and many people. I can help you find out whatever you need." He touched his fingers to his forehead and was off and through the hatch.

Joss leaned in toward Bax as the tour boat lined up behind the other boats waiting at the lock. "Well, wasn't that convenient. 'Let's go on a boat tour and get oriented?'"

"Serendipity is a wonderful thing."

Joss gave him a narrow-eyed look. "Remember the whole talk about partners? If you were looking for specific information on this trip, you should have told me."

He digested it for a moment. "You're right," he said finally. "And I'm sorry. The thing is, I don't always have a goal, at least not one I'm conscious of. Sometimes I just do things on gut instinct, because they seem right. All I can say is I'll tell you what I can, when I can."

"I think that's good enough for me," Joss said. "And now, I suppose, we need to figure out where Pelikan is, right?"

Bax grinned. "You read my mind."

11

THE CEILING of the Stockholm convention center exhibit hall arched high overhead as Joss and Bax dodged the foot traffic in the aisles at the stamp expo. She'd known that philately was a popular hobby, but it had never occurred to her that thousands of people would flock to a stamp convention on a gorgeous summer Saturday in Stockholm, where warm weather was fleeting. It had also never occurred to her that so many stamp dealers existed in the world. Unlike her grandfather, who specialized in investment and did a small storefront trade, most of the exhibitors did the bulk of their business with casual hobbyists.

"What is the name of your sister's friend, again?" Bax asked her.

"Ray Halliday. Booth 1057," she read from her exhibit guide.

Bax scanned row signs hanging overhead and pointed. "Down there."

The booth for Halliday Philately was large and colorful, with a backdrop covered in blowups of famous stamps. Joss stopped to stare into a glass case displaying tongs and humidifiers for removing stamps from envelopes.

A spare-looking man in a white polo shirt approached them. "May I help you?"

"I'm looking for Ray Halliday," Joss told him.

He smoothed back his slightly frizzy red hair. "That's me."

Joss put out her hand. "I'm Joss Chastain, Gwen Chastain's sister. This is my friend Bax."

"Yes, of course." He shook hands with both of them. "Gwen e-mailed me you might be stopping by. Why isn't she here?"

"Too much going on," Joss said. "Someone had to mind the store."

"And you're the lucky devil who got stuck coming to Stockholm."

Joss grinned. "Someone had to suffer. Gwen said you might be able to help us with some information."

"Sure, whatever I can." What looked like a father and son stopped in the booth and Halliday glanced at Joss. "Give me a minute, will you?" He crossed to the pair and began chatting with them.

Bax glanced at him. "So how well does Gwen know this guy?"

"I gather she's been doing business with him for some time. She trusts him."

"She also trusted Oakes," Bax pointed out.

"So did my entire family. There's always the chance that someone's going to screw you over," Joss said. "Halliday sounds like a person who keeps his mouth shut and might be able to give us information that we need. It's worth taking a risk."

"If you say so."

Joss glanced over at Halliday. The discussion with the father and son had turned animated and he was pulling out stamp albums to show them. Finally, he broke loose and crossed back over to Bax and Joss. "Listen, I'd love to talk with you but I need to take care of these two first. You know how it goes."

"The customer comes first," Joss told him. "Don't worry about it."

"What about if we talk over dinner tonight, instead? Are you free?"

Joss looked at Bax and nodded. "Sure."

"Great. Say, seven-thirty at Fredsgatan 12? It's this great restaurant near the Royal Academy of Fine Arts. It'll be my treat."

"Too good an offer to turn down," Joss said. "We'll see you then."

THERE WAS SOMETHING fascinating about seeing a woman dress for the outside world, Bax thought as he watched Joss slide into a low-cut red and gold patterned dress. Seeing her go from bare skin and a towel to the silks and satins and little pots and bottles of mysterious girl stuff that smelled so good…he couldn't help but be intrigued.

She walked over to stand in front of him and turned around. "Can you zip me up?"

There was a familiarity to the gesture that floored him temporarily as he pulled up the zipper, watching the dress mold itself to her body. Unzipping a woman's dress was about sex. Zipping it was about…it was about intimacy, he realized in sudden discomfort. He'd been on that particular battleground before and the scars were still tender. Time to back away.

"All set," he said briskly and breathed a sigh of relief as she walked to the vanity area. Still, he couldn't keep from watching her apply her makeup and hold her jewelry against herself to choose exactly the right look. He didn't recognize the feeling as proprietary because he'd worked so hard to avoid any emotional connection to a woman—to anyone—for so long.

The phone rang. Bax looked at Joss, who nodded, and he picked up the receiver. "Hello."

"Ah, Johan. Keeping a close eye on your client, I see." It was Markus.

"Wouldn't you?"

"Your job appears to have extra benefits this time around...although it is unwise to overindulge."

"I'll keep that in mind. What do you want?"

"I have spoken with my employer and he has decided to meet with you."

"With the two of us, you mean."

"Yes, of course," Markus said impatiently.

"All right. Where?"

"Mr. Silverhielm's city office."

Bax snorted. "Neutral ground, Markus. You know how this works."

"One would think you do not trust us."

"One would be right," Bax agreed. "Neutral ground, a public place."

"Such as?"

Bax considered various candidates and rejected them. "How about Skansen?"

"You wish to be a tourist, now?"

"I think it would be a good location. In fact, the more I think about it, the more I like it." An outdoor museum that collected together historic buildings from all over Sweden, Skansen was public, open and on a Sunday afternoon would very likely have just enough people to prevent any funny business while affording some empty space to talk.

"Mr. Silverhielm will not find that satisfactory."

"If he wants the goods, he will. Tell him it's a chance to get back in touch with his culture."

Markus's only response was a snort. "A moment,

please." There was quiet murmuring in the background, then Markus returned. "Mr. Silverhielm says he will be indulgent. This time. Where in the park shall we meet?"

"How about at the temperance hall?"

"How very appropriate—9:00 p.m.?"

"Daylight."

"This is Stockholm in August, 9:00 p.m. is daylight."

"Broad daylight. Let's make it earlier, say seven."

"Private business needs to remain private, you know that."

"It'll be private enough, I guarantee." And every concession he pushed Markus into gave him that much more authority.

"All right, seven at Skansen. See that it is just the two of you."

"See that it is just the two of you."

"For a well-known figure like Mr. Silverhielm, bodyguards are an unfortunate necessity," Markus said smoothly.

"Not at the meeting," Bax persisted.

"It is a matter of safety."

"My point, exactly. He should be safe enough with you watching over him."

Markus chuckled. "You flatter me. Very well, no bodyguards, then. Do we have a meet?"

"We do."

"Until tomorrow."

"We'll see you then." Bax hung up the phone and turned to Joss, who stared at him.

"So?"

"A meeting at Skansen. Markus and Silverhielm. Now we just have to figure out what happens next."

Bax rubbed his knuckles along the edge of his jaw. He had a germ of an idea, but no real understanding of how to make it work. Somehow, they needed to tempt Silverhielm into bringing out his one-penny Mauritius, and do it without risking the Blue Mauritius. "Maybe we'll get a fix on what happens next when we talk with Gwen's friend tonight. Speaking of which," he glanced at his watch, "we've got about half an hour to get there."

"Then I guess we don't have time to fool around, do we?"

She smelled of seduction and his body tightened. "Depends on how efficient we are."

She twined her arms around his neck. "Oh, I can be very efficient when I want to."

THE RESTAURANT was open and airy with slate-violet walls and minimalist decor. The food at Fredsgatan 12 was minimalist, too, Joss discovered. The menu dispensed with quaint notions of starter and entrée, serving up exquisitely flavorful and astoundingly expensive dishes of just a few bites each. "You'll want four or five dishes," their severely dressed server said breezily.

"Get whatever you like," Halliday said expansively as he chose a bottle of wine. "Dinner's on me."

"We can't do that," Joss objected, staring at the menu.

"Of course you can. It's a business expense. I've done some good business with Chastain's. Buying you dinner is the least I can do."

"I take it you had a successful day?" Joss asked after they'd ordered.

Halliday nodded. "Good traffic, actually."

"I wouldn't have thought it," Joss said. "The weather is so gorgeous now I expected people to stay outside enjoying it."

"Ah, but true collectors are a different breed. It's all about the acquisition. Nothing else matters nearly as much, not even a sunny Saturday in August."

Interested, Bax leaned forward. "Tell us more about the psychology of a collector."

"Psychology? Pathology, more like it, depending on who you're talking about."

"Oh come on, surely it's not that bad," Joss disagreed.

The waiter appeared with the wine. "It depends," Halliday said, nodding at the bottle the waiter displayed to him. "You get all kinds. There are the harmless ones, like the pair who were in my booth today. They're excited about it and they enjoy it. It's something a father and son can do together. They learn about history and geography and enjoy themselves, but it doesn't run them. You can see the place it holds in their lives, just like you can see it in the eyes of the other ones." He took a sip of the wine the waiter brought for him and nodded.

"What other ones?" Bax asked.

"You know, the obsessives. For them, it's not about the process. It's not about the learning, it's not about gradual growth of the collection. Their obsession is having, and having more than anyone else." Halliday watched the waiter fill their glasses. "You'll see them throw away all their money on stamps, go into debt, even, pay tens or hundreds of thousands for a stamp, just to have it."

"But Gwen has plenty of customers who pay those prices as an investment," Joss objected, then sampled her wine.

Halliday shook his head. "Different thing. I'm talking about the ones who have to have. For some of them, nothing is too much. I had a client a couple of years back who was fixated on the Inverted Jenny. You know, the U.S. airmail stamps where they printed the plane upside down? He couldn't get enough of them, had a standing order for me to buy one any time I found it available, no mater how inflated the cost and no matter how many he already had."

"Are collectors always experts?" Bax asked.

"Some, not always. Sometimes they're so busy obsessing over having that they never really learn all the details. At least, not the kinds of details known by those whose passion is in the collecting process."

"Interesting. So talk to me about forgeries," Bax said as the waiter set their first dishes before them. "Do you see a lot of them out there?"

"Oh, some. They're always out there for the people who aren't smart."

"Like the obsessives?"

"Hopefully the obsessives have a trustworthy dealer to take care of them. Besides, any moderately intelligent person buying a stamp these days expects to see certification on the property."

"Of course, certifications can be forged, also."

"They can, for the person who's sufficiently determined. You hear about it occasionally."

"Are most forgeries made from scratch?"

"Fewer than you'd think. Some of them are antiques, and collectable themselves, ironically. Most of what you see as forgeries is really doctored up versions of existing stamps. The change in value of a stamp in good condition versus one in fair condition is pretty steep. You get stamp doctors who can add back gum and things to make a stamp look mint."

"What about forgeries of rare stamps?" Bax asked, watching him intently.

"How rare?"

"Oh, say, a Blue Mauritius."

Halliday gave Bax a long look. "The whereabouts of all the existing Post Office Mauritius stamps are known. A person coming up with a forgery would be taking a big gamble."

"What if a person wanted to gamble?" Bax asked softly. "Could you get me a forgery?"

"You've got a lot of nerve asking me a question like that," Halliday began angrily.

"Ray," Joss put her fingertips on his arm, "you know what happened with my grandfather's stamps. Gwen and I have hired Bax to help us. Please." She moistened her lips. "We need your help."

Halliday slowly studied her, then moved his gaze to study Bax. "All right. Well, first, a convincing forgery would require a good plate. One way to do it would be to find a person who could produce a new plate from a photograph. They use lasers, I understand. They'd have to doctor it, color match the inks, get the right paper and gum. It's not an easy process."

"But doable?"

Halliday nodded slowly. "I suppose. Another way is to do a reprint from the original plate."

"I would have thought they would have long since been destroyed."

"You'd be surprised. The original plates for the Post Office Mauritius pair still exist but they're not in a museum. They're reputed to be in the hands of a private collector. Perhaps they are. And perhaps that collector might rent them out to an ambitious forger for the right price."

Halliday took a sip of his wine. "Of course, even with the original plates, you'd have the same problems of inks, paper and gum. It's not a simple thing to find what you seek."

"Could you help us?" Joss asked, fighting the urge to hold her breath.

Halliday stared at her. "Perhaps you'd better tell me what this is all about."

DUSK WAS DARKENING to evening as Bax and Joss walked back to the Royal Viking. "So, what did you think of Fredsgatan 12?" he asked her.

"The food was wonderful, but I feel like stopping somewhere to get dinner, now. Do you know I calculated that the two scallops in my fish dish cost about twelve dollars each?"

"Maybe lemon juice is more expensive here."

She stuck her tongue in her cheek. "That must be it. Anyway, it was nice of Ray to treat us. We owe him."

"We'll owe him even more if he can find that forgery."

The last shades of evening were falling away as they walked toward the waterfront. "So just exactly what are you cooking up with a forgery, assuming Halliday can get one?" Joss asked, giving Bax a speculative look.

He shrugged. "I'm not sure. We're currently playing a very dangerous game with our friend Silverhielm. If our talks move forward, at some point he's going to expect us to come across with a stamp. I don't mind bluffing with the real Blue Mauritius, but we'd damned well better cook up some way to keep it safe from him."

"But how is having either a real or a forged Blue Mauritius going to help us get the one-penny Mauritius?"

"I haven't figured that out, yet." He grinned. "Feel free to chime in if you think of something."

It was that certainty that an idea would crop up that she admired. "Hey, it was my idea that got us this far."

"And it was a good one," he told her, sliding an arm around her shoulders.

It felt immeasurably cozy. "Could we try playing 'you show me yours, I'll show you mine'?"

"Possibly, though it would take some doing to get them to fall for it. Silverhielm doesn't strike me as a risk taker. He likes to have the game rigged in his favor, I think."

"Well, what if we get him thinking that it is?"

Bax considered. "Could work. Now we have to figure out practical implementation."

"Maybe we'll learn something when we meet with them. Have your sources told you anything more about Markus or Silverhielm that might help?"

They crossed another of the ubiquitous public squares and headed to the waterfront. "Just that Markus is working for him as a trigger man. Markus can be a very effective scare to pull out of your pocket."

"But you and he are buds, right?" There was something between Markus and Bax that she didn't quite understand.

Bax shook his head. "Never make that mistake. Nothing comes ahead of the job for Markus. He'll take care of his client, first and foremost."

"But he talks like you're friends."

"It's hard to tell with Markus. Maybe I just amuse him."

"And he still has no idea you worked for Interpol."

"Not as far as I know."

It seemed extraordinary to her that Bax could have lived this separate life, a separate life that he still maintained. How much of the person she knew was real? "How did you wind up working for Interpol, anyway? That's rare, isn't it? I mean, you'd need to know a lot of languages and European customs and everything."

"I grew up in Europe, remember? I speak Danish, Dutch and German fluently and bits of a couple of others."

"So you just picked them up as you moved around?" Walking through the warm twilight, it seemed natural to talk.

"Kind of. I seem to be a natural linguist, but it helped being exposed to so many different languages when I was young. Speech patterns aren't set then, so it's easy to learn different ways to think about the same thing."

"But you speak English without an accent." Ahead lay the cream and blush baroque palace of the opera house with a statue of a king on horseback before it.

"My father and the people at the embassies taught me. Besides, we moved back to the U.S. when I was about sixteen. I worked hard at getting rid of my accent."

"How did your mom take leaving Europe?"

"She died around that time, so I don't have an answer to that." Something in the tone of his voice warned her not to pursue that line of questioning further. He dropped his arm and moved away.

"So then, what, you went into the military?"

"The FBI, eventually."

"What did your father think of that?"

"He didn't like it, but then he doesn't like much that I do." The rancor in his voice was startling. "We aren't exactly a typical father and son."

"Sometimes being different can be good," Joss said, thinking of her own family.

"When it comes to my dad, being apart is good," he said with finality.

People lived what they learned. Joss reached out to tangle her fingers in his. "Being together has its moments, too."

For an instant, his fingers were still, then they softened. "So I've seen."

12

THE LONG SUMMER afternoon stretched out as Joss and Bax entered the back gates of Skansen. They ignored the funicular and began to walk up the winding path that led from the meadow below to the top of the bluffs that held the outdoor museum.

"Why did you choose this as a meeting place?" Joss asked. "Aren't we taking a chance being in the middle of all of these buildings? Silverhielm could have some of his people in here."

"Almost certainly. Then again, we're only here to talk, not to make a handoff or do anything where force would benefit them. I think Silverhielm's going to want to have additional people in place just to feel like he's got his extra measure of control, but they're going to essentially be aboveboard. The temperance lodge is in the open. We should be okay there."

Ahead of them, as they reached the top, clustered the wooden buildings of a nineteenth-century family farm.

Back in the previous century, Skansen had been conceived as a way to preserve the history of Sweden with a collection of typical buildings from all regions of the country and all time periods. Now, it stretched across acres of the island of Djurgården, dirt lanes leading from one to another of the dozens of buildings. During the day, crowds attended the festivals, filtered through the outdoor market in the square. Park employees in authentic costumes demonstrated the techniques of bakers, printers, metalsmiths and so on. During the day, Skansen was bustling with activity.

Now, although the park was ostensibly open, the grounds were largely deserted. They found their way to the temperance lodge, a low, red building surrounded by a wooden fence.

"Did temperance ever take off in Sweden?" Joss asked as they came to a stop by the information sign.

A corner of Bax's mouth twitched. "You're talking about a country that has a museum of alcohol. I'm thinking not. Here we are." His voice changed. "There."

She turned to see Markus and Silverhielm walking toward them, flanked by two bodyguards.

"No bodyguards, Markus," Bax reminded him as they came close.

"They are here to enjoy the culture," Markus said with a faint smile.

"Let them enjoy it elsewhere."

Markus nodded at the two men, who hesitated a moment and walked down the path toward another area.

"Good evening, Ms. Astin." Silverhielm held out his hand to take hers and kiss it as before.

He'd dispensed with the formality of a suit, but only just. Instead, he wore a dark blue jacket—cashmere, perhaps?—over khakis, with a white shirt unbuttoned at the collar, sort of a King-Karl-watches-polo outfit.

Markus wore a jacket as well, for the same reason, she assumed, as Bax—to hide a gun.

Her stomach tightened.

"Good evening, Mr. Silverhielm."

"Please, let us dispense with formality," he said comfortably. "You shall call me Karl and I shall call you Josie. And this is your friend?" He looked at Bax.

"This is my associate, Johan Bruhn," she told him.

"Ah. Markus tells me many things about you, Mr. Bruhn."

"Johan," Bax said.

"I hear you are a man of no small talent. Perhaps we should discuss that at some point."

"Perhaps. For now, though, we are here to discuss Josie's business and your business with Stewart Oakes."

"Ah yes, this business. Come, Josie." They began to stroll down the pathway that led to the reproduction nine-teenth-century village, Markus and Bax following. "Such an embarrassment that Stewart Oakes confessed to the theft of such valuable stamps, he and his associate. A person dealing with Mr. Oakes would, of course, assume that he'd obtained the goods he brokered by honest means."

"Unless," Joss said, "that were impossible, in which case a client would have to know he might take extreme measures to attain the prize."

Silverhielm shook his head sadly, folding his hands together at his back. "Truly reprehensible. The news accounts were not clear about which issues were taken and which were recovered. Perhaps they were more detailed in the U.S."

"The papers were not, but I have the luck to have had a…close relationship with Stewart's associate." She let satisfaction creep into her voice as she glanced at the white and periwinkle wildflowers lining the sides of the lane.

"Mr. Messner, correct? I understand both he and Mr. Oakes are in jail at present."

"True. The last time Jerry—Mr. Messner—was at my apartment, he happened to leave a valuable piece of property with me for safekeeping." They turned up a steep cobblestone street. "A valuable piece of property that I believe you have some interest in. After all, just because the law caught up with Stewart and Jerry doesn't mean that your transaction has to be a complete disappointment."

Afternoon shadows stretched across the lane. Silverhielm examined the now-dark windows of the metalsmith's store and turned to her.

"So bold of you to ask for additional money to deliver the property I already own, is it not, Josie?"

"Think of it as a delivery fee." She gave him a brilliant smile. "After all, I wasn't a part of the original negotiations, and yet I have gone to the trouble and expense of flying to Stockholm to reach out to you."

"And how did you come to know of me?"

She spread her hands. "Pillow talk, Karl. You understand."

"But you are no longer sharing a pillow with Mr. Messner, I see."

Joss gave him a cool look. "Mr. Messner left me high and dry. A woman has to find a man who can take care of her."

"So you now share your pillow with Mr. Bruhn."

"Now you're the one who's bold." They approached the deserted town square with its array of wooden picnic tables. "What matters is the service that I can potentially render to you. After all, Stewart was unable to complete your agreement. If I hadn't stepped in, you would not have the opportunity to obtain your commissioned property. Because I took the time to come here, you have the choice of whether to receive it or not, depending on what it is worth to you." Joss sank down on one of the wooden benches. Below and beyond them, the lights of the Gröna Lund amusement park spread out against the water.

Silverhielm sat at the table next to her. Markus and Bax lingered nearby. "So you might have one of the objects that Stewart promised me?"

"Well, yes, but obviously a certain amount of risk and cost have been associated with getting the property over here. If I were to hand it over to you, for example, instead of the authorities, I'd expect compensation."

"You must understand, I have already paid a substantial commission to Mr. Oakes for his efforts. I naturally expected a positive result from the investment."

"Things don't always go as planned, though, you know that." A wave of screams erupted from the Power Tower at Gröna Lund as a group of thrill-seekers went into extended freefall. "I understand that you have a long-standing interest in owning a Post Office Mauritius pair. Wouldn't you like to see that interest brought to fruition?"

Something hot and proprietary flickered in his eyes and she knew she'd guessed right. Not just a collector, not just an investor. An obsessive, one for whom owning the object of desire was everything.

"So you have it, then."

"The Blue Mauritius? Yes."

His gaze became bright with avarice and he let out a slow breath. "It would bring me a good deal of pleasure to have the Blue Mauritius."

"The proper deal would bring me a good deal of pleasure, too."

"I do not like to have terms dictated to me." The Silverhielm she'd glimpsed in Slussen emerged.

She suppressed the urge to shift away from him. "You can dictate all the terms you like," she said instead. "I'll just exercise my right to say yes or no."

"I see. What is to stop me from, for example, directing my associates down the lane to bring their weapons to bear on you to force a 'yes' answer?"

"If you were going to do that, you'd have done it already." Bax stepped up and sat next to Joss. "Stop wasting our time. We've got something you want, something you're willing to pay for. We want two hundred thousand for it, cold cash."

"Kroner?"

Bax just snorted. "Dollars. I'm sure you can get a favorable exchange rate."

"'We want,' you say?"

Bax looked at him calmly. "I have a commission coming."

"Of course. I shall consider this proposal."

"Nothing to consider," Bax told him. "It's a fifth of the market value of the stamp. You're getting a bargain. Either you pay us or Josie takes it to the authorities, it's as simple as that."

"To the authorities?"

"Or, perhaps, to another collector."

Silverhielm's nostrils flared. "The stamp is mine. I will have it."

"Easy enough. All you have to do is meet our terms."

The Swede gave him a black look. The two bodyguards appeared at the edge of the lane where it opened out into the square. "I will not answer this now."

"You want time to think about it, take it. I'm sure it's easy to find a Blue Mauritius at a discount rate. Shoot, you can just have your goons break into the postal museum and take theirs. You'll get it for free."

"Do not mock me," Silverhielm said coldly.

"Then don't mock us. We know you've got money. That's not an issue. The only issue is whether you're willing to pay us what we want. That figure wasn't a top line bargaining number we're working down from, by the way. That's our number, period."

"It is a fortunate liaison you've made, this 'we.'" Hostility crackled in Silverhielm's voice.

"Yes, isn't it?" Joss interrupted and rose. "I think Johan is right, the conversation is over. Contact us when you've decided to get serious."

THEY WALKED AWAY from the town square toward the nearby front entrance of Skansen. Joss ignored the tickle between her shoulder blades and tried not to imagine the red dot of a laser sight dancing around the area between them.

It was easier once they'd gone down the hill toward the noise and life of Gröna Lund. "Thank God that's over," Joss murmured. She wanted to be among the lights, she wanted to be among people. Anything but around the grinding tension of the meeting they'd just had.

"You did well," Bax told her, resting his hand lightly on the small of her back as they went through the exit gates. "You handled him just right."

"Except for the part where he started threatening bodily harm." She'd been calm when it was going on. It was only now that she trembled.

"You're not used to it, that's all." They turned down the road that led back toward the mainland. "It was a bluff. He was expecting you to back down. Guys like him, they like the cat and mouse game. They're not happy if they can't flex their muscles."

Her shoulders felt like they were up somewhere around her ears, tormented with iron pincers as they walked through the wash of lights from the front entrance of Gröna Lund. "We'd better get the goods from our buddy Ray or we're going to be in trouble."

"We'll figure something out."

Again, the confidence. Joss shrugged, trying to relax, but the tension only got worse. It wasn't enough to know it was over. She needed to believe it. She needed to let it go.

She needed to scream her head off.

"Hey, come on." Seizing Bax's hand, she pulled him across the street toward the ticket kiosks of Gröna Lund.

"What are we doing here?"

She dug kroner out of her pocket and handed it to the cashier. "I need to get rid of some stress."

"I'VE BEEN TO an amusement park maybe twice in my entire life," Bax said. They stood in the line, waiting their turn on the roller coaster billed as Sweden's scariest. "There's a big amusement park in Copenhagen called Tivoli. I went one time when we were visiting my cousins."

He sounded just a bit uneasy, Joss realized, amused. "I'll make sure nothing happens to you," she reassured, patting his hand as the line moved. Slowly, they inched forward. Because it was the end of the weekend, the queue was shorter, but not by much. It was summer, after all.

"I always loved amusement parks," Joss said. "It was the one thing I really missed in Africa."

"No amusement parks there?"

"Not where we lived. I'd always make my parents take me to Great America when we went back to San Francisco each year, though. I dragged my mother and Gwen on the rides whether they wanted to go or not."

"And you always wanted to go on the scariest, craziest, most death-defying roller coasters, and over and over again, right?"

Joss grinned. "Maybe you do know me after all."

They'd reached the head of the line and the attendant waved them forward. A little frisson of anticipation ran through Joss as they sat in the car and pulled down the safety restraints.

"How did I let you talk me into this?" Bax muttered as

the air brakes hissed and the car rolled slowly forward. "I haven't been on a ride like this since I was about ten."

"Really? Well, then you're due."

A wave of pure, giddy pleasure swept over her as the car shot off without warning and they whipped up the first climb. There was no time to think, only time to feel. Only time to live in the moment. As the car crested the hill and began to drop, she threw her hands up in the air and screamed her lungs out. G-forces pulled at her and she could feel the crazy grin stretching her face. It was wonderful to be scared silly, completely, harmlessly silly in a way that didn't include guns and threats. The pit of her stomach dropped out as the car whirled into a sideways turn up in the air at a dizzying height, with the ground far below and only the slender rails restraining them.

This time, she swore she heard a whoop from Bax over her own giddy scream, though she couldn't be sure.

Joss was still laughing when the car wheeled into the station, even as she pushed her hair back out of her eyes.

She looked over at Bax. His hair was in disarray, his collar was flipped up from the wind of the car's passage. For the first time since she'd known him, that tense, watchful look was gone from his face.

"Satisfied?" he asked, taking his hand off the safety bar and flexing his fingers.

Joss grinned at him. "Don't give me that. You had fun and you know it."

He gave a sudden laugh, looking younger than she'd ever seen him. "You're right. Let's go again."

13

BAX STOOD IN LINE at the café next to Karl XII's *torg* wearing shorts and a T-shirt, still damp from his five mile run. When he went too many days without working out, he started to feel sludgy and slow. Not healthy, for a man in his line of work.

He was still too hot to think about going back inside for coffee, though. And even if he were, he had a pretty good idea that the café at the Royal Viking would disapprove of his current state. So he'd stopped at the outdoor café, instead.

The server turned to him. *"Hej."*

"Hej," he replied, ordering coffee in Swedish.

"You've picked up the language quickly, but then you were always very good in Danish," said a voice behind him. Bax turned to see Markus.

"I'm very good in English, too. Do you want coffee?"

"Yes, thank you. I see you have been running."

"I've got nothing else to do while I'm waiting for you and Silverhielm to get your acts in gear. Besides, Stockholm is a beautiful city. I may as well see some of it while I'm here."

"But you saw it all when you were here before."

Bax paid for the drinks and handed Markus his cup. By unspoken accord, they walked out to the tables.

"Back then my tastes were less…refined, shall we say."

"And now your tastes run more to tour boats than strip clubs?"

It didn't surprise him that they'd been watching. "And did your man like the tour?"

"He did not join you. He would have enjoyed the strip club more." Markus stopped to doctor his coffee with cream.

"I'm sure."

"You never cared for them, though, did you?"

Bax shrugged. "Not my call. When that's where the boss wants to set up to do his business, you do it."

"But he is your boss no longer."

"No." Bax eyed him. "You've changed as well."

"Yes. I have, as you Americans say, traded up."

"A smart man."

"You are a smart man also, Johan and you puzzle me. Your current client is not exactly up to your usual standards."

They reached a table and pulled out chairs to sit. "Do you make a study of my clients?"

"You have a certain reputation among our community. Or had. You disappeared." Markus took a drink of his coffee.

"I went to Miami for business and wound up staying on." And he had an acquaintance who would back up that story, if necessary.

Markus gave him a steady look. "For a man with your talents, I am sure there is work everywhere you go."

"As there is for you."

"Yes, but I prefer the familiar. So how did you wind up with the woman?"

Bax gave him an amused look. "You certainly get right to it."

"Do you blame me? You were not, I assume, surprised to find me working for Silverhielm."

"Not a bit."

"No," Markus agreed. "I have worked for many like him in the past, several that you know of."

"Several I didn't understand how you could tolerate."

"The price was right. And you, I could see you winding up in Miami. Or in Las Vegas, wasn't that where you met her?"

"It was."

"There are a number of men in that city who would find your services useful and pay you handsomely. Yet you are with the woman. Why?"

Bax grinned. "You've seen her and you have to ask that?"

"I have seen many beautiful women but none who would stand between me and money."

"Who says she stands between me and money? I stand to make a nice profit once we pull off the exchange."

"A trifle and you know it," Markus said contemptuously. "You are too smart to let your appetites control your professional life. Why are you here?"

"A favor for a lady, a free trip back to Europe and a nice fat commission."

"I don't believe that."

Bax took a swallow of his coffee. "And a chance to set myself up for my next job."

Markus looked at him consideringly. "That, I am more likely to believe. How did you find out about the stamp?"

"I happened to be at the right place at the right time and overheard a few things."

"Including my employer's name?"

"Including that. Including a description of someone who sounded a lot like you. I thought it couldn't hurt to come over and check it out. At worst, it is a paid vacation. At best, a chance to do a little career networking."

"Ah, now we come closer to the truth."

Bax let the humor fall away. "You and your employer have indicated an interest in me."

"An interest in your talents, yes. Mr. Silverhielm would like to know if they are for hire."

"He doesn't know the first thing about me."

"But I do."

"And that is enough?"

"In such matters, yes."

And suddenly Bax felt as though he were back undercover, when the objectives were clear but day to day life was ambiguous.

"What would I have to do?"

Markus smiled faintly. "Provide your usual sort of services."

"Does he have something specific in mind?"

"It is difficult to say. Mr. Silverhielm has his fingers in many pies, you might say. He wishes to have you on his team. I think you will not find his terms ungenerous."

"How not ungenerous?"

"He prefers to tell you such things himself."

"When?" The dance, the constant dance frustrated Bax.

"Perhaps in a day or so."

"First, we exchange the stamp."

"Of course. But there is no reason we cannot move forward down both paths, is there?"

Now it began to make sense. "Don't think that by offering me a job you'll have an easier time getting the Blue Mauritius."

"Of course not." Markus snorted. "I know better."

"So Silverhielm's ready to name a time and a place?"

"Always impatient."

"My client is impatient," Bax corrected. "Where and when?"

"You set terms for the last meeting. It is our turn."

"So what do you choose?"

Markus watched the steam rise off his coffee and glanced up at Bax. "Our territory. Mr. Silverhielm's home."

"Out on the archipelago?"

Markus didn't show surprise, but then again he wouldn't. "You have done your homework."

"As you no doubt expected."

"Then I shouldn't need to give you directions or arrange for your transportation."

A challenge, perhaps. Or a test. "We'll find our way."

Markus rose, taking his coffee with him. "Mr. Silverhielm will expect you on Saturday evening at seven-thirty. We will make our exchange and perhaps talk a little business."

"I look forward to it."

JOSS WAS AT the bathroom mirror putting on lipstick when her cell phone rang. She walked out into the bedroom to grab the slim phone from the bedside table. "Hello?"

"Joss. Ray Halliday."

She counted to three. It didn't do to look too eager. "Ray, how are you?"

"Today's the last day of the expo. I'm doing great."

"Ready to go home?"

"You know it. Hey listen, can you get over here before ten?"

Joss blinked. "You mean to the convention center?"

"Yeah."

She checked her watch. "It's already nine. Bax is out and I'm not sure when he'll be back. Can we be a little later?"

"Not really. There's someone I want you to meet before the show starts. He might be able to help you out with…your problem."

She chewed the inside of her lip. This was an opportunity they couldn't afford to squander, whether Bax was there or not. "I don't know where Bax is, but I can come over now."

"Great. I'll see you then."

The last thing she wanted to do was run out while Bax was gone. This was just what they'd talked about. Bax would go ballistic if he came back and found her gone, Joss knew that. She dialed his cell phone number, only to hear the answering ring across the room, on his night table. Okay, so calling him was out. Now what was she supposed to do? Hang around, maybe miss the meeting with Ray? Or go to the meeting and fill Bax in later?

It was no contest. Reality was, she'd made the decision the minute Ray asked her to come out. The important thing was that she do what was necessary to get the stamps back. If it meant taking a risk, so be it. If it meant letting Bax down, she'd deal with his anger. It was what he got for forgetting his phone.

To salve her conscience, she scribbled a hasty note and left it on the bed. He wouldn't like it, but it was the best she could do. Shoving a handful of kroner and her transportation card in the back pocket of her jeans, she grabbed her key and cell phone and headed out the door.

It was still early enough that the ornate lobby was nearly empty. The people with morning plans were gone. Those checking out hadn't come down yet. In the front café, a trio of men in sober chalk-striped business suits held a breakfast meeting. A woman with a dog on a leash walked toward the elevator. On one of the gold padded benches by the door, a guy in jeans and a tweed jacket read the newspaper. And Bax was nowhere in sight.

Joss stood for a moment. She couldn't afford to wait for Bax to return, she thought desperately. In her shoes, he'd do the same thing. She checked her watch again. Be here in an hour, Ray had said.

It was time to go.

Outside, puffs of white clouds dotted the cerulean sky. In a perfect world, she'd have made the leisurely walk to the central train station, enjoying the clean streets and the morning cool of the air as she went. Today, she didn't have time. Instead, she headed directly for the Tunnelbana station a few blocks from the hotel. The subway would take her to Central Station and a fifteen-minute ride on the commuter rail would bring her to the convention center.

At least the morning rush hour was over. She wouldn't be fighting with a mob of commuters, not that all that many commuters probably lived in this exclusive tourist district. Indeed, she found herself alone as she clattered down the stairs to the station. Behind her, she heard the soft slap of footsteps. Okay, maybe the commute wasn't quite over, she thought as she walked onto the empty platform. Even in Sweden there were laggards.

The glare from overhead fluorescent lights reflected off the concrete of the platform. Joss blinked and frowned. Something was strange. The footsteps, she realized. They'd stopped without anyone ever appearing in the station. Perhaps the commuter had decided to go back home and to bed, she speculated. Then again, she hadn't heard the sound of someone climbing back up to the street.

The hairs on the back of her neck prickled.

It was ridiculous, of course. It was broad daylight, mid-morning. No one was going to bother her, not down here.

Still she breathed a little sigh of relief when she heard the distant rumble of the approaching train. Clean and open though it was, the empty station was a little too creepy for her. Any second, a train, other people, would be here. And maybe once she was on the train, she could stop wondering about those footsteps.

The rumbling intensified. It swelled to a roar, crescendoed, and a bullet of silver burst along the tracks. Shining and sleek, the cars slid smoothly to a stop, the doors snapping open.

Only a handful of people sat in the car nearest to her, newspapers open on their laps. Just working people on their way to the office. Just another normal day. For a moment, she felt incredibly foolish. She'd been dealing with the cloak-and-dagger world too much. Bax's constant alertness had rubbed off on her.

With an inner smile, Joss moved to board the train. Then the faint echo of a shout from outside the station had her looking reflexively toward the stairs that led to the street.

And she saw the tweed-jacketed guy from the hotel walking toward her.

BAX WAS WAITING to cross at the light, the Royal Viking just ahead when he caught the flash of scarlet far down the street, the scarlet of Joss's jacket below the dark cloud of her hair. She was walking quickly, head down. On the building before her he saw the encircled black *T,* the sign for the Tunnelbana.

Consternation surged through him. She knew better than to run out on her own. So what did that mean? Was it just an errand? Was it something too important to miss? Had Markus ignored him and gotten to her? For an instant, Bax stood indecisively. She was too far away for him to reasonably expect to catch up with her, yet he didn't want to let her go.

Then his gaze snagged on a man paralleling her course.

A man who kept pace with her from across the street, turning his head and shoving his hands in his pockets when she glanced up.

Doing his best to be inconspicuous.

Bax was walking before he realized it, breaking into a run when he saw Joss disappear into the entrance to the T-bana station. The man sped up now, crossing the street and moving swiftly after her. An errant breeze off the water caught at his jacket, molding it against him, outlining a bulky shape at his hip that had nothing to do with the human anatomy, a bulky shape that was deadly metal.

And Bax began to sprint.

IT PROBABLY didn't mean anything, Joss told herself as the train rumbled out of the station. After all, if the guy in the tweed jacket was staying at the hotel, it made sense that he'd go to the nearest T-bana stop. But why alone, and so suddenly after he'd been loitering in the lobby? What if it weren't just coincidence that he'd decided to put down his paper and go for a ride?

What if he was following her?

It was something she simply couldn't afford. And so, when she got out of the train, she purposely took her time walking down the platform. He stepped out ahead of her and she stopped to study one of the enormous street maps of the area that stood against the wall. It wouldn't hurt to stay behind and keep an eye on him. It was what Bax would do.

The walls of the tunnels were rough hewn, rising up to shadowed arches high overhead. All the lights in the world couldn't make the platform bright. For some reason, she thought of an old movie version of H.G. Wells's *Time Machine,* with its Morlocks and subterranean dangers.

Ahead of her, Tweed Jacket walked briskly to the end

of the platform and out of sight. She really was getting paranoid, Joss told herself. Clearly, he was just a tourist headed out for the day. Why shouldn't he be alone? She was worried about nothing. If Bax thought there was a risk of them being tailed, he surely would have said something.

Then again, he hadn't been expecting her to go out.

Joss made her way to the end of the platform. Tweed Jacket was off to whatever adventure he was having next and she was off to the convention center and the meeting with Ray. She turned into the first of the series of tunnels that would lead her through the levels of the Tunnelbana and eventually to the commuter rail station.

The Blue Line that she'd ridden in on was the deepest of the three lines that intersected at Central Station. She worked her way along moving walkways that carried her up gradual rises until she reached the long escalator that would bring her toward the higher platforms.

Here, the walls were plastered with ads for kitchen tools and department-store sales, interspersed with scenic tourist-board photographs of Götland. Joss looked across at the line of matching ads flanking the down escalator opposite her. Idly, she glanced back, down the steep slant of the moving stair.

And saw Tweed Jacket riding the escalator below her.

14

BAX BURST INTO the room at the Royal Viking. It was empty, as he'd expected. As the T-bana station had been empty when he'd raced down the stairs, lungs burning, only to find the train long gone. Over his head, an electronic sign in mocking red had told him to expect a train in four minutes. He hadn't bothered to wait. With no idea of where Joss was going, there was no point.

Instead, he'd run back to the hotel.

Now, he grabbed the note from the bureau, reading it with a curse. He crumpled it and threw it down, snatching up the cell phone. There was no answer to his call. Small surprise. Joss was probably too far underground to get a signal. If the phone wasn't ringing, she wasn't about to answer.

Or maybe she couldn't.

He refused to give in to the cold crush of fear that filled his gut and instead concentrated on what he could do. The note said she'd gone to the expo. Bax tore off his running clothes and reached for jeans.

THE ESCALATOR moved inexorably upward. Casually, Joss stared at the advertising signs across the way, watching Tweed Jacket with her peripheral vision, her heart pounding. The instant she'd turned to see him, he'd shifted as well, looking downward, making himself innocuous. He was there, behind her, where he had no business being. She'd walked off the platform behind him, she'd made sure of it, and now he was behind her again.

He had to be one of Silverhielm's men.

Run. All of her instincts screamed for her to flee as adrenaline flooded her system. It was the wrong thing to do, though. Losing control would only make her a target.

Instead, she made herself stand casually, looking as oblivious as she could manage. The longer she could go with him thinking she hadn't made him, the more options she would have. His feet made a dull, metallic thud on the escalator steps as he moved closer to her. She had to find a way to ditch him so that he'd stay ditched. The last thing she wanted to do was lead him to Ray.

She emerged onto the platform of the Green Line and found herself amid a crowd of people. Relief surged through her. People were protection, even if they were jostling and pushing to get to the train just coming to a stop in the station. The crowd could offer her camouflage, a chance to get away.

If she hurried.

Joss began to rush, pushing aggressively through the crowd, making him work to follow her. Making him abandon caution. If he were worried about losing her, he'd take chances, he'd make a mistake. She passed the end of the train, just steps from the escalator that would take her up to the level of the train station.

And spun to run back down the platform, dashing through the closing doors of the last subway car.

Tweed Jacket lunged after her, but it was too late. All he could do was stand on the platform and watch the train slide away.

IT WASN'T a big deal, Joss told herself as she walked into the lobby of the convention center, trying to ignore the residual shakiness in her legs. She'd lost him and she was safe, and that was all that mattered.

The expo hadn't quite opened yet so she pulled out her cell phone. It was nearly ten o'clock. Time to find Ray. She punched up his number and waited for him to answer. "Ray? Hey, it's Joss. I'm out in the lobby." The missed call tone of her phone beeped in her ear but she ignored it.

"Great." His voice crackled out of the phone. "Get a seat at one of those round tables over by the windows and I'll be right out."

"All right."

"Hey, are you okay? You don't sound so good."

"I'm fine." She was, now. It had taken her several stops after she'd left Central Station on the green line before she'd recovered enough to look at her transit system map and figure out where the heck she was going. Making sense of the tangle of colored lines with her rattled brain took another couple of stops, leaving her barely enough time to work out the sequence of transfers that would get her to the commuter rail without going through Central Station, where Tweed Jacket would doubtlessly be waiting for her.

Now, though, anger was replacing anxiety. Now, the need for action drove her. She didn't feel shaky, she felt energized and mad as hell. Edgy and tense, Joss found a table and then paced restlessly beside it, staring out at the greenery outside.

The missed call was from Bax, but she didn't get a response when she rang. Frowning, she switched it to mute and shoved it into her jacket pocket.

"Glad you could make it."

She turned to see Ray behind her, standing next to a portly man in an expensive suit.

"Good to see you, Ray," she said, shaking hands with him.

"I've got a person here who might be able to help you with your problem."

Person. Not friend, not colleague. An odd way to put it. "All right." Joss put her hand out. "I'm—"

Ray shook his head. "No names," he said brusquely. "You guys talk and see if it gets you anywhere. I'm going into the exhibition."

The portly man took a seat at the table and looked at her calmly. His name badge was flipped backward so she could only see the name of the convention center and nothing else.

Joss sat down in a chair to face him. "So, are you exhibiting here?"

The man shrugged. "I am just walking the show, meeting with clients," he said with an accent that sounded vaguely Germanic.

"What do you do?"

"I specialize in reproductions of famous stamps."

"Forgeries?"

His eyes chilled. "No. Legitimate reproductions. I do not attempt to pass them off as true rarities. They are marked clearly on the back."

"Do you sell a lot of them?"

"There is a market for reproductions. They are for those who want the thrill of owning a stamp beyond their means."

"And what if I wanted a reproduction of a famous stamp that wasn't marked on the back?"

He drew himself up. "I could not, of course, help you. I am a legitimate businessman. I do not contribute to fraud."

"Of course, if the buyer buys one of your reproductions and pastes it onto an envelope, the mark wouldn't show," Joss said thoughtfully. "He could pass it off as authentic, if he wanted to."

He shrugged. "The world is a perilous place for the gullible. My job is to manufacture and broker properly marked reproductions. What happens to them after the sale is beyond my control."

All very neat and convenient, she thought. Ray's treatment of him suddenly made sense. "What if I wanted a version of a famous stamp that I could pass off as the real thing?"

"I am sorry? I do not understand."

"What if I wanted a pair of extremely good reproductions?" Joss kept her voice low, mindful of the exhibit attendees who were starting to circulate around the convention center lobby. "Something good enough to fool a knowledgeable amateur. They wouldn't have to pass an expert, but they'd have to be very, very good. Front and back."

"And what are the stamps of interest?"

"The Post Office Mauritius pair."

He nodded, digesting this. "It would be difficult," he said finally. "I myself cannot do such things. As I said, I am a legitimate businessman. I have heard of a man in Amsterdam who perhaps accepts these sorts of commissions, however."

"How do I reach him?"

The German gave her an oily smile. "I could, perhaps, make inquiries. How soon do you need these…reproductions?"

"Two days, perhaps three."

"Just a moment, madame." He rose and crossed the room, pulling out his cell phone to make a call. Minutes went by as Joss watched him.

If he could be trusted, and she wasn't at all sure he could be, he could help her get the forgeries. There was still the matter of cost, of course, not to mention timing. Late would be as bad as not at all. She wished passionately that Bax was there with her. He would know how to handle the German. Since he wasn't, though, she'd have to do her best.

The German walked back to the table and settled in his chair. "It is possible I have a way to contract this man in Amsterdam. Of course, such work as you require would take some investment. All the more so for such a rapid turnaround."

Which included his commission, no doubt. "Can I talk with him directly?"

"Of course, but he is a very cautious man. The nature of his business, you understand." He made a dismissive gesture with his hand. "You must travel to him, meet him at the spot of his choosing. And it must be you alone. Do not attempt to bring another with you."

"Impossible. I've got a partner."

"You must leave the partner behind. Or take the partner with you, but give up your hope for the stamps."

"It's a simple business deal."

"Madame, what you ask is not simple at all."

She could already imagine what Bax would say, but she didn't see that there was a choice. "All right, if that's the way he wants it."

"He insists, I'm afraid."

She tilted her head a bit and looked at him. "And what do you get out of all of this?"

"Merely the satisfaction of bringing two interested parties together."

"Merely?"

"Why, yes. Of course, it is a risk for me to give you this

name. It is a risk for me to be associated with this business at all. I am a—"

"Legitimate businessman," she finished for him.

"Indeed. However, if you wanted to make the arrangements proceed more smoothly, you might offer a token of your appreciation. After all, I still need to give you the name and location of the Amsterdam contact, and there are meetings to arrange…"

A shakedown, in other words. Joss's eyes narrowed. "What do you want?"

"I will leave that to you, but if your need is great, a thousand kroner would be a small price to pay. For my trouble, you see, and for international telephone calls."

"A legitimate businessman?" she asked sardonically.

"It is a risky thing I do for you."

"And I'm sure you've never sullied yourself with this sort of business in the past."

"Certainly not, madame."

Joss dug in her pocket. "I wasn't prepared for a shakedown. Would you take," she fumbled in her pocket, "five hundred?"

"I am not, despite what you think, a greedy man." The bills disappeared smoothly into his pocket. "And in exchange, the information. Go to Amsterdam on Wednesday morning."

"He can't come here?"

"He is a man with very special skills and connections. Such men are very rare. If you wish to do business with them, you must go to where they are."

"Amsterdam."

"The choice is yours, madame." He gave a shrug. "Perhaps your need is not so great."

She thought of Silverhielm and of the real Blue Mauritius, currently at risk. "What do I do?"

"It is very simple. When you reach the city, call this number." He handed her a small slip of paper. "When someone answers, ask to speak with Mr. Kant. They will instruct you where to go."

"How much money does he want?"

"I cannot say for sure. Perhaps two hundred times what you paid me."

More than twelve thousand dollars, she thought in shock. "For a forgery?"

"Madame, please." He looked around quickly to see if anyone was watching. "It is no small thing you seek. There is great risk involved."

Translation, they knew she needed it and they could gouge her. "How can he expect that much?"

"He expects nothing. You are the one who seeks something. If I were you, I would go prepared."

Joss nodded, thinking quickly. They'd have to fund this from Operation Recovery, as Gwen had called her poker tournament winnings. They had the money and Gwen, of all people, would appreciate anything that reduced risk to the Blue Mauritius. Still, it was hard to think of paying so much for something that had no intrinsic value.

Then again, if it let them get the one-penny Mauritius back, it would be worth it.

"All right. Are you going to let him know I'm coming?"

"He expects you."

"Can I count on your confidence?"

He shrugged. "Of course. After all, I do not know your name. Also, I do not wish to have my name associated with such questionable activities."

Although moral qualms certainly hadn't stopped him from pocketing the money earlier. She had no doubt he'd collect more. "Thank you for your help."

"I am happy to be of assistance, madame. I wish you a safe journey."

Show up safely with your money, more like.

He rose. "Good morning."

"Good morning." She stood to watch him go.

And looked up to see Bax staring at her from the entrance, face taut with some emotion she couldn't name.

15

ANGER. HE WAS SURE it was anger whipping through him as she walked out of the glass doors to meet him and he moved to hold her, just hold her. He pressed his face against the soft tumble of her hair, breathing in her scent, absorbing the reality of her against him, healthy and whole. Until that moment, he hadn't known just how certain he'd been that something had happened to her.

And just how much that would have hurt.

It hit him like the brutal, unforgiving shock of falling into a pool of very cold water. That wasn't the way it was supposed to go. She was a client, nothing more. He was too smart to get emotionally caught up in her and lose his focus.

So he loosened his hold on her and stepped away. "What were you thinking, going off like that?"

Joss blinked at him. "Ray called and wanted to see me. You were gone. I left you a note."

"I saw it. That doesn't answer my question. What was so important that you couldn't wait?" he demanded.

She walked past him into the semicircular entrance area with its cul-de-sac and line of taxis. "This isn't the place to talk," she hissed.

He stalked after her, staying several paces away to remove himself from the temptation of touching her again. To forget the metallic taste of fear that had filled his throat when he'd reached the empty T-bana station. "You took a damn fool risk," he ground out once they were on the shaded pathway that led to the commuter rail station up the hill.

"I took a calculated risk," she countered. "I wasn't meeting Markus again. I was meeting someone we knew and it had to happen now. And I tried to reach you. You didn't take your phone, you didn't say when you'd be back. Am I supposed to read your mind?" She stalked away from him and turned back in frustration. "Why don't you just admit that you're no better at this working together thing than I am?"

And that quickly his anger ebbed away.

"Look." Joss took a deep breath. "I'm sorry I scared you. I knew you wouldn't like it but I thought you would understand."

"You had a tail. I saw him as you were walking down the street."

"You saw? How? Where were you?"

"Markus stopped me after my run. I was walking back from the *torg* when I saw you. I couldn't catch you before you walked into the station." And he remembered watching helplessly as she disappeared into the station with the tail behind her.

"I thought I heard something as I was getting on the train but I wasn't sure. That was you? It made me turn, and then I saw the same guy who'd been in the hotel lobby."

Bax raked a hand through his hair. "It scared the hell out of me, getting to the station and finding it empty," he said unwillingly. "I didn't know what had happened to you."

"It kind of threw me for a loop, too," she confessed. "But I figured out a way to ditch him. Left him standing on a platform in Central Station," she said in a proud tone.

"No kidding?" Despite himself, he was impressed. "So you made it here without being followed?"

"I'm pretty sure. I saw that I missed your call while I was on the T-bana but I couldn't get an answer."

"It's okay," he told her, realizing that for the moment, anyway, it was. "So what did Ray have to say?"

Joss moved away to sit on a nearby bench. "Actually, he mostly wanted to introduce me to a friend. Or not a friend, but someone he knows. I don't think he thinks very highly of him, quite frankly."

"The one who was walking away when I came in?"

"Yes. He makes reproductions of famous stamps."

"Forgeries?"

"Reproductions marked on the back. Legal forgeries, I suppose, but they're not good enough for what we want. He knows someone, though."

"What's it going to cost us?"

"A lot," she said, and told him. "It's not so much that we can't afford it. I'll call Gwen and have her wire it."

"When's the handoff?"

Joss hesitated and his radar went up. "A couple of days. It's not exactly a handoff. We've got to go pick them up."

"Where?"

"Amsterdam."

He considered it. "You're looking at a one hour flight. It's not the end of the earth. We can do it the same day."

Joss looked down at the ground. "It's not that simple," she told him.

He had a bad feeling he wasn't going to like it, not a bit. "What's the catch?"

"I'm the one who's got to go get them."

"ABSOLUTELY NOT," Bax thundered.

Joss stared at him. A moment before, he'd seemed like

he was releasing the whole control thing. Now, he was back to telling her what she could and couldn't do. "I've got to go. We've don't have a choice."

"You're talking about walking into God knows where with a fistful of cash. You don't know these people, you've got nothing to trust but the word of a man Ray Halliday doesn't like very much. What if they try to rob you? What if it's all a scam? You don't have the experience and training to deal with it."

"I dealt with being tailed, didn't I?" she retorted. "And you taught me self-defense."

"I taught you a few emergency moves. Don't make the mistake of thinking you can deal with a professional. I don't want to see you get hurt," he said abruptly.

That was it, she realized. He was scared for her. It was just coming out as anger.

"Then tell me what to do. Get me as prepared as possible. If you stay here, or if you go out, even, Silverhielm's men will be busy watching you. It'll be easier for me to slip out alone than if we were together. You've got to let me do this," she pleaded. "If I don't, it'll screw everything up."

It took fighting every instinct he had for him to say yes, she could see that. The fact that he nodded, finally, meant that he put an enormous amount of trust in her.

Now all she had to do was pull it off.

PELIKAN WAS warm and dark, a hall lit with overhead clusters of luminous globes. It wasn't a restaurant so much as a beer hall, with heavy, square pillars that held up the twenty-foot ceiling. The walls above the walnut wainscoting were dark gold, some of them painted with jungle scenes, some merely darkened with a patina of age. Parquet tile covered the floor, making the room ring with a hubbub of sound.

Bax scanned the crowd, looking across the ranks of tables. "He's not here."

"What about the bar?"

On the other side of the wall lay Kristallen, the bar part of Pelikan. The two shared an entrance, but little else. Crowded Kristallen focused on electronic DJ music for the hip crowd. Cigarette smoke spiraled upward toward the ceiling. A shout of laughter erupted at the far corner and Bax looked over to see Oskar.

The young boat mate scrubbed at his hair as he leaned over to whisper to a pretty blond girl next to him. She turned in mock anger and punched him in the shoulder. He laughed again, and murmuring to her, he leaned in to steal a kiss. A flush stole over her cheeks.

Bax could tell the minute Oskar saw him, his gaze sharpening as he set down his beer mug. He said something to his friends and rose to walk down the bar toward them. The blond girl followed him with her eyes.

"*Hej.* So you have come to enjoy Pelikan. Welcome. Come have a drink with us."

Bax shook his head. "We were hoping to talk. Can we buy you a beer?"

"Of course." Oskar glanced down the crowded bar. "Let's go next door and get a table. It will be easier to hear."

They were able to get a table, that much was true. If anything, though, it was harder to hear in the echoing hall of the main room. Then again, Joss thought as the waitress led them to a table in the corner of the restaurant, that wasn't necessarily a bad thing. A blanket of sound made it difficult for anyone else to hear what they had to say.

It was a cozy spot. Bax immediately pulled a chair around so that they could sit, heads together. Expertly, he flipped a five hundred kroner bill onto the table in Oskar's direction. "We need to talk and we need to know it won't go further. Are we agreed?"

Oskar moved his hand away from the bill without touching it. "It is a question of what the talk is about. I don't break the law."

"This is not about breaking the law."

He relaxed fractionally. "What is it about?"

"Will it remain between us?"

Oskar gave Bax a long, searching look. Bax looked back at him impassively, seeking neither to convince or to intimidate. Finally, Oskar gave a slow nod. "It will."

"Good. We need a boat."

Oskar laughed. "All this secrecy over a boat?"

"There's more but we can start with that."

The waitress appeared and they ordered beer.

"We need a speedboat," Bax resumed, "one that can do sixty or seventy kilometers per hour."

"Such speed can be dangerous. Do you know anything about piloting such a boat?"

"I've got experience and I know how to navigate. I don't know the archipelago, though, so I'll need charts."

"Where are you going?"

"A private island."

"Ah, yes, I remember. Beyond Bullerö. Which one?"

"It's called Silverholmen."

For a moment, Oskar was perfectly still, then he leaned back and studied Bax. "So you want to go to Silverholmen. Are you invited?"

"We are, though I want to go out there a day or two before our invitation to check out the area."

"Karl Silverhielm is a formidable man."

"How do you know that it is Silverhielm's island?"

"I have heard stories. And are you a friend of his?"

"Would I be renting a boat to spy on a friend?" Bax asked softly.

"No."

The waitress appeared with their drinks. For a moment, they were occupied with the ceremony of beer mats and distributing mugs, but finally she was gone. Oskar gave Bax a frank look. "Are you sure you understand who you are dealing with?"

"I think so."

"He kills those who interfere with him."

Bax took a drink of his ale. "I'll take that chance."

"Are you willing to risk Josie, too?"

"I'm not his to risk," Joss spoke up. "It's my choice and I'm ready to do it."

"You don't understand what he's like. He is dangerous."

"You seem to know him awfully well," Joss observed, looking at the tense lines of Oskar's body.

Oskar stared at them. "You say I am not to talk of this conversation. What of you? What is your interest in Silverhielm?"

"He has something of ours, something we want to get back."

"And you're willing to cross him for it?"

"I'm eager to cross him," Joss said. "I want to get it back and I want it to hurt him."

Oskar shook his head. "You are both crazy, you know?" He circled his finger by his temple. "My advice to you is go home. Do not do this."

"That's not an option," Joss returned.

Oskar stared at them both moodily. "Let me tell you a story and see if you are still of this mind. I worked for Silverhielm, or rather I worked for a delivery company that brought goods to him. For a while."

"How was that?"

There was no humor in Oskar's smile. "It worked out as you would expect. Silverhielm was the barracuda and we were the herring. In the beginning, we delivered once a week, groceries, mostly. Some fuel for his generators. Then he offered to invest in the business, to help it grow, he said. A service for the archipelago. My boss was so eager, falling down to say yes." Oskar shook his head, an expression of pity mingled with contempt on his face. "You don't give a man like Silverhielm anything. My boss did not understand that. Not so smart, you understand? Or maybe too greedy."

Bax knew what happened to small, greedy players when they got involved with the Silverhielms of the world. "When was this?"

"About three years ago. At first, everything was just as Silverhielm said. My boss bought more boats, advertised to hire more pilots." He looked from Joss to Bax. "But you can guess, I am sure, what happened. Silverhielm sent over some people. Hire them, he said, and hire my dispatcher. Soon, we were making many more deliveries...and pickups."

"Smuggling." Joss said aloud. "They were smuggling."

"Congratulations. You are very fast. My boss did not believe for six months, until he saw one of the pilots hand off a package. He complained to Silverhielm, told him to stop or he would go to the police. They found him a week later in Lake Mälaren."

"Silverhielm?" Bax asked.

Oskar shrugged. "No proof. No proof of the smuggling, no proof of the murder. People saw him that night with a stranger in a bar. The bartender said he had only one drink but the police said that tests of the body showed he was very drunk. Maybe he stumbled into the water, police said." Oskar took a swallow of his beer. "Maybe not. Silverhielm bought the rest of the business."

"Didn't you tell them what you knew?"

"I had left the company by then. My statements were not enough to help, they said."

"Why did you leave?" Joss asked.

He gave them an opaque glance. "In the beginning, I made the deliveries to Silverholmen."

It was the foot in the door Bax had been hoping for. "Did you get into the house?"

"Not at first. His people came to the dock and took everything." Oskar moved his mug in small circles on the table, making little patterns on the scarred wood. "After a couple of months, though, they gave me a handcart and had me take the boxes up to the house."

"How much did you see?" This was what they needed, a layout of the house and the island. They needed to know what they were walking into.

"Mostly the kitchen, but sometimes I had to bring office supplies."

"Silverhielm has a home office?"

"With a desk the size of Gamla Stan. There is a fax, computer, copier, everything."

"A safe?" Joss asked.

"Probably, but I never saw it."

"Did you ever see him?"

"Oh yes. On the day I quit."

It was there in his voice. This wasn't the story he'd set out to tell them, but it had become the story they needed urgently to hear. "Why did you quit?" Bax asked.

For a moment, he was silent. A noisy group of students at the table behind them clanked glasses and shouted in a boisterous toast.

Oskar shifted. "I usually made my runs at the end of

the day, when the office was empty. One day I arrived earlier than usual. I put the groceries in the kitchen and started to deliver a box of printer paper to the office. There is a back passage there from the kitchen. I was by the door to the office when I heard loud voices. There is a peephole in the door and I looked."

He stared down into his beer, swirling the glass around. "Silverhielm was in the room along with some of his men. One very tall and blond. His eyes are flat, you understand? They were holding a man in a chair with his leg propped on another chair. And then Silverhielm said to the blond man 'Show him, Markus, why he should not have held back from me.' And Markus used a club to break his knee into small pieces."

Joss drew a breath in through her nose. Bax didn't move.

"That was the day I quit." Abruptly, Oskar looked up at them. "These are the men you are dealing with, do you understand? They are not to be trifled with."

"Neither am I," Bax said quietly, holding Oskar's gaze.

A second passed, then two. "I believe you," Oskar said finally. "So you are determined, it seems. How can I help you?"

"We need to know the layout of the house."

"Very well. Hand me a napkin." With a pen, Oskar began to sketch on the soft paper. "I can mark the charts to show you the way across the archipelago. You will require perhaps forty-five minutes to get there."

"And you can help me rent a boat?"

"I will supply you with my own. She is very fast." He pointed to the sketch with his pen. "The coastline of the island is curved, with a little inlet here. That is where the dock is, to one side of the house. A line of rocks stops the waves. What is the word?"

"A breakwater?"

"Yes. There are other rocks, maybe thirty meters out. Watch for the buoys. They mark the channel."

Bax nodded.

"The island is rock that rises steeply. From the dock, you must climb stairs to reach the level of the house."

"Can you see the house from the dock?"

"Only the roof. At the top of the stairs, a stone path leads to the house. It passes the main entrance here," he drew an *X* on the side nearest the dock, "and continues to a yard on the side away from the sea. The generator shed stands behind the main house. A door, here, goes to the kitchen."

"How far?"

"From the dock? A hundred and fifty meters, maybe more. Behind the house is grass down to where the rocks fall away to sea, you understand? And that side of the house, all windows."

"How about the inside?"

"I know only the kitchen and the office." He sketched them in. "The office faces the ocean. All windows on one side."

Bax nodded. "We'll need the boat on Friday during the day and Saturday evening, both. And can you mark charts for me to get out to the island?"

"Yes. Be careful. Silverhielm has a racing boat he uses to travel to the island. Do not think you can outrun him." Oskar tapped his fingers restlessly on the table. "I cannot take you out on Friday. I have work, you understand. In the daylight, you should be okay. The archipelago looks very different at night, though. I can pilot you Saturday, if you choose."

"Would you go back there?" Joss asked him.

"If it might ensure your safety, yes. They have no reason to be suspicious of me."

"Think about it. If you have not changed your mind Saturday, we would appreciate it," said Bax.

Oskar looked at them soberly. "Be careful. I do not want to see you dead, my friends."

16

JOSS THRUST a handful of kroner to the cab driver and got out, checking her watch as she walked into the SAS terminal. Her flight was in less than an hour, which was pushing it as far as the timing went. Then again, she was flying without luggage within the European Union and they'd bought her ticket online the night before. All she had to do was get a boarding pass and go to the gate.

Whoever was following her—and she assumed someone was—wouldn't know what flight she was on, couldn't tell without following her to the gate. To pass security, they'd need a ticket of their own. The line for purchasing new tickets was satisfyingly long, Joss noted as she walked to the check-in kiosk. Even if they were smart and bought the ticket by phone, she'd still be through the security gates before they could turn it all around.

All in all, a job well done, she congratulated herself as the kiosk printed out her boarding pass. She might be an amateur, but she was learning to ditch tails with the best of them. Now all she had to do was track down her forger.

"HELLO?"

Joss stood in the Amsterdam airport, watching a trio of KLM stewardesses walk briskly by with their wheeled bags. "Is Mr. Kant there?"

There was a short silence. "Where are you?" A man spoke in heavily accented English.

"The airport."

"Good. Make your way to a tavern named Polder. Be there at one. Sit at the bar. Someone will contact you."

She tried to guess his age, but it was impossible to tell from the clipped sentences. He was not old, not young. Just a man.

"Who should I look for?" she asked. "Is there a name?"

"Do not worry. We know you already."

"But I—"

He disconnected with a click.

The whole venture might have been risky but rather than being nervous, she was actually fairly calm. Better than calm. They were finally doing something besides watching and waiting. It was exhilarating, finally taking action. So what if it was risky walking into a meeting with total strangers, wearing a money belt stuffed with a small fortune? She could take care of herself. She had the self-defense moves that Bax had taught her and a squared-off steel rod about the size of a felt tip pen that could be used for a variety of interesting purposes. More than that, she had painfully earned street smarts that had gotten her out of more than one pickle in the past.

She was going to make it work, Joss vowed. No matter what.

BAX RAN. He ran across Gamla Stan, through Stortorget square, past the Nobel museum without noticing. He crossed the bridge to Slussen on Södermalm and fought off the memory of standing at the Katarinahissen with Joss their first day in Stockholm. She was in Amsterdam, out of his reach, out of his ability to protect.

To have gone with her would only have brought attention to them both, attention they couldn't afford. He hadn't liked it a bit, but he'd had to let her go. Now she was there and there was nothing he could do but wait for her to return.

And so he ran.

He'd always thought best when moving. Something about working his body pitilessly let him focus more completely on the task at hand. And the task currently at hand was getting the one-penny Mauritius back from Silverhielm.

Today, though, running didn't help. It just sent his thoughts moving in circles. They had entrée to Silverhielm's home, they had bait in the form of the Blue Mauritius. They had his trust, to a certain measure, or Markus wouldn't be recruiting Bax. The problem was getting the one-penny Mauritius out of the safe and into their hands. It would take the forgeries, inspiration and a fair amount of luck.

Inspiration, would come eventually. Luck, Bax could make. The forgeries were the big question, which brought him back to Joss.

She was resourceful, he reminded himself. The impromptu self-defense lesson he'd given her had taught him that. She knew enough dirty tricks that she had at least a fighting chance if anything funny started coming down. She'd promised to have her cell phone at hand. There was little more she could do to be prepared, nothing more that he could do save be with her, and this time he couldn't. He had to trust that she could manage the situation and come safely away with the goods.

This was what came of working with a partner, you were forced to trust them. The familiar thought came to him but oddly, he didn't feel much conviction in the sentiment. If he thought about it, what bothered him wasn't so much that he was trusting Joss to get the forgeries instead of doing it himself, or that he was working with a partner. What bothered him was that he didn't know if she was okay.

Which was natural, he told himself as he moved onto the ring road that encircled most of Södermalm. She was his client and, for now, his lover. Deeper involvement than that was out of the question, though. He wasn't built for anything serious, he'd learned that the hard way. Of course, he was concerned about Joss, and he'd be concerned until he'd closed the case and gotten paid.

But when that was done, so were they.

THE BAR wasn't pretty. It was neither quaint tourist bait nor worn and comfortable the way Pelikan had been. What it was was a dive, pure and simple. Cigarette smoke clouded the air. The floor felt sticky under her feet. The clientele consisted mostly of older lushes or hardened men with flat gazes, hunched at the bar or the handful of tables scattered at the front. When Joss walked in, they all turned to look.

Being stared at had never bothered her in the past. She'd always enjoyed being the center of attention. There was nothing that would be fun about being the center of attention for this group, though, unless fighting off the groping hands of men who smelled of cheap whiskey and stale cigarette smoke was someone's idea of a good time. It certainly wasn't hers. Scanning the room, she wondered which one was the forger, and tried to imagine handing over the money to any of them.

With a silent prayer that her real contact was yet to arrive, she slid onto a stool a few seats over from a guy the size of a small mountain who looked like he'd recently done time in a maximum security facility.

Anticipation—and nerves—fizzed through her. I can do it, she'd told Bax. Now she had to make good on that promise. She had to make the meeting come off, she had to come home with the forgeries in hand. She had to make it work.

The ex-con stared her way. He wore a dingy plaid shirt with the sleeves ripped off to show his thick biceps and blue tangle of jailhouse tattoos. More muscle than fat, but plenty of both. Joss gave him a dismissive glance. She didn't have time for him unless he was her contact, and in that case she was going to fly right back to Stockholm and tell Bax to come up with a Plan B, thank you very much.

"Can I get you something?" The bartender stopped in front of her. She had dyed raven hair, pale skin and lipstick so dark it looked almost black in the dim lighting.

Although Joss wanted a quick shot of tequila, it probably wasn't a good idea. "Just water for now, please. I'm waiting for someone." She scanned the bar again, studying the faces of the patrons, gauging whether their interest was purely male or held something more.

"Hey you, American?" asked the ex-con in a thick accent.

Joss looked away. There were times for a polite brush-off, but this was not one of them. The last thing she wanted was for some half-crocked criminal to be coming on to her when her contact came in.

Not that her forger wasn't a criminal, but she hoped he was a little more civilized than this.

"Hey, American," said the ex-con, shifting closer. "A drink?"

"No thanks," Joss muttered.

He pulled at his shirt to point to a set of Harley Davidson wings on his meaty chest. "Look, American."

Joss put her hands on the bar and opened her mouth to

reply when the bartender said something to him in Dutch that had him spitting out a curse and turning away.

"What did you say?" Joss asked.

"I told him you could date a convict in America if you wanted one."

Joss looked at her. "Thanks. I think."

"Don't mention it."

Joss checked her watch and drummed her fingers on the bar. The voice on the phone hadn't said when her contact would appear, only for her to wait. She glanced at her watch again.

"You said you're here to meet someone?"

Joss glanced up to see the bartender again and gave a shrug. "Yes, but I don't know what he looks like."

"He did not tell you it would be a man," she returned.

Joss blinked. "Excuse me?"

"Mr. Kant. The voice on the phone. He said only for you to come here and you would be contacted. I am the contact."

Joss stared. "I was expecting a guy," she said finally.

"Clearly. But as you can see, your options here are limited. Now, do you want to meet our friend or don't you?"

"Of course I do." There was a rushing sound in her ears.

Goth Girl smiled thinly. "Good. Go outside. There is a building on the opposite corner, a dark red. Buzz 2C and you will be let in. It is the third door on the second floor."

Joss rose to walk out when a hand clamped on her wrist. "Hey, American," snarled the ex-con. "Too fancy?"

The bartender spoke sharply to him in Dutch. He ignored her and tugged Joss toward him. He smelled sour and sweaty.

"Let go," Joss snapped, adrenaline flooding her system. Across the bar, men were looking up. No one was coming to her immediate rescue, though, she saw. No one wanted to tangle with this mountain of a man. She'd have to fend for herself. Taking a breath of mixed fear and fury, Joss flattened out her hand and chopped the ex-con across the Adam's apple, the way Bax had shown her. The edge of her stiffened hand bounced off the elastic feeling lump of his neck.

He gave a choked bellow and grabbed for his neck, releasing her.

"Hey," the bartender cried, but Joss ignored her. Instead, she bolted for the door, slamming out into the afternoon sun.

17

THERE HAD BEEN no reason to go through the whole bar routine, Joss thought as she stomped angrily across the street to the ruddy stucco building. They knew who she was, she'd been vouched for. It was a waste of time, and an irritating one at that.

She was in a working-class neighborhood of stark, utilitarian buildings that looked like they'd seen better days. The area held none of the charm and warmth of central Amsterdam. In the doorway of the red building, the directory showed no name next to unit 2C. Joss pushed the bell.

The door buzzed immediately and she pushed it open, her pulse speeding up just a bit. The entryway smelled musty in the warmth of the summer day. She climbed the stairs slowly, listening carefully, the self-defense rod out and in her hand. When she reached the right door, she knocked.

She'd expected someone different, was her first thought as the door opened inward. Someone who looked menacing. Someone who looked more criminal. Certainly she hadn't expected someone who looked like he could have been an eighth grade math teacher. She released the rod and brought her empty hand out of her pocket with an inner smile.

Slight and spare, he peered at her nearsightedly through thick glasses. He wore an ink-smudged blue canvas printers' apron over a white shirt. He didn't look like someone she'd need self-defense moves to overcome.

"I'm looking for Mr. Kant," she said.

"Ah yes. Come in, come in." He stepped back from the door.

It was clearly a working studio. There was a drafting board, shelves laden with inks and tools. On a solid wooden table sat a compact, old-fashioned printing press, and next to it a machine that looked very much like the perforator that she'd seen at the postal museum in Stockholm.

He smiled faintly at her inspection. "Sometimes the old tools are the best."

Joss turned to look at him. "Old tools to make new things?"

"Indeed. So you have come from Stockholm," he said. "What is it that you seek?"

Of course. Force her to declare herself so that if she were in law enforcement it would be entrapment. He was just doing what any smart criminal would. "I need a reproduction Post Office Mauritius pair. A very, very good pair. They should be able to pass inspection by an experienced amateur. They don't need to convince an authenticator."

He nodded, his dark hair gleaming under the lights. "You realize, of course, that these are the most famous stamps in all the world?"

"Yes."

"Then you understand that producing the type of reproduction you seek is not a simple thing. There is the ink, the paper, the gum. And there is the matter of the plate."

"I thought the original plate for the Post Office Mauritius pair still existed."

He raised his eyebrows. "I see you have done your

homework. The owner is not, however, prepared to participate in making reproductions, even for a very handsome sum."

And he'd probably offered that sum, from the sound of it. "So what do you do without a plate?"

"I do not need the original. I have the technology to make my own." He opened a door and flipped on the light. The room behind it was as high-tech as the workshop was old. A large blue metal box sat on a steel table, next to a computer. Waffled tubes ran to a humming box in the corner. Power cords snaked to a wall outlet. "This is a laser etching system. I scan a photograph of the stamp and the laser produces a new plate in copper. Very high quality. Very precise."

And undoubtedly expensive, Joss thought. "Impressive. So you can do the job, it sounds like."

"Oh, yes."

"How much do you want for it?"

He pressed his lips together as though he were considering a geometry problem. "It is risky, you understand."

"Your price?" she asked with an inward sigh.

"Fourteen thousand euros."

Fourteen thousand, she thought in shock. It was well over what the contact had told her, well over what she could afford. And well over what she had on her. "No way. That's too high."

"The Post Office Mauritius set is very valuable," he countered. "Of course such a fine reproduction should be of commensurate value. I seek merely a percentage of their price at auction."

"Your figure is higher than your broker suggested."

"My broker is not always privy to my production costs. Developing the correct ink colors for the Post Office Mauritius set, for example, has required visits to the Stockholm

Postmuseet. The papers are very specialized, and must be hand-treated to age them. Even the gums are specialized, and of course all of my printing equipment is rare and costly."

"But surely you have some of these materials in house."

"I have all of them, madame. I must recover the cost it required to amass them, though." He looked at her placidly.

The neighborhood was not particularly nice, nor was the building, Joss thought. He might make money on his various ventures, but he wasn't exactly prospering. It was worth taking a chance. "I'll pay you seven thousand," she told him.

"Ridiculous," he blustered. "This is precision work. My price is a fraction of the cost of the real stamp."

"I'm not getting the profit of the real stamp."

"You will be getting something. Thirteen thousand, then."

"Eight," she countered.

"It is impossible to do it for that price," he snapped.

"Then I'll go elsewhere." Joss turned to the door.

"There is no one else who does what I do." He raised his voice. "You are not just buying the stamps, you are buying my skill and experience."

"I'll take my chances." She laid her hand on the knob.

"All right. Twelve."

Joss stayed in place. "Nine." She held her breath.

"Eleven," he demanded. "Not one euro less."

She turned back to him, her face wiped clean of any expression of triumph. "Fine. How soon can you have them ready for me?"

"How soon do you need them?"

"Tomorrow? Thursday at the latest."

"That's impossible," he exploded. "Even Thursday is just two days from now."

"I have to have the stamps."

"This is an art," he protested. "It requires not just skill but time to produce a convincing reproduction."

"And you are a skilled and experienced man. If I don't have the forgeries by the day I need them, I may as well not have them at all, in which case I will not need your very expensive services."

He shook his head.

Joss studied him. "I would, of course, be prepared to add an expediting charge to your fee. Say, a thousand euros?"

He gave a grudging nod. "It is possible, I suppose."

"I thought it might be."

"I will need a deposit before I begin work. Three thousand now, the rest when you pick up the stamps."

"Of course," she said smoothly. "Tomorrow at the end of the day, then?"

"Tomorrow," he agreed.

JOSS HELD her cell phone to her ear and waited for the line to pick up as she walked down the avenue, headed back toward the city center.

Bax answered. "Hello?"

"It's me," she said.

Neither one of them considered the fact that Bax didn't have to think twice to recognize her voice.

"How'd it go?"

"Smooth as silk."

"No problems?"

"None," she said, conveniently leaving out the gorilla in the bar. "He came in high but I managed to bargain him down."

Bax laughed. "A smart shopper. So when are you going to get them?"

"Tomorrow at the end of the day, he says." She stopped on the corner and waited for the light.

"That will be cutting it close."

"He has to make a whole new plate. He was talking a week, I got it to two days."

"Not bad, Chastain," he said.

Pleasure warmed her. "I try."

"So it's what, two-thirty? What are you going to do in Amsterdam all by yourself for a day and a half?"

"I don't know. Wander, I suppose. It seems like a great city," she said, looking around. She'd come back into the city center, where the full charm of Amsterdam emerged. "I wish I had someone to play with."

"Do you want me to come over?"

It sounded perfectly splendid, but she was learning to be responsible these days. "We probably shouldn't spend the money."

"True. On the other hand, there's nothing to stop me paying my own way. I've done everything here I can at this point. I'm only going to be sitting around and Amsterdam is one of my favorite cities. I could be there in two or three hours."

"You mean it?" she began. "That would be a gas. We'd have to get a hotel, of course."

"Sure." There was tapping in the background.

"What are you doing?"

"I'm going online to get a ticket and a hotel. How would you like to stay on the Gentlemen's Canal?"

"I don't know, would you have to be a gentlemen when we're there?"

"I suspect there's some waffle room." He clicked keys some more. "Okay, we've got a room in the Huygens House, on the Herengracht." He spelled it for her.

"I was thinking somewhere cheap out by the airport. We're spending twelve thousand on the forgeries."

"This one's on me," he told her.

"Bax, you can't blow your money right and left like that."

"I'm not blowing it. Consider it a barter agreement. My flight gets in at 7:00 p.m., so I can probably be there by eight. I expect to find you in bed, naked, when I get there."

One corner of her mouth tugged up into a smile. "If you play your cards right." She sobered. "Of course, we do have one problem. What if you get followed?"

Bax's only response was a snort.

"Okay, forget that question."

"Good. I'll call you from the airport."

"I'll drag you to do tourist things," she warned him.

"I live for the Anne Frank House," he told her.

She disconnected with a foolish smile on her face. He was flying in to see her. He could have stayed in Stockholm but he wasn't. He was coming over to be with her.

BAX SAT in the back of the cab, watching the gabled buildings of Amsterdam pass by as they headed to the hotel. And to Joss. He'd seen her only that morning, so why was it that it felt like it had been days?

The decision to head to Amsterdam had been sheer impulse, an impulse that made him a little nervous now. One minute, they'd been talking about the case. The next, he'd been on a plane headed south over the Baltic.

Not because staying in Stockholm would have left him at loose ends, necessarily, he thought as the car stopped. He was perfectly happy prowling the city on his own. It was just that being with Joss would give him a chance to keep an eye on her, to be around in case of trouble. And being in Amsterdam would be no hardship—it was his favorite city in all of Europe. He wasn't getting in over his head with her. He was too smart for that. This was just a little bonus.

He got out of the cab, slinging his satchel over his shoulder, a little rush of expectation running through him. He bounded up the steps to the front door of the little hotel. He knew where he was going. Nodding at the proprietor, he didn't stop but climbed the steps to the second floor, looking for the room Joss had described to him over his mobile phone as he'd walked through the airport.

And then he was at the door and she was flowing into his arms, all silky, fragrant and soft against him. She wasn't a creature of his imagination anymore. She was here, safe in his arms. And for a moment he didn't let himself think about anything, she was all he wanted.

Dropping his satchel, Bax kicked the door closed with one foot and lifted her in his arms. "I thought I told you to be naked," he growled against her neck, then kissed the sweet rises of her breasts.

"Forgive me, master," she said, flipping open the towel she'd wrapped around herself to shield herself from prying eyes.

He knew the way desire for her could tear at him. Day after day, over and over he still got the slow thud of arousal in his blood every time he looked at her, driving him to bury himself in the tight heat of her body. At this moment, though, he wanted only to hold her, to feel her warm and close against him. Clothes were an impediment, a barrier that he dispensed with impatiently.

And then he buried his face in her neck and held on for all he was worth.

The need, when it came, was slow, gentle. It wasn't about the wild rush they usually encountered but a tenderness he hadn't known he had a capacity for. It was a coming together more than just a coming, and when he slid inside her and he heard her soft sigh, it was as though all the disconnected parts of his world made sense.

And as they rocked together, it was the gathering connection that bound them gently.

JOSS SAT on the bed, her legs folded, turning a euro coin over idly in her hands. Lovemaking, a romantic walk down the canals to dinner and now, a quiet evening. She felt lazy and satisfied as a tabby cat with a dish of cream.

All was right in her world. They were getting the forgeries, they had a meet planned with Silverhielm just three days away. Things were coming to a head. Soon, if all went well, they'd be getting the stamp and everything would be back in place. She could return to San Francisco, her grandfather could come home without facing ruin.

And Bax would fly off to Copenhagen.

A shiver of cold whisked through her and she blinked. Having him here, now, next to her felt so right. The hours before he'd arrived, she'd drifted around the streets and canals of Amsterdam. She'd taken in the sights, but it had all felt empty. It wasn't the same without someone to enjoy it with. It wasn't the same without Bax, his wry humor, his seemingly endless store of knowledge.

It wasn't the same without the feel of his hand in hers.

Knowing he was on his way had made it easier. In a week or two, she wouldn't have that. In a week or two, they'd go from essentially living together to leading separate lives.

It wasn't a surprise. That had been the plan from the beginning. She'd known she'd have to do it.

She couldn't imagine it.

Joss swallowed, shaking her head blindly. And the sudden knowledge snaked through her. This couldn't be. Surely she was smarter than that. She couldn't have been this foolish, she, who'd always skimmed blithely through relationships without so much as a bobble. She who'd always held the upper hand. She couldn't have been foolish enough to fall in love.

At first, the plan had been simple: sleep with him to get his cooperation. Indulging in her attraction was just a side benefit, and the fact that they'd been incredible together in bed had been a rather wonderful present.

Now, though, everything had changed. She'd lost control of the situation. She'd let her feelings get involved. How could she have let herself fall for Bax? Bax, of all people? Bax, the loner. Bax, who made it clear he was only in it for the job.

And yet, he'd seemed to slide easily into the togetherness they'd been forced into recently. Granted, their affair had started out as physical, but for all the moments of flash and fire, there were many more of sheer closeness.

She needed to say something, she thought, glancing over at him where he sat reading a book on Amsterdam. She needed to talk to him, see if there was a chance of continuing their relationship after the case was over. It was a simple enough question. Plenty of people did it. People dated all the time. Okay, they'd be coming at it sort of backward, but what was wrong with that? It wasn't like there was a rule book or anything. Whatever worked was the right thing to do.

Nervously, she began toying with the coin, rolling it between her fingers. "So, we've got the forgery and we'll be getting the stamp back soon, right?"

Bax looked over and watched her manipulate the coin. "Sure. All we have to do is figure out how to make the switch."

"What are your plans after that? After we get back to the States?" Don't be a wuss, she told herself. Tell him. "Because I'd really—"

"Do that again," he interrupted.

Joss blinked. "What?" She looked down at her hands.

"That's right," he muttered to himself. "You know sleight of hand."

"Yeah, so?"

"We might just have found our way."

"What do you mean?"

"The switch. You get Silverhielm to give you the stamps to look at and then you switch them for the forgeries."

"It would be risky."

"Not really. Besides, you're a pro." Energized, he sat bolt upright, the book set aside, forgotten. 'We can do this," he promised.

And Joss nodded and watched the moment slip away.

18

THE WIND WHIPPED through Joss's hair as the speedboat skimmed over the waves. Out here, on the Stockholm archipelago, the world was sky and water, rock and tree, both pristine and beautiful. Occasionally, they passed another pleasure boat or an inhabited island. Mostly, once they'd gotten out of Stockholm's inner harbor, they'd had the archipelago to themselves.

Joss adjusted her sunglasses. For more than half an hour, Bax had had the little speedboat going all out, setting it to autopilot while he squinted at charts and checked the landmarks that Oskar had written down for him. Occasionally, he muttered to himself but she couldn't hear a word of it over the roar of the engine. Since there was nothing she could do, she just leaned back and enjoyed.

The day before their meet with Silverhielm and it was unseasonably hot for Stockholm. Joss had started out wearing her jacket, but by the time they'd reached the dock to pick up the boat, the jacket was off and tied around her waist, leaving her in just a tank top and jeans. Even that had been sticky and uncomfortable.

Now, the wind blew the heat away. She felt the hot press of the sun on her shoulders and cheekbones, but the passage of air made it pleasant instead of oppressive. In the distance, the white shape of a ferry forged its way toward the horizon. Nearby, a gull skimmed low over the water.

Bax reached out to the controls. Abruptly, the boat slowed until it was going just fast enough for him to keep it aimed at the swells.

"Are we there yet?" Her hearing was so numbed by the sound of the engine that her voice sounded strange to her own ears.

"Near enough that we should slow down and make sure we know where we are." He checked the compass and the GPS unit and pointed to the low-lying islands to either side of them. "That should be Kymmendö and that over there is Mörtö, which puts us right about here." He pointed to the map. "Silverholmen is about another five or six miles. Call it half an hour."

"Thirty minutes to go five miles? I thought Oskar said this boat topped out at seventy-five miles an hour."

"Kilometers," Bax corrected, "kilometers per hour. That's about fifty miles an hour flat out. It doesn't matter, though. I want to go slow enough that we can stop as soon as we're in sight. This is our chance to get a nice, quiet look without them knowing we're out here."

Already, the heat was settling over her as though she were standing in front of an oven. "So what do you want to do besides roast for the next half hour?"

He handed her a bottle of water and picked up his binoculars. "Stay cool."

"HERE ARE YOUR keys to the room and to the minibar. Please enjoy your stay with us." Nils Andersson stood behind the polished mahogany counter of the Royal Viking hotel and handed the room folio to the American woman with her tightly permed hair. He liked working at the Royal Viking. It always impressed the women he met, especially when he lied and told them he was a manager.

Anna, the sunny clerk at his side greeted the guest in

front of her with a brilliant smile. Nils wished he could impress the lovely golden Anna with her tilted nose and her midnight-blue eyes, but she knew he was only a junior clerk. Besides, she looked down on him for the rules he broke. Like everyone didn't break a rule once in a while.

He was aimlessly skimming down the list of registered guests on the computer when a tall blond man caught his eye.

The man jerked his chin in a beckoning gesture. Andersson froze. He leaned to Anna. "Can you cover for me for a moment?"

"Nils, you just had a break. Mr. Hogberg will not like it," she protested, but he was already disappearing into the offices behind the counter. There were people more important than Mr. Hogberg. A moment later, he came out the side door that led into the lobby.

"Good morning, Nils," said Markus Holm.

"Are you trying to get me fired?" he snarled, walking toward the door to the luggage room with Markus following. "You have no business here. Go."

"I have business with you," Markus countered. "Mr. Silverhielm did you a favor. I would think you would want to return it."

"A favor?" he whispered. "They break me, these payments you extract."

"You have not been injured, have you? Your knees work well? Your hands? Your eyes?"

Andersson swallowed. "Yes," he faltered.

"I thought so. Few in the position you were in can say as much." Markus stepped closer to him, eyes cold. "You should be grateful."

"I am grateful," Andersson said huskily. "What do you want?"

"Please."

"What?"

"Please tell me what you want."

Andersson cleared his throat. "Please tell me what you want."

Markus smiled benevolently. "Only a small favor."

"What?"

"You have a guest in the hotel, Josie Astin. I need to get into her room and I need to get into the safe."

"I can't do that," he said emphatically. "It is not allowed. I would be found out. I would be fired."

"It won't be found out." Markus's voice was soft.

"You cannot guarantee it."

"Ah, but I can guarantee that if you do not assist me, information will be laid in front of your employers that *will* get you fired. I can guarantee that your life will get very uncomfortable, indeed."

Andersson gave Markus a look brimming with equal parts fear and resentment. "What if the guests walk in on us?"

"The guests just set off from the Nybroviken in a motorboat, headed for the archipelago. They will not return to the hotel for some minutes, probably hours. I only need a small amount of time."

Andersson stared at him, balancing one fear with another. Markus waited serenely.

"All right," the clerk said finally, his eyes shifting back and forth. "I'll do it."

BAX PICKED UP his camera phone and pointed it toward Silverholmen to take a photograph. The boat idled in the swells.

"What are you doing?"

"I'm sending this to Oskar to see if we're in the right spot." A few minutes went by and the phone rang. He heard Oskar's voice in his ear.

"Hello, my friend. Are you enjoying yourself?"

"Just doing a little sightseeing. I was wondering if we've hit that fishing spot you were talking about."

"Yes, it looks like you are there. Watch out for the shoals to the north. They're marked on the chart but you come up on them more quickly than you would think."

"All right." Bax picked up his binoculars with one hand and studied the waters ahead.

"Remember, some of the fish are very alert, so you should be cautious to avoid alarming them."

"I'll try. I have not seen the barracuda who lives around here."

"Stay away from the island. I'm told he swims near there."

"Don't worry, I have a very strong line," Bax said.

Oskar laughed. "It sounds as though you are well prepared. Good fishing, my friend."

"Thanks. I hope to hook him."

CHECKING THE HALL in both directions, Nils used a passkey on the door to the room. "Inside," he hissed, "quickly."

The room showed the disorder impossible to avoid with two people living in close proximity. A woman's jacket and trousers were draped over one of the chairs; books were piled haphazardly on the desk.

Markus looked at Andersson. "And now, I need to get into the safe."

Andersson slipped the master key from his pocket and handed it to Markus. "You know I will be fired if this is discovered," he muttered resentfully.

"Worse things can happen." Markus snapped on latex gloves. "I can demonstrate, if you like." He opened the armoire that held the safe and adroitly used the master key. With a click the door opened.

Humming, Markus began to poke through the safe, pulling out a woman's purse, some kroner, a packet of documents. No envelopes, he noticed with disappointment but no surprise. It was impossible to imagine Johan being sloppy enough to leave the Blue Mauritius in a hotel safe. Still, it was always worth checking.

He picked up the kroner and Andersson stepped up behind him. "You can't steal anything. The safe stores the time it was opened. I will be caught."

Markus stopped and turned to him. "Nils, it is time for you to go."

"I will not." Nils swallowed. "I have to stay here while you are in the room."

"Then go sit on the chair by the window." The tone was kind, the look was not. Andersson jumped to obey.

Shaking his head, Markus spilled the contents of the safe on the bed. "And who are you this month, Johan my friend?" He opened up the blue passport to see a photo of Bax. "John Baxter. Very good. And your companion?" Markus reached into the small handbag and pulled out the wallet and passport, appreciating for a moment the faint whiff of Joss's perfume. The wallet, he noticed, was small, with no credit cards or bank card such as most people usually carried. It did, however, include a driver's license. He looked at it and stilled. "How very interesting," he murmured.

"I cannot be gone from the desk for long," Andersson reminded him. "They will demote me to night shift. Haven't you found what you came for?"

Markus flipped open Joss's passport. "Much, much more," he said to himself. "All right, back to the front desk with you, Nils," he said briskly, putting the wallet back into Joss's purse. "I am done for now."

"Now? Will you be back?"

"Perhaps." Markus took his time returning the objects

to the safe, adjusting things carefully so that they looked as they had when he'd opened the safe. Johan, he knew, would notice.

"You must go," Andersson muttered, herding Markus back out into the hall like a nervous sheepdog.

"And so I will, Nils, and so I will."

SILVERHOLMEN WAS gorgeous, Joss thought, all rounded gray rock and green birches against the sapphire-blue of the sea. Small waves sent up occasional plumes of spume as they hit the shore. A few smaller islands dotted the sea around them, none even remotely large enough to be inhabited. Silverhielm had chosen his island getaway carefully. The nearest people would probably be ten miles away, maybe more. Out here, he'd have his privacy and then some.

Out here, he could do as he chose.

They'd come upon Silverholmen from the northwest and now circumnavigated it slowly. It was shaped a little like a lopsided lima bean, perhaps a mile and a half across at its widest. Birches and pine and heather covered much of it, at least what she could see. The house, Oskar had told them, was on the southern shore.

Slowly, Bax brought the boat around the island to come upon the house from the southeast, from the Baltic side rather than the Stockholm side from which boats normally approached.

Joss pushed her hair back out of her eyes and tried to ignore the heat. "Were Oskar's directions off or did you overshoot it intentionally?"

"It seemed like the best way to come up on them without being spotted. They may have guards watching the water with binoculars from the house, but they're not likely to monitor the northern exposure as carefully. And it doesn't hurt to have a feel for the whole island."

"In case everything goes south and we need to run that way?"

"If everything goes south and we're cut off from the boat, it won't matter whether we get loose on the back side of the island. We can't walk back to Stockholm. Eventually, they'll find us." He lowered his binoculars and looked at her. "Everything won't go south, though. This is just habit. The more prepared you are, the fewer surprises you have." The boat chugged along and slowly the trees thinned and the house came into view.

As they'd navigated the archipelago, she'd seen homes of glass and wood that looked to be made of air, homes built in traditional long-house styles that blended by virtue of their humbleness, homes that brought Swedish Modern to the age-old archipelago. In all this variety, though, she'd never seen a house like Silverhielm's.

It wasn't an island home, it was a transplanted manor house, suited to one who imagined himself lord and master of his world. Massive and baroque, it made no concession to its environment but dominated. The facade rose straight up, built of gray stone blocks, stolid and imposing. On the western exposure, they could see the ornate portico, designed as though for dukes and duchesses to roll up and alight from their coaches. Even the bottom floor, with all its windows overlooking the sea, was broken up with heavy columns and carvings.

Behind the house lay a stone terrace with steps down to the green lawn that rolled out to the shore. Stone lions sat in frozen vigilance on either side. It was the sort of manor house a member of the nobility might have built back in the eighteenth century. It said, Joss thought, a great deal about its owner.

"So do you think this was really the house he had in mind?" she asked.

"Of course. A man like Silverhielm always gets exactly what he wants."

"He must have an incredible view," she murmured.

Bax slowed the boat to an idle and threw an anchor overboard. "Always nice to have good scenery when you're ordering people kneecapped."

"Now, there's a thought I can do without."

"I'm glad you heard that story. You need to understand that Silverhielm is a genuinely ruthless man. It doesn't do to underestimate him."

Joss thought of the singlemindedness and disregard for anything but his own desires that it must have taken Silverhielm to build this sort of house out on a lonely island. Somehow the sight of the mansion, along with Oskar's story, made Silverhielm's character all too real. "It's too bad we couldn't just sneak on and swap out the forgeries without him knowing. He'd be happy because it's all about the owning, not the stamps themselves. We'd be happy because we got the stamps back."

"Why do you care about what he thinks?"

She didn't answer right away, but picked up the binoculars and scanned the island. "So what do you think he's going to do when he figures out we've scammed him?"

"That's a good question." Bax rose to pull one of the fishing rods they were using for cover out of its holder and opened up a container of chum. "I don't imagine he'll be happy."

"Will he come after us?" she asked, dreading the answer.

Bax drew his arm back and moved it forward in an arc, sending the baited hook sailing far out over the water. "He'll have to find us first."

"I don't think it'll be that much of a challenge for Markus to find us, do you?"

Bax finished adjusting the reel and turned to look at her. "So what are you saying?"

"Maybe we're better off finding a way to a standoff."

"We already have. The standoff we'll have is that we'll have the stamp mounts with Silverhielm's fingerprints on them, proof that he had them. Rolf, for one, would love an opportunity to send in a team with a search warrant. I think we can keep Silverhielm quite busy enough if we get the one-penny Mauritius back."

"If?"

He kissed her. "When."

"SO, HOW WAS YOUR visit to the Royal Viking?" Silverhielm leaned back in his expensive leather executive chair, staring out the windows of his Slussen office at the pastel buildings of Gamla Stan.

"Interesting," Markus said easily.

Silverhielm turned to face him. "Did you find the Blue Mauritius?"

"Of course not. The Blue Mauritius is most likely in a bank vault somewhere in Stockholm. Johan is well aware of the vulnerabilities of hotels and hotel safes."

"Did you find anything?"

"Indeed. Johan's current identity, for one."

"That is of little interest to me."

"He changes them at will," Markus agreed. "I did find out something far more useful, however. The identity of his lovely companion."

Silverhielm picked up a pencil and began tapping it against his desk blotter. "She is not Josie Astin?"

"No. The beautiful Ms. Astin has been lying to us. She is not the girlfriend of Stewart Oakes's thief. She is actually Joss Chastain, Hugh Chastain's granddaughter.

Silverhielm said nothing, but the pencil he held

snapped in two. "She is not here to sell the Blue Mauritius."

"Unlikely, but not impossible," Markus agreed. "Joss Chastain has no money, no permanent home, few records." He shrugged. "She may be here for profit. It is also possible that she is here to recover the one-penny Mauritius."

"Preposterous."

"It would explain why she has engaged the services of a man like Johan, however."

Silverhielm nodded. "We could have a family rebel, selling for her own profit. Why would she not tell us?"

"Afraid of suspicion, perhaps? It is more likely that she wishes to take the stamp back, as her sister did."

"Sentimental fools."

"Indeed."

Silverhielm put his elbows on the arms of his chair and steepled his fingers in front of him. "I do not care for being lied to. I will not be made a fool of. Or cheated." Anger vibrated in his voice as he glowered into space, his face ruddy. Minutes passed.

"Do you wish to cancel the meeting?" Markus asked.

Silverhielm exhaled and shifted his shoulders. He smiled slowly. "Not at all. It promises to be even more amusing than I'd anticipated. I will get the stamp, we will have some sport." His eyes turned cold and implacable. "And the very attractive Ms. Chastain will not leave Silverholmen alive."

_19_

THE SUN BEAT DOWN on them from its zenith. Joss sat on one of the bench seats along the side of the boat and trailed her fingers in the water. More than two hours had passed since they'd dropped anchor. Bax had merely kept his binoculars trained on the house. Despite her awareness of the importance of the surveillance, it was getting old. She was bored, tired, hot, restless and wholly impatient for something to happen.

"So you've monitored the guards and you've seen the layout. What are you looking for now?"

He shrugged. "I'm not sure. When I'm not sure, I watch and I wait. We know that they have a daytime patrolling schedule. I don't see Silverhielm's cigarette boat."

"The racing boat, you mean? Do you think he's in town?"

"Maybe. In that case, he'll either stay in his townhouse or come back out here. It might be nice to hang around and see what he does."

"That wouldn't be until five or so, right?" Joss checked her watch. "That's about four hours from now."

"About."

"And we've been here for two hours already."

"You were the one who wanted to come on the stakeout." He gave her a glance of amusement mixed with sympathy. "Welcome to the exciting life of a detective."

He was right, Joss admitted, but it didn't do anything to ease the oppressive heat. She was sticky and uncomfortable in her jeans, and the light breeze that had eased things that morning seemed to have died away. There wasn't even a shade over the cockpit of the boat. "So we're basically going to just sit here and wait."

"Yep."

Joss moved over to the captain's chair next to Bax and sighed, wishing she hadn't worn a black tank top. On the horizon, another ferry chugged its way north, bound, perhaps, for Finland.

She was so hot.

"Are there sharks out here?" Joss asked.

"You mean besides the ones on the island?"

"Besides them. Could I take a swim?"

"No. I don't want you in the water if we need to leave suddenly."

She fanned herself with one hand. "This is killing me."

"You look like you're dying. Here." Bax handed her another bottle of water. "We can stop when we get closer to Stockholm and you can swim all you like. Once we're done here."

"All right." She wouldn't act like a surly child, she told herself. If he could tolerate it, she could, too. "So how do you keep from getting bored on a stakeout?"

Bax shrugged and brought the binoculars back up to his eyes. "Oh, try to reconstruct *Goodfellas* in my head scene by scene. List the players on my all-time World Cup team." One corner of his mouth twitched. "Try to figure out the best sex I've ever had."

Joss snapped her head around to stare at him. "The best sex you've ever had?" she repeated dangerously.

His grin widened. "Uh-huh."

"If you're smart, your next comment will be that this

time that topic hasn't been particularly useful because you haven't had to think very much about it."

"Oh, this time around I've had an indisputable winner."

"Oh, really?"

"Yes, really." He leaned over and kissed her on the nose. "Of course, when we get back to the hotel, I might need to verify it." He raised his binoculars again and began watching the island.

The minutes ticked by and Joss picked at her sweat-dampened shirt. The heat of the sun baked her legs through the denim of her jeans. If only she'd worn shorts, she thought with a sigh. If only she'd thought to *pack* shorts. Sweden was north, for crying out loud. It wasn't supposed to hit the nineties all the way up here. It was like having a heat wave in Alaska.

On Silverholmen, the grass baked gently in the heat.

She had to do something.

Impatiently, Joss stood and unsnapped her jeans. Bax swung around to look at her. "What are you doing?"

"Don't let me distract you. I just want to cool down."

"I see."

"I forgot my bikini." She lowered the zipper and slid the denim off her hips. "I figured I'd improvise."

"You're stripping in broad daylight?"

"Who's going to see? The people on that ferry?" She pointed to the horizon. "I think they'll survive." She kicked off the jeans and stripped off her tank top, sighing in bliss as the faint breeze hit her sweat-damp skin.

"You'd better hope the Swedish coast guard doesn't show up and bust you for public exposure."

"I'll see them long before they get here." She reached back to unfasten the black lace of her bra and shrugged her shoulders to slip it off. "I'm just so hot. I thought if I took off a little clothing I'd be more comfortable." She slid her hands down to her hips, to the straps of her lacy thong, and paused. "You don't mind, do you?"

When he only stared, she hooked her fingers in the sides and began dragging the scrap of lace slowly down her hips, leaning over to pull it over her thighs, her knees and down to her ankles. "Oh, that's much better." She straightened to toss the thong on top of the pile of clothing she'd discarded. Sitting back in her captain's chair, she propped her feet up on the dashboard and poured water over herself.

Bax set his binoculars down slowly.

"Of course, there's always a risk of sunburn." Joss reached out for the bottle of sunscreen they'd brought.

His eyes followed her hand as she squeezed a line of sunscreen along first one leg, then the other. With a wicked smile, Joss slid her palm over the sleek lines of her thighs, stretching her legs up like a dancer. "I don't know why you don't at least take your shirt off." She nodded at the dark blue polo jersey he wore. "You must be baking."

Pouring out more sunscreen, she stroked her hand up and over the flat of her belly, spreading the cream over her waist, along the swell of her hips.

Utterly still, Bax just watched her.

Enjoying herself now, Joss slid her hands up higher, over the soft swells of her breasts. They filled her cupped hands, firm against her palm. To please herself, she caressed the skin, squeezing the nipples. "Aren't you hot?" she murmured.

In almost one motion Bax tossed down the binoculars and reached for her, pulling her against him and capturing her mouth with his. She chuckled deep in her throat in giddy delight. Once again, she'd made him lose the control he prized. Once again, she'd tempted him to give in to desire.

He dragged her to her feet with one arm, letting the other hand rove as he pleased, from her breasts to her ass to the slippery cleft between her legs. Arousal, pleasure flooded through her.

"You drive me nuts," he growled.

"That's why I do it," she whispered, her words filled with desire.

Bax stripped off his shirt, then leaned back against his captain's chair and reached for his belt.

"I can do that," Joss murmured, and brushed his hands aside. She unthreaded the strap from his buckle and found the button of his jeans beneath. "If you're not worried about the coast guard, that is." She pulled the zipper down and drew him out, already hard and pulsing. "After all, I don't know what they might think if they came across this." She brushed his silky soft cock over her cheek, licking the length of him like some erotic ice cream cone. "I could tell them that you're injured and I'm doing triage before applying first aid."

She swirled her tongue around his glans until she heard his rapid intake of breath. The first slick, faintly salty drop of precome emerged, and she spread it down the hard length of him with her fingertip. "Or I could tell them you've got a cramp and I'm applying warm compresses." She slid his cock swiftly into her mouth and he groaned.

It was incredibly arousing, seeing him, tasting him, feeling him, hearing him groan as she pleasured him and pleasured herself. There was no telling what would happen once they'd gotten the stamp back and the case was over. Bax might be true to his word and move on. She might never hear from him again. But she had him now. Now, of all moments, he was hers, hers to play, hers to pleasure. And if this had to be the end of it, this memory of sun and salt air and the gently rocking boat and the purity of pleasure would stay with her always.

She put a hand to her breast and caressed herself even as she felt him harden against her lips, knowing he was watching, knowing it would turn him on. When he dragged her to her feet, she went willingly, but she didn't move to the cushions of the bench seat that he urged her toward.

Instead, she pressed him into the captain's chair. As a breeze whisked over her, she straddled him and looked down at his hard cock, shuddering in the diamond formed by the overlap of her thighs and his. "Of course, if the coast guard does show up, maybe we're better off if we hide the evidence." And she rose to slide him inside herself, catching her breath at the feel of it.

Bax bent his head to her breasts, brushing his chin against first one nipple, then the other. The light scrape of his afternoon shadow against the hard nubbins of flesh made her murmur in pleasure. He reached a hand down between her thighs, rubbing his thumb against her clit until she cried out at the touch.

Joss clutched his shoulders and leaned into him, rising and falling, feeling him get harder and thicker, going deeper, so deep that it forced a cry from her at the intensity of each plunge.

And then his hands were on her hips, moving her up and down, setting the rhythm, setting the pace. The sound of the water, the rock of the boat, the slick rub of the base of his cock against her clit took her up, and up, the tension coiling up in the center of her. And then she broke, shuddering, leaning back from the waist to push herself hard against him for one final stroke that combined with her final contractions to bring him to a swift, hard orgasm in the sun.

"SO IS THIS what they taught you at Interpol, to have sex on a stakeout?" she asked him lazily, trailing her fingers over his chest.

They lay on the deck of the boat, cushions underneath them.

"Absolutely. It was part of the orientation class."

Joss made a husky sound of delight. "You must have had some instructors."

"They couldn't hold a candle to you." He stroked a hand down her back. "Actually, you may very well have ruined me for the future. I'm going to compare every single stakeout I'm on to this, and believe me, cold coffee and stale sandwiches in a car at night don't come anywhere close."

"So I win the award for best stakeout companion?"

"You win the award for best everything." He gave her a long, lingering kiss that carried much more than even he realized.

Joss stretched her arm above her to look at her watch. "Three o'clock. I suppose we should get dressed before Silverhielm comes home. If he comes home. Him and his goons."

"And Markus."

"Anyone who blows away someone's knees counts as a goon to me."

Bax frowned. "It's hard to say what he is, but he's not a goon."

"What is it with you two?" Mystified, Joss tapped her fingers on his chest. "I know you said before that you didn't like him, but you do. I can hear it in your voice."

"I don't even know that it's liking. It's more that I understand him."

"I don't see how. He's a bad guy, Bax. You were the one who told me that."

"There's a reason I understand Markus. There was a time when I wasn't a very good guy, either."

"I find that hard to believe."

"Believe it."

There was something hollow about his voice. Joss turned on her side to face him and propped herself up on one elbow. "When?"

"Right after my mother died, my dad and I were at each other's throats. I was sixteen and thought I knew it all. He wanted to run me like I was one of his buck privates."

"And you didn't like that at all."

"Now there's a surprise." He gave a wry smile. "He got put on the night shift, which was perfect for me. I got to running with a rough crowd, got in some trouble."

"What kind of trouble?"

"Little scrapes. I ignored the rules when they stood in my way."

"Like what?" She'd never been much for rules herself.

He moved his shoulders. "We ran wild, did some joy-riding, got our hands on some beer a few times. The more I did it, the more it made my father crazy and I liked that. The more I did it, the more I wanted to do."

"That doesn't sound like a kid headed to the FBI. What happened?"

"One night I took one too many chances and got caught with some kids who were breaking into a store. I was outside, across the street, but I got picked up too. They didn't charge me. I wound up sitting across from a youth counselor named Tom McDowell." He remembered the cramped office with its battered metal desk. Tom hadn't looked kindly and caring. Tom had looked like a hardass. Bax had given tough right back to him, but he'd been scared down deep, scared that he'd gone maybe too far. And Tom had seen.

He'd kicked away the cockiness that Bax had held around him like a shield, kicked away his pride in being a rebel. And as the weeks went on, he'd showed Bax that there were other things to have pride in, things that really mattered.

"The next step was getting arrested and winding up with a parole officer. But Tom didn't let me slide that far. He turned me around."

She traced her fingertip over the frown line in his forehead, erasing it. "He saw something of value in you."

"He was young and idealistic. I was lucky enough to be his project."

"His success story, it sounds like." She kissed him.

"I like to think so." When he'd confessed to Tom that he liked the idea of investigating, Tom hadn't laughed, he'd helped him look up the different ways to do it for a living. The day Bax graduated from the FBI academy, Tom had been there. They'd stayed in touch ever since. "He was the one who pointed me to the FBI after I'd gotten my head on straight. Luckily, I hadn't gotten in trouble bad enough to close any doors."

"And the FBI led to Interpol?"

"Eventually. The States never really felt like home to me. I always thought they would, but somehow…"

"I know what you mean."

"You do, don't you?"

"We're a lot alike, Bax."

In more ways than he'd expected. He nodded. "You get it. I thought Europe might be better for me, but I didn't quite fit in there, either. So I wound up back in San Francisco."

"And now you're trying Europe again. Isn't that why you took this job, to get back to Europe?"

"Partly."

"What was the other part?"

"I couldn't resist you."

This time, he kissed her hard and desire flared again. Roughly, he pulled her down to the deck of the boat. He wanted her underneath him, slick and strong, lean and taut.

Foreplay was irrelevant. The arousal of each fed off the other, their bodies straining together, the taste, the touch blending until the feel of her slickness against his fingers aroused him as much as the stroke of her palm against his hard cock. When she moaned, he felt the shudder of pleasure. When she quaked, it made him groan.

Then he rolled on top of her, lying between her legs, feeling them wrap around him like silken bonds. He slid his cock into her swiftly and they cried out together. He was into her up to the root, a part of her, connected as though they were one. And with every stroke, as he drove himself into her, he felt completed.

Part of a oneness he couldn't name.

He could say he was a loner, at this moment they were bonded in ways that went beyond physical. This time when he was inside her and they were moving together, pulling each other along toward climax, he didn't close his eyes and concentrate on his own pleasure. He cupped her head with his hands and stared into her eyes, watching her lips part as she gasped, watching her face come alive as he moved in her.

And as he saw her reach orgasm and begin to quake under him the crystal clear realization broke through him.

He was a man who'd lived through life-threatening situations. He was currently in a dangerous situation facing a dangerous man, without a clear idea how to make it work.

But he'd just realized the most dangerous thing of all. He was in love with her.

20

Joss RUBBED LOTION into her hands and listened to the sound of the television coming from the other room where Bax sat on the bed. He'd tuned in to a soccer game. Or football, she corrected herself. After all, she was in Europe.

"I hadn't realized you were a sports fan," she commented idly, leaning her head out of the bathroom.

"I'm not."

She watched him a moment. It was the first night since they'd been in Stockholm that they hadn't either been working or completely wrapped up in each other. Granted, they'd made an afternoon of it, but he'd definitely been acting a little strange since they'd been back. It made her edgy and unsettled, even more than her own feelings did.

She didn't want to be unsettled. She'd been unsettled for the past seven years. Enough, already. It was time for all of it to stop. It was time to build a life, a home, a career.

And she very much wanted Bax to be a part of it.

Nerves skittered in her belly. She'd never been vulnerable in a relationship before. She never wanted to hurt anyone, but you couldn't fake feelings. She wasn't faking the feelings now. If things ended, she would be the one getting hurt.

It gave her a queasy feeling in the pit of her stomach.

She had a choice, of course, you always had a choice. Do nothing, let him go, perhaps, and in time—maybe an aeon or two—the feelings would die away. Or maybe Bax would come to her and she wouldn't even have to say anything.

But doing nothing and waiting for things to happen was the coward's way. It had never been hers. She had to say something, pure and simple. She had to take her chance. And if she pancaked, at least she'd know she'd tried.

Joss stared at herself in the mirror. It would be okay, she told herself silently, remembering the way it had felt out on the archipelago, remembering the way it had felt in Amsterdam, where he'd come for her. It wasn't just her imagination. It was real. He cared for her, she knew he did.

She just needed to tell him how she felt.

Swallowing, she shook her hair back and walked out of the bathroom to sit on the bed in her silky robe. Unconsciously, she twisted her fingers together. "We had a good day today."

"I guess."

She cursed herself for making small talk instead of telling him what was on her mind. "We've been working pretty well together, haven't we?"

"Block the freaking ball," Bax barked at the goalie on television.

Joss stared at him. "Is everything okay?"

"Sure, fine," he said shortly, staring at the screen.

She nibbled on the inside of her lip and took a breath. "You know, I was thinking. This detecting stuff is kind of fun. I could get used to this."

"Oh, come on," he said disgustedly in response to a play, and then flicked a glance at her. "Don't get too excited. This isn't a real case. We're not investigating anything, we're just trying to figure out how to swindle Silverhielm out of something that's not his."

"Sure." She nodded. "Real investigating must keep you busy."

Bax just watched the soccer game tensely.

"Have you ever thought about getting someone to help you?" Her voice was elaborately casual. "You know, someone who could do the office stuff and maybe help you with some of the leg work? Someone you could train?"

Bax picked up the remote and punched at the button to mute the sound. "Joss, what's this all about?" he asked abruptly.

She blinked. "Well…"

"You've obviously got something to say. Say it."

Nervous, they were both nervous over tomorrow. This had to be said, though. She couldn't wait.

Now's your chance, she told herself silently. Do it. "I want to learn to become an investigator," she blurted. "I could work for you, doing whatever you needed me to. Maybe just secretarial stuff, or phone calls, street canvassing when you need to talk with a lot of sources. Whatever you want." With every word, she talked faster. "You know, learn how the business works from the ground up. Take away the dull stuff so you'll be more efficient."

For a long moment, he just watched her, some light of bewildered longing in his eyes. Everything would be okay, she wanted to tell him. She loved him. They could make it work. She moistened her lips and opened her mouth. "I—"

As though to ward off her words, he shook his head. "It's a nice offer, Joss, but no. Thanks."

"Wait a minute," she began.

"I've told you before, I work alone."

"You're not on the case alone now, though," she reminded him. "We've worked together just fine."

"Have we? We were on a stakeout today and I spent half

the afternoon focused on you instead of watching the island. That's not what I call working."

She stared at her hands and nodded her head as though
to the beat of music only she could hear. Then she turned
to him. "Okay, what's going on, Bax?"

"What do you mean, what's going on?"

"You've been acting strange ever since we got back.
What got you so ticked off? So we fooled around on the
job? Well, you were there, too," she reminded him, an edge
to her voice. "And you didn't seem all that worried about
it at the time. If you're going to get ticked, get ticked at
yourself as well as me."

"It doesn't work. Having you around is screwing things
up." He punched at the remote and turned the sound back
up.

"So what was all that the other night about what a good
job I was doing and how important I was? Or was that just
a load of crap?"

His eyes skated off to the side. "Joss, you're the client.
Of course I'm going to tell you you're doing a good job."
A muscle at the side of his jaw worked. "Reality is, if I
were working alone, I'd probably have the stamp back by
now."

"Give me a break, Bax."

"What's that supposed to mean?"

"It means that it's taken two of us to pull this off, working together. Together, remember that? And it's been good,
like it was this afternoon, until you got ticked off. Like it
was in Amsterdam, and you came over there voluntarily,
remember? That wasn't about work, it was about us."

"Amsterdam? Amsterdam was about taking care of you."

"Excuse me?" Her voice wavered.

"I wasn't going to leave you over there on your own. I
came over to make sure you didn't get in trouble."

It sliced into her, wicked and unforgivable. "No. You came for me. You told me you did."

"You thought what you wanted to think."

"This isn't really about me coming to work for you, is it?" she asked, her voice a little wobbly. "This is about us, period."

"What 'us'? There is no us. That was a game we were playing, remember? A role to fool Silverhielm? It was never supposed to fool us, too. We're on the job and when it's done, we're done."

It was a cold, hard verbal slap and it silenced her momentarily. She'd always been the one who ended relationships, she'd always been the one who walked away without being hurt. Now, she was the one sitting here with her heart sliced open and he was just staring at the television.

At first it was just pain, harsh and undiluted.

And then the pain flamed back into anger. "There is no us? You are so full of it, Bax. Who do you think you're kidding with this, huh? You don't want anything going forward? You don't want us to see each other once this is over, fine, but don't sit there and try to pretend that nothing's happened here." Her voice rose in fury. "Even if you can't be honest with me, be honest with yourself."

"I am being honest."

"Oh yeah? What about this afternoon?" she demanded. "Not the sex, the other part. The part where we talked. The part where you told me things."

Now he did turn and look at her. "That was a mistake," he said bleakly. "I had no business telling you that stuff. I had no business spending the afternoon making love to you instead of paying attention to the case."

And because he had, he was trying to get as far from her as possible. It frustrated her, infuriated her and it hurt. Oh, it hurt. "What are you afraid of, getting close? You think because your father could never connect with you and your mom that you're hardwired to be that way, too? You think that because you grew up a loner that that's what you have to be your whole life?"

"You've got no idea what you're talking about," he said angrily. "You don't know what it's like to watch someone you love get hurt over and over again because they can't stop needing someone. My mom spent her whole life trying to open up to him and getting shut down every time. I saw what needing him did to her. I watched what it did to me."

"But that's them, that's not us. Let it go," Joss pleaded, reaching a hand to his face. "I care about you. I want to build something with you."

Bax jerked away and rose. "Sure. I've fallen for that one before, too. Her name was Stephanie." The first woman he'd ever loved, the first woman who'd ever loved him back. But time had told the lie of that. "She wanted to be there for me, too." He remembered staring into her beautiful face as she begged him to let her in. He'd done it, in incredulous wonder that everything could come together so easily, be the way it was supposed to be.

And he'd been so wrong.

Bax shook his head. "She wanted me to open up. And like a stupid schmuck, I did. And you know what? Surprise, suddenly I wasn't the man she'd fallen in love with. I wasn't the bulletproof tough guy. I was just a guy."

"You're the strongest man I've ever met."

He smiled humorlessly. "Not to her, not after that. She didn't really want to know me. No one ever really wants to know anybody. We're all happier with our fantasies."

"Bax," Joss whispered. "What did she do to you?"

"Oh, dropped that little bombshell before she walked off with a guy she met in a bar one night when we were out for a drink. A couple of weeks after I'd asked her to move in with me. Doesn't exactly make you want to get involved," he said, tossing the words at her shocked face.

She struggled to take it all in. "She was a witch. It wasn't about you, it was about her."

"It doesn't matter. Actually, she did me a favor. She taught me the most important lesson I ever learned—you can't depend on anyone but yourself."

"Just because one woman was an idiot doesn't mean every woman is." Impotent anger filled her words. "It doesn't mean that I am."

"And you telling me the same things she did doesn't mean that you aren't."

"Can't you trust me? Can't you try?"

He wanted to, part of him suddenly wanted to very badly. But he couldn't get there. It had been too hard, too long. "I believe you think you feel something for me, Joss, but it's not love. It's sex, it's excitement, it's danger. You want an answer to your life and you think I'm it."

"That's not true," she shook her head blindly. "I care for you Bax. I love you."

"You just think you do. You're not in love with me, you're in love with salvation."

"I don't need you to save me," she flared. "I just need you to be with me."

He hesitated. "Look, Joss, I can't be your fantasy man and I can't be your answer. We came into this knowing the score. Let's keep it that way."

"I'm not sixteen, Bax. I know what I feel."

"And I know what I know. It's over, Joss. We get the stamps back tomorrow and then we say goodbye."

"We won't have to," she spoke, almost inaudibly. "You've already said the only goodbye that matters."

_21_

THE DAY DAWNED gorgeous and clear with an exquisite sunrise over the water by the Royal Viking. Joss stood at the window and looked out toward Karl XII's _torg._ She had no frame of reference for the misery she felt. She had never experienced it before. She'd had breakups born of anger and frustration, breakups fueled by incompatibility, breakups driven by lack of desire. Always, though, she'd felt a sense of relief after, a lightness at the idea of being on her own again.

Now, all she felt was despair.

Bax had become a necessary part of her world. Only two weeks had gone by since they'd first met and yet she felt that he'd always been there, that his presence made her days and nights complete in a way she hadn't realized she'd needed.

And she had no idea what to do next.

They'd spent the night lying in the same bed. They might have been inches apart, but the reality was millions of times that distance. Eventually, Joss had dozed off into dreams in which everything was right again. She'd woken to find herself wrapped in Bax's arms, and for a moment in the warmth and sleepy comfort, she'd forgotten that everything wasn't all right, that everything was as wrong as it could be.

Her jolt into full wakefulness had woken Bax as well.

With the light of dawn just beginning to slip through the windows, he'd risen to pull on his running clothes and leave, without a word. Without a backward glance.

And in the empty room, she'd risen to stand by the window and watch him run away from the hotel, as he was running away from her.

BAX LISTENED TO the thud of his feet and waited for the run to do its work. In the aftermath of his breakup with Stephanie, he'd logged enough miles that he'd run the D.C. marathon and finished in the top one hundred. Whenever his thoughts would start chasing themselves in circles, he'd lace on his shoes and hit the streets or the trails, driving himself relentlessly. Running was Bax's escape, and that day should have been no different.

Except it was.

He turned the corner by the Opera House and found himself on Fredsgatan, just down from Fredsgatan 12. And suddenly he was hit by memories of walking there with Joss in the gathering evening, her fingers tangled with his.

Bax shook his head and sped up. *Block it out, block it out.* He didn't want to feel what he felt for Joss. There was no place in his life for letting another person in, for letting another person into his heart. For needing.

He knew what happened when you did that. He knew the danger.

His life was fine just as it was. So maybe it wasn't filled with people, but he knew what he could depend on. He knew who he could depend on—himself. When you started depending on other people, you put yourself at risk. Some people liked that. For his part, he could skip it.

He sped up, feeling the good burn in his quads and calves. Concentrate on the body, concentrate on the pain there. *Focus, focus, got to focus.*

Because if he stopped concentrating on physical pain he'd have to start registering the way it had felt to see the mute anguish on Joss's face the night before and that morning. And he'd have to start thinking about the loss he was going to feel when she was gone.

A SHOWER, clothes, coffee. The basics of life, the routine. If she clung to those, she'd get through this. She was strong enough, she knew it. She was tough enough.

And at the moment, there wasn't anything else to do but keep on, so Joss sat in the café at Karl XII's *torg* and held her coffee cup. She felt grainy and slow and out of sync with herself. More than ever before in her life she wanted to leave a place behind, but it simply wasn't possible just then. Not when the meeting with Silverhielm loomed. Once it was over, she could run to ground and lick her wounds, but for now, she had to stay with Bax to maintain their cover. No matter how excruciating it was.

"Hey."

She turned to see him behind her. He'd clearly just finished his run. His shirt was patchy with sweat, his unshaven chin, dark. He'd never looked better to her. But he wasn't hers, not anymore.

Bax set down his coffee and sat at the little table. He looked at Joss, but his eyes were hidden behind his sunglasses. It made him look even more remote and impassive than ever. "How are you?"

"Fabulous. I can't think when I've been better," Joss said, her voice brittle and hard. "Gee, this is fun. We ought to do this more often."

His jaw tightened briefly. "All right, dumb question. I'll just get right to it."

"Please do."

"We need to talk about what happens tonight."

"We finish the job. Isn't that what you've been waiting for?" Finish it and separate. So easy to say.

So difficult to do.

"Look, you've been waiting for this to be over, too. You can get back the one-penny Mauritius, close on what we came here to accomplish."

"Sure. So we've talked about the plan. What's your concern?" she asked, working to keep her voice as emotionless as his.

"You and me."

For an instant, hope bloomed. "Go on."

"Look, things are different now between us. You know it and I know it."

"And what do you want to do about that?" What had he come to talk with her about? What did he want from her, for them?

"Nothing," Bax said aloud. "It is what it is, but we can't go to Silverhielm's and let that show."

"Oh," Joss said tonelessly. He was talking about work. Of course. Foolish of her to expect anything else. "What do you want from me?"

"I want your assurance that when we go there tonight, we'll act like everything is normal, everything is like it was."

"Even though it's not." She searched his face for signs of regret, but his expression was so controlled she couldn't see anything at all.

"Exactly."

"So, why the big show? All couples have fights and break up. Why pretend?"

"Because tonight of all nights, we don't want them wondering about anything. Everything needs to go smoothly. I just wanted to be sure that you can carry it off."

It was like he was trying to pull a response from her,

trying to get her to plead with him one more time. "What, are you afraid I'm going to wail and weep and gnash my teeth?" Joss snapped, undone. "I can blow it off just as easily as you can, Bax. You're not as unforgettable as you think you are."

He stared at her for a moment and his mouth tightened. "I never thought I was," he said softly.

THE SINGLE red light flashed on the end of Silverholmen dock in the gathering dusk. Oskar slowed the little cruiser to a crawl and began to thread his way in through the breakwaters. He glanced at Bax.

"Just about there," he said.

Bax nodded. "You remember the drill."

"Yep," Oskar said cheerfully. "Stay alert and out of sight."

"The guards may come to talk with you."

"And I will tell them that you insist I stay with the boat."

"No matter what. Even if they tell you that I've sent word for you to come in. If anything changes, I'll come tell you personally. Otherwise, stay here. We may need to leave in a hurry."

"I have no desire to spend any more time with Silverhielm's men than I have to."

"Do you think they'll recognize you?"

Oskar shrugged. "It is possible, although almost a year has passed. Anyway, they have no reason to care if I am here. I did not leave under suspicious terms."

The long, wooden finger of the dock projected out from the steep gray rocks of the island. At the landward end, a short path made a sharp turn to the stairs that threaded up the side of the ten-foot bluff to reach the level of the back lawn and the house beyond. From where they sat on the boat, only the upper part of the house was visible.

Oskar piloted the boat up to the dock, stopping as close to the end as he could. On the other side bobbed Silverhielm's cigarette boat. And at the end of the dock, waiting for them in a charcoal shirt, jacket and trousers, was Markus.

"You made it, I see," he said.

Bax jumped to the dock to dog the bow line around a cleat, then moved to do the same with the stern line. "I wouldn't miss it." He brushed his hands off briefly and shook with Markus.

Meanwhile, Oskar shut down the engine and positioned a couple of fenders to protect the boat from contact with the dock.

Joss stepped up onto the side rail of the boat and reached out for Bax's hand. In deference to the occasion, she'd worn a little black silk jersey dress with a plunging neckline and long sleeves that ended in belled cuffs. The hem hit her at midthigh. Heels and dark hose added the finishing touches. It wasn't, perhaps, the best costume for walking down a dock at dusk, but it might distract Silverhielm at a crucial moment. Every bit of carelessness they could achieve was a benefit.

"Your pilot is welcome to come up to the house and stay with our men," Markus said, talking to Bax but looking at the boat. "Oskar, wasn't it?"

Oskar tilted his head in acknowledgement. "You have a good memory."

"So I do. How very clever of you, Johan, to find the one person in Stockholm who knows the route to Silverholmen well."

"I suspect there are others," Bax observed. "A man like Silverhielm is very popular."

"But private. It is not everyone who is invited to visit his home."

"Then we should consider it an honor."

"Indeed. Shall we all go up to the house?"

Bax glanced at Markus. "Oskar will stay here with the boat, thanks."

"That would not be Mr. Silverhielm's choice."

"I don't see why not. Oskar has delivered goods to Silverholmen in the past. He is trustworthy."

Markus considered and finally nodded. "You are right, of course. So, we will leave young Oskar here and hurry up to the house. Mr. Silverhielm has something very special planned."

FACETED CRYSTAL sparkled in the flickering light of dozens of candles. Decanters of doubtlessly expensive wine sat on an antique sideboard. The thick napkin on Joss's lap was of creamy white linen, as was the snowy tablecloth. The fork and knife she held had the heft of solid silver.

Stylishly ornate, the dining room suited the exterior of the house. Formal baroque carvings surrounded the high ceiling with its painting of Norse gods reclining on clouds. An elaborate chandelier formed of hundreds of crystal drops shimmered overhead. Paintings of hunting scenes adorned the wood-paneled walls. In one, a tusked boar bled, torn at by a pack of dogs.

It made Joss feel faintly sick.

"A toast." Silverhielm held up his glass. "To accomplishing long-held goals."

"To long-held goals," they echoed and crystal rang.

"The world is fraught with disappointment," he remarked, sitting. "What a happy occurrence, then, for a situation to occur in which everyone is satisfied."

"It's just a matter of having a common goal," Joss told him.

His eyes held some private amusement. "And so we do."

The butler began serving the dinner in silent ceremony. Course followed course, with wines to match the herring appetizer, the crab bisque, the stuffed lobster and the venison in port wine sauce.

It was surreal, Joss thought, watching Silverhielm slice off a piece of meat so rare that blood oozed out onto the white plate. How could he play the expansive host, catering to the comfort of his guests, when she knew the kind of acts he was capable of? What would he say if he knew why they were really there, she wondered, watching him chew the meat.

And what would he do?

"So BUSINESS does not have to be all labor," Silverhielm remarked, taking a drink of his port. "There is always time for pleasure."

Dinner had given way to dessert, which had given way to brandy and cognac in the opulent living room with its deep, soft couches. A wall of French doors overlooked the water as the last rays of the setting sun gave way to the full moon. Markus sat in a chair against the wall, observing everything, saying nothing.

"Your house is exquisite," Joss told Silverhielm, doing her best to sound sincere. "As is your chef."

"He is very talented," Silverhielm acknowledged. "He is not my first chef, of course. The first chef, I found, used the kitchen budget to attempt to cheat me. I took it poorly, as you might imagine."

Joss swallowed. "Where is he now?"

"It is of no concern." Silverhielm swirled his brandy. "Will you have some more brandy?" he asked Joss.

"No thank you. I had too much at dinner. I'm wearing high heels. If I don't watch it, I won't be able to walk," she joked.

"Then slide them off. Come now, it is my house. I demand that you be comfortable." He stepped over and lifted one of her feet by the ankle, slipping her shoe off. "And the other?"

"I can get it," Joss said hastily, trying not to shudder at his touch.

"Now, some brandy for you." He picked up a snifter from the tray the butler had left and brought it over to her.

Joss took the balloon glass, cupping her hands around it. Without shoes, she felt a bit naked.

"And now," Silverhielm rose, "it is time to get to our private business, Ms. Astin."

"Josie," she corrected.

"Of course. So, if you will join me, Josie?" He put out his arm in a courtly fashion.

Bax stood as well. Silverhielm eyed him.

"Oh, I do not think that is necessary. This is a friendly meeting. Markus can keep you company here."

Bax looked at Joss. "All right with you?"

"We'll be fine," she told him. "Won't we, Karl?"

He led her into the hallway outside of the living room. "But of course."

MARKUS ROSE from his chair. "Come." He walked to the open door to one side of the room. "We can play billiards while we wait."

"Sure." Bax followed him into the dark green room with its carved mahogany table.

"Did you consider Mr. Silverhielm's offer any further?" Markus asked as he picked up a cue. "I think you will find his terms very generous. He rewards loyalty."

Bax began pulling balls from the leather net pockets of the table and setting them in the wooden triangle of the rack. "I have a job to finish here. When would Silverhielm want me to come on board?"

Markus chalked his stick and adjusted the position of the cue ball. He stroked the cue twice and slammed it against the cue ball so that it knocked the colored balls all over the table. "Perhaps now."

"PLEASE, SIT," Silverhielm said, relaxing back into his cordovan leather chair.

Joss sat looking past him to the deepening dusk and thought of the man who'd probably sat in this chair moments before getting his knee shattered. She suppressed a shudder.

"So, here we are at last," Silverhielm said.

"Here we are," she agreed.

"And you have the Blue Mauritius?" His eyes glinted with avarice.

"Of course." Her palms dampened just as she raised her purse into her lap.

"A momentous occasion, Ms. Astin. One I have waited for. I do not deal well with frustration, as you might imagine."

Was it her imagination or was there just a breath of malice in his voice? "Isn't it good that I came to see you, then?"

"Indeed." He opened a drawer and brought out a mat and a pair of stamp tongs. "I do not wish to wait any longer. The Blue Mauritius, please."

"The money," she countered, ignoring his clipped tone of command.

He smiled as though at some private joke. "You do not trust me? I thought we were friends."

"I still need to see the money."

"Very well." He pressed a button in his desk and a section of his bookcase popped ajar. "It is, perhaps, too dramatic, but for a man like myself, security must be of paramount concern. Always, there are those who attempt to cheat me."

Behind the bookcase was a panel that slid aside to reveal a wall safe. Like her grandfather, Silverhielm apparently believed in keeping his precious belongings close at hand.

Unlike her grandfather's, those belongings were guarded by killers.

He opened the safe and moments later returned with a banded stack of bills and a leather stamp album. "Two hundred thousand dollars U.S., as you requested. Would you like to count it?"

"That won't be necessary." She didn't really want his money. Taking it would be tantamount to stealing. All she wanted was her grandfather's property.

"Ah. You do trust me, then. I'm flattered." He opened the cover of the stamp album. "Well, then, I will show you the prizes of my collection. Of course, you are not a stamp collector so perhaps they will not please you as much as they would some."

"I appreciate rarities as much as the next person," Joss corrected him. "You have the other half of the Post Office Mauritius pair, right?"

"I suppose your ex-boyfriend would know that, would he not?" There was laughter in Silverhielm's eyes.

"I suppose he would."

"Here it is."

Joss let out a breath as he turned the page to display an orange stamp, the stamp that was a twin of the one she'd seen in the safe at the Postmuseet. "May I look at it?" she asked reaching for the album.

But Silverhielm raised a hand. "The Blue Mauritius, first, if you please."

Reaching into her purse, she pulled out the stiffened glassine envelope that held the Blue Mauritius.

"You have taken proper care of it?" he asked sharply.

"See for yourself." She slid out the transparent mount that held the stamp, then laid it on the mat in the center of the desk.

Silverhielm set aside his stamp album and reached out to move the mat directly in front of him. For a moment, he just looked at the stamp reverently. Using the tongs, he reached inside the mount to pull out the Blue Mauritius, his hands shaking just a bit. From a drawer, he produced a loupe and inspected the stamp at length. Finally, he let out a long breath. "It is genuine." He leaned near, brought his fingers almost into contact with the colored square of paper.

It made her sick to see it in his possession. Her only comfort was that it wouldn't be for long. "Of course it is genuine. And now you have them, side by side."

He blinked for a moment as though coming out of a trance. "Yes," he said briskly and reached for the album to pull out the one-penny Mauritius. Using stamp tongs, he reverently picked up the Blue Mauritius and slid it into the empty slot. "So long," he whispered. "So long I have waited for it to be mine."

Hands below the level of the desk, Joss reached into her purse and palmed the forgeries. "May I see them?" she asked, rising to lean over the desk.

Just then, a tone sounded. Silverhielm's eyes flickered over to his computer and in that instant Joss palmed the Post Office Mauritius pair and substituted the forgery.

"I can see why you're so fascinated by them," she commented. Silverhielm's gaze, she noticed, slid to her cleavage and she remained standing and leaning over his desk to look at what was now the forged Post Office Mauritius pair. Finally, she sat.

"So, I have the stamps and you have the money. I think

this calls for a toast," he said, raising his glass. "To the Blue Mauritius." He took a drink. "My dear Ms. Chastain."

"YOU KNOW where I stand on this." Bax squinted along his cue and popped the six ball in. "I have a client already. Until this job is done I can't switch."

"Perhaps the job will be finished more quickly than you had planned."

Bax flicked a glance at Markus and set up his next shot. "What's that supposed to mean?"

Markus smiled slightly and nodded his head forward a fraction. "I commend you on a most excellent charade. We initially had no idea of your client's true identity." Markus stepped up to the table as Bax straightened. "Fortunately, Mr. Silverhielm is a practical man who appreciates skill. Things may not go well for Ms. Chastain, but you may find yourself in a position to profit from your audacity."

Bax gave him a hard look. "What?"

"It means that you have a choice. Mr. Silverhielm, of course, has brought you here falsely—he has no intention of giving you or Ms. Chastain any money for the one-penny Mauritius. But then, you have come here falsely yourself. The fate of Ms. Chastain has already been settled. What happens to you has not."

Only through years of training was he able to keep from reacting. Joss was alone with Silverhielm, with a man capable of just about anything. And to get to her, Bax had to go through Markus, not to mention assorted other goons around the house. He needed to figure out a strategy but the fear for Joss kept rising up to choke him. Push it down, he told himself. Put all the emotions away and concentrate. "So what are you asking me to do? Beg for my life?"

"I know you won't. That's the kind of man you are."

Markus crossed to the other side of the table, keeping his distance, Bax noticed, keeping balanced. "Of course, the more important question is what kind of man is Mr. Silverhielm?"

"I'm sure you'll tell me."

"Indeed. He is a man who wants always to have his way. He is very vicious when he is crossed. Just as you and Ms. Chastain have crossed him. He would like to kill you. But I believe he would also appreciate someone like you on his side. And I can make that happen."

"In exchange for what?"

"A show of loyalty to your new employer, perhaps." Markus leaned his cue against the table. "Ms. Chastain's punishment is likely to be messy if not attended to with proper care. You have always been so neat." Markus reached into his coat toward the holster Bax was sure was there.

Their eyes locked.

"I believe it is your shot, Johan."

"WHAT DID YOU SAY?" Joss stared at Silverhielm.

"Did you really think we wouldn't find out who you are?"

Her heart began rabbiting in her chest. "I told you who I am."

"Come now." He thumped his glass down. "It is an embarrassment to both of us for you to try to maintain this falsehood. You are Joss Chastain, the granddaughter of Hugh Chastain."

"The rightful owner of that Post Office Mauritius pair you're so proud of," she snapped, unable to keep quiet.

"The Post Office Mauritius pair I won't be paying for now," he said smoothly, picking the stack of bills from the desk and slipping them into a drawer. "You were a fool to think you could fool me, Ms. Chastain, even with the help of Mr. Bruhn. It may interest you to know he's agreed to come to work for me, so you won't find any assistance from that quarter."

It was a trap, they'd been drawn into a trap on this remote island.

Or she had.

Joss moistened her lips. "He wouldn't betray me," she whispered, as much to herself as to Silverhielm.

"No? I think he would. But it is of no matter. You are on my private island, surrounded by my employees. I have the upper hand. Then again," he raised his eyebrows, "I always do. I don't like being cheated."

It stiffened her spine. She glared at him. "You stole those stamps from my grandfather."

"On the contrary. The thieves are already in jail." He smiled faintly. "Your fine American criminal justice system at work."

Her fingers tightened on the stem of her balloon glass. "You stole them."

"The Post Office Mauritius pair is mine," he snapped, goaded into anger.

"Then have them." She rose and flung the contents of the snifter over the album on the table.

Silverhielm roared and snatched at the stamps as Joss whirled and ran for the door.

It was as she'd gambled. He was more interested in saving his million dollar babies than in running after her.

She ran down the hall toward the living room, her stockinged feet slipping on the hardwood floors. Bursting into the living room, she stared at the empty couch. Gone? They couldn't be, he wouldn't have abandoned her. She looked around wildly.

And saw the light coming out of a door across the room, partially ajar.

She burst through the door to see Bax standing on the far side of a pool table. "Bax, we've got to go, *now*."

"Not so quickly, Ms. Chastain," said a soft voice from behind her.

She turned to see Markus Holm standing against the wall, his gun pointed directly between her eyes.

22

BAX FROZE, pool cue at his side, and stared at the two of them.

"Now is the time to choose your side, my friend," Markus said. "The girl can do nothing for you. Silverhielm can offer you money, a job. And, of course, since I am the only one in the room with a gun, I can offer you something more immediate. You have only to walk away."

Joss stood transfixed.

Bax shook his head. "I can't do that."

"That is a pity. I approve of honor, as you know. But I approve of intelligence more."

"It's more than honor, Markus."

Markus looked at him with curiosity. "More than honor." He moved the gun slightly in Bax's direction. "More than your life is worth?"

Bax returned his gaze. "Yes."

"Why?"

"Because I love her," he said calmly.

Joss snapped her head around to stare at him.

Markus shook his head in disgust. "When did you become a fool, Johan?"

"I'm not sure. Maybe the day I met her." His reply was to Markus but it was Joss he spoke to, even as he calculated ways and means to get the two of them out of there alive.

Markus studied him. "I could shoot her."

"I'd come for you."

"I could shoot you, too, of course. Probably first. Perhaps now."

"You think so?" Bax asked. "Is your memory really that short?"

Their eyes locked together and the seconds ticked by. "So," Markus said at last, "you wish my debt repaid."

Bax said nothing.

A slight smile played on Markus's lips. "It is perhaps not so great a price as you now think." He nodded to the French doors that let out from the living room to the terrace and the lawn beyond. "I will let you go and count to ten. You and the lovely Ms. Chastain will get a chance to escape with your lives and you and I will be even. Go." He jerked his head and lowered the gun. "One…"

And they went.

Markus replaced his gun in his holster and walked out into the living room. "Two," he said softly to himself as footsteps sounded from within the house.

"Stop them," Silverhielm roared from the hallway. "She has the real stamps." He burst into the living room and stopped, staring first at the open doors and then at Markus, who stood impassively before him. "Where are they?"

Markus nodded toward the lawn, toward the two running figures.

"What have you done, you fool?" Silverhielm demanded.

Markus looked at him serenely. "Nothing that will matter."

"Go after them. Warn the others."

"Don't worry," Markus said, reaching in his pocket for a walkie-talkie. "It is taken care of."

BAX RAN ACROSS the slick grass with Joss. Moonlight bathed the scene in a deceptively calm wash of silver. Beyond the grass, the sea was a presence of darkness broken by the distant haze of light that was Stockholm. If Markus were true to his word, they might have time to make it to the boat before the others pursued them. They might be able to make it to open water.

For now, they needed to reach the staircase that hugged the side of the low rock bluff. Once they were on it, they'd be protected from anyone running toward them, at least until their pursuers got close. He grabbed the hardwood banister and took the stairs two at a time, listening to Joss behind him. Then they hit the landing at the bottom, turning around an outcrop toward the dock.

Only to come to a scrambling halt.

Small lights on the railings silhouetted a guard at the landward end of the dock as he leaned against the railing, nodding his head a little, not looking up. The light offshore breeze brought them the scent of the smoke from his cigarette. Out at the other end of the dock, by Oskar and the boat, the red light flashed. Waves slapped quietly against the pilings.

Joss tapped Bax's arm. "He has a headset on," she whispered. Bax nodded, edging forward. The closer he could get without warning the guy, the better. He couldn't see a gun, but he knew there had to be one. A staticky buzz like that of a walkie-talkie broke the silence. Even as the guard slid off his headset to answer, Bax pounced.

The guard was bigger than he was, solidly built in a way that suggested more muscle than fat. Size wasn't everything, though. Bax was on him before he could raise his gun, chopping at the hand that held it. The revolver spun away.

"Run to the boat," Bax bellowed to Joss, then stepped in to catch the guard with a punch to the eye, pain exploding up his arm. The punch should have decked the guy but he only stepped back, shaking his head. Not a good sign, Bax thought, trying to step in before his opponent had gotten himself set. A fraction of a second later, Bax found himself bouncing dizzily off the dock railing, struggling to keep his feet while his ears rang.

The guy was definitely quicker than he'd anticipated. And so were the others, judging by the shouts he heard.

"Watch out," Joss screamed.

Bax looked to see the guard moving in again, sending a looping roundhouse toward Bax's temple. Ducking to get inside of it, Bax summoned up a fast uppercut and snapped the guard's jaw shut. The man stood for a moment, then his knees softened and he sagged toward the ground.

Bax vaulted over him and pounded down the dock to the boat.

"Oskar's gone," Joss shouted from inside the boat.

Cursing, Bax unfastened the bow and stern lines. He gave the front of the vessel a shove and jumped in.

"Did you hear me?" Joss cried. "Oskar is gone."

"He's not all that's missing," Bax said grimly. The keys, as he'd feared, had also been taken and they'd disconnected the GPS unit. Silverhielm's men had been thorough. Bax reached under the dash to fumble for the ignition wires. And the boat drifted slowly away from the dock, turning back toward Stockholm.

Figures appeared at the edge of the bluff and a bullet ricocheted past him with a whine.

"Get down," Bax shouted and ducked himself.

"Bax, we can't leave," Joss shouted. "What about Oskar?"

Bax ignored her and squinted to see the wires in the moonlight as he untwisted them. He couldn't think about Oskar, he couldn't think about feelings. Compartmentalize. The key to survival was focusing on action and admitting no distractions.

A spark jumped from one wire to the other and the engine chugged once. Pumping the gas, he touched the wires again and the engine caught with a roar. With a spin of the wheel, he headed the boat back toward Stockholm.

Joss caught at his arm. "What are you doing?" she demanded.

"We have to get out of here." He grabbed her, shoved the throttle forward and the boat leapt out of the water.

"We can't just leave him behind." Her voice rose in fury. "They could do anything to him."

Bax glanced back to see figures spilling over the edge of the bluff and clustering around the fallen figure at the head of the dock. Another shot whined past them. "There are people shooting at us, in case you hadn't noticed. We have to leave him." He stared at the water ahead, trying desperately to see his path. The moonlight threw a silver glaze over the water, making it easier to see land but harder to see hazards. He aimed the boat away from the islands and tried to remember landmarks from the previous day. "If we stay here, they'll take us, too and we'll be no good to him at all."

"We're no good to him if we just let them have him. What kind of a man are you?"

As cold and calculating as he could make himself be. "We can't help him right now, Joss. The only way we can help him is by getting back to Stockholm and Rolf."

"And if they hurt or kill him in the meantime?"

"That's a risk we have to take. Don't you finally understand who we're dealing with, here?" Bax glanced back as a roar started up behind them and he cursed. "Do you hear that engine? They're coming after us in that goddamn big cigarette boat. We'll be lucky to make it back in one piece, but we're guaranteed to die if we try to go back to Silverholmen alone." She opened her mouth to protest, but he rode right over her. "We don't have the tools, Joss, and you're not helping me by being hysterical."

Her mouth clamped shut and she glared at him. Good, he told himself, and tried not to care. If she was angry she'd be focused. "Fine," Joss snapped. "What do you want me to do?"

The conversation wasn't over yet, he knew that. At some point, there was going to be hell to pay. First, though, they had to survive. "Concentrate on getting back to the hotel in one piece and then we can figure out what to do. We've got a mile on them, maybe two, but they can out-run us and they've got guns. Here," he stepped back. "Take the wheel for a minute. Aim for that light over there." He pointed.

"I've got it," Joss said.

Bax reached up under the dash and searched for the gun he'd duct taped in place earlier that evening. "Okay." He brought it out. "It's not much fire power, but it's all we've got. You cock it by pulling back the action, like this. The safety is right here." He showed her. "If you want to help, when that boat pulls up to within eight or ten feet, try to take a shot. See if you can get them to keep their heads down." He took the wheel and adjusted their course. "Sit down and steady it on the gunwales. Remember to squeeze the trigger, don't pull."

"What about extra ammunition?"

"There's another clip." He handed it to her. "If we're not out of trouble by the time you've finished them both off, we're not going to be."

She nodded and took the gun from him.

And in that moment, compartmentalization be damned, he loved her.

JOSS STARED tensely back at the lights of the cigarette boat as it drew inexorably nearer. They'd moved through the line of barrier islands on the outer archipelago. Ahead of them, the inner islands formed a funnel of land that would bring them into the narrow, tree-lined pass that led to the Stockholm harbor. She felt their speed drop a little.

There was a whine and a corner of the little boat's windshield exploded into shards.

"Get down," Bax hollered. "They're within firing range."

Joss dived down on the deck of the boat and scrambled over to the gunwale, her anger and fear forgotten. Survival was all that mattered now. "They're a good half a mile away."

"So they've got a rifle." He slalomed the boat a bit to make them less of a target. "It's getting shallow and tricky in here. They're going to have to come down off the plane, soon, and that's going to bounce them around more. Make them less accurate, slower. But we're going to have to slow down, too." Another shot whined past them.

The entrance to the pass was tantalizingly near yet frustratingly distant. The gun felt heavy and useless in her hand. Turning, she searched for an answer in the darkness.

And felt a surge of hope. "Bax," she shouted, "the ferry." Coming up from their left, the white boat looked like a waterborne chandelier, the deck lights shining out over the water as it steamed majestically along toward the Stockholm inner harbor. "Could we use them as a shield in the pass?"

He stared at her a moment, then understanding broke.

It was a chance, she thought. If they could get ahead of the ferry before they went into the narrow waterway, the cigarette boat couldn't get to them, Silverhielm's men couldn't shoot them. If they could head off the ferry they might be safe.

Another shot whistled by them. Bax made a minor adjustment in their course and inched the throttle forward, his expression hard and focused as they rocketed through the dark waters. The ferry steamed along, closer and closer to intersecting their course. Would they get there in time, was the question. Behind them sounded the relentless engine of the cigarette boat.

Ahead of them lay the pass between the island of Nacka and the island of Ingarö. The ferry began its long, slow turn across in front of them, aiming at the pass.

And everything began to happen way too quickly.

One minute, they were behind the white ship. The next, Bax was whipping the boat around the ferry, skimming terrifyingly close to the rocky margins of the islands. The high, white side of the ferry towered over them mere feet away as they surged past it. The coastlines flowed in toward them.

Joss's hands tightened on the gunwale. If Bax miscalculated, they'd be wiped out like a bug on a truck windshield. And if he lost his nerve... Another shot from their pursuers whizzed past them, ricocheting off the white side of the ferry and clipping the edge of the speedboat's gunwale. Reminding them of what lay behind.

Foot by foot, they neared the ferry's bow. Time stretched out, the seconds crawling by. Then Bax shoved the throttle all the way up. The speedboat jumped forward and shot ahead of the ferry, slipping in front of the white painted prow with only a few feet or so to spare. The ferry's airhorn blared in protest.

Then they were in the narrow pass, the solid bulk of the ferry behind them and no room for the cigarette boat to get by. They'd made it. They were safe.

For now.

23

Joss was a pacer from way back. Sitting still made her want to scream. When she was upset, she had to move. Stay away from the window, Bax had told her, so she moved from the bathroom to the bed and back, four steps, turn, four steps, turn. It kept her from going crazy.

It kept her from worrying about Oskar.

Across the room, Bax cursed. "Dammit, Rolf." He tossed Joss's cell phone on the bed. He'd been using it to stay off his own, which remained stubbornly silent. "Your big chance to nail Silverhielm and where are you?"

Four steps, turn, four steps, turn. "Forget about Rolf," she told him. "Call the police directly."

"I've been trying to. It's nearly midnight. The people I need to talk to aren't exactly at their desks."

"You swore to me that if we got back here we could find a way to help Oskar." She rounded on him, her voice tight with anguish. "We have to do it."

"They'll call, Joss. Trust me."

"Why should I trust you about anything? You left him there, just to save your own skin."

"Looks to me like your skin is in one piece, as well. They're not going to do anything to Oskar. At least not yet."

"How do you know?"

"Because Oskar is leverage. You don't hurt leverage, you use it."

The electronic burble of the phone broke into their conversation, silencing them momentarily. Joss stared at Bax. Stiffly, she walked over to pick up the receiver.

"Hello?"

"Ms. Chastain. Did you enjoy your trip back to Stockholm?" It was Silverhielm.

"Perhaps if someone hadn't been shooting at us."

"It added to the excitement, did it not? By the way, please pass my compliments to your associate for his maneuver with the ferry. I'm told it deeply frustrated our captain."

"You didn't call to discuss his piloting skills."

"Of course not. I called to discuss a meeting. After all, we have something of yours and you have something of ours. Your forgeries were good, but not good enough."

"We don't have anything of yours." An edge entered her voice. "The Post Office Mauritius set is stolen goods. They belong to my grandfather."

"An interesting assertion. Would you care to hear what your young friend Oskar thinks?" There was a muffled curse by the phone.

"What are you doing to him?" Joss demanded.

"Nothing permanent." Silverhielm's voice was smooth and lightly amused. "We can do worse, though. You know that."

"What do you want?"

"A swap. You bring the stamps, we will bring Oskar. If the stamps are authentic, we will release him to you."

"And what is to stop you from killing us as you tried to do on the way back to Stockholm?" she asked hotly.

"I want only the stamps."

"I don't believe you."

"Whether you do or don't is irrelevant, Ms. Chastain." An edge entered his voice. "We are wasting time and your friend does not have much of it."

"If you want the stamps, you will see to it that nothing further happens to Oskar," she said steadily. The blood pounded in her temples but she felt curiously calm.

"He will not be harmed, I assure you. What is your decision?"

"Let's do it now."

"Tonight, then."

"Where?" She motioned to Bax, who leaned close enough to hear.

"The Djurgården, behind the restaurant Ulla Winbladh."

Bax shook his head violently again and held out his hand for the receiver. "Silverhielm? You know who this is. I want someplace inside, neutral ground."

Joss put her ear near enough to the phone to hear Silverhielm's reply. "Neutral ground? But what is the Djurgården?"

"A good place to get shot. Inside, Silverhielm, where there's people."

"My Slussen office, then."

"Stop wasting my time," Bax said impatiently. "Neutral ground. You come in with Oskar, you and Markus alone. If I like the look of things, Joss comes in with the stamps. We trade, everyone goes home happy."

"Very well. Erik's Gondolen, in Slussen," Silverhielm said finally. "One hour."

Bax tensed as though to protest and Joss could almost see when he decided not to. "All right. We'll be there."

He hung up the phone.

"But that's the bar in the building where Silverhielm's office is. It can't possibly be neutral ground."

"It won't be."

"Then what are you thinking of, setting up a meet there?"

"I'll tell you."

GONDOLEN LOOKED like the sort of place Silverhielm would like. Stylish and sleek, it oozed sophistication, from the dark and light wood parquet floor to the wavering chrome bars of the railings that separated the bar area from the restaurant.

Bax had been there for more than half an hour, using the faint reflections of the windows to monitor the people moving in and out. The goons had been there before him, sitting uncomfortably at a table near the entrance of the bar. They tried, he'd give them that. But even in an upscale establishment like Gondolen, where sport coats were de rigueur and not merely worn to cover up guns, they stood out. It wasn't just the dress. They were too big, too bulky, too rough-looking.

Bax checked his watch. Almost showtime.

A moment or two later, Markus and Silverhielm walked in. They didn't look around but came directly for him. Bax took another swallow of his beer. "Right on time, gentlemen."

Silverhielm looked around. "Where is Chastain?"

"No Ms.? You're losing your manners."

"And you will lose your young friend if you are not careful." Silverhielm dropped his hands to rest on the back of the wood barstool. "Where is she? Where are my stamps?"

"The stamps, and Ms. Chastain, are in another location." Bax finished his drink and set the glass on the bar. "Where is Oskar?"

"Your young friend will appear when the stamps appear."

Bax rose. "He appears now. You, Markus, Oskar and I go together to the meeting place or I don't take you."

Silverhielm's face darkened. "I will not be threatened."

"Do you want the stamps?"

"Do you want to ensure that nobody dies?"

"I'm doing my best. Now are you coming?"

Markus spoke up. "It would be well to let him have his way this time."

The back of the chair creaked under Silverhielm's fingers as he glowered. Finally, slowly, he released his hold. "All right. We will take my car."

"We walk," Bax interrupted.

"What?"

"It's only half a mile. We'll walk." He gave a friendly smile. "Safer that way."

"And where are we going?"

"You'll find out when we get there."

Joss sat in Pelikan, at a table near the entrance, her back to the wall that separated the beerhall from Kristallen. She glanced at her watch. Midnight, the witching hour. She wished she were a witch, that she could make Silverhielm and his men into rabbits, or their guns into harmless water pistols.

Instead, she could only wait for them to arrive.

In her purse was the glassine envelope that held the Post Office Mauritius pair. Nothing had ever mattered to her less. Bax hadn't been able to reach Rolf Johansson for assistance, so their best chance of saving Oskar was for her to hand over both of the Post Office Mauritius stamps. It didn't matter. Next to a man's life, stamps and money meant nothing.

At this hour, both Kristallen and Pelikan were still busy with the usual young crowd, but things were beginning to wind down. The electronic music from Kristallen throbbed against the wall behind her shoulder blades. She heard a shout and looked over to see Bax walk in, followed by Silverhielm, Oskar and Markus.

Oskar's face looked pale and pinched. A dark thread on his neck looked like dried blood. From the stiff way Oskar held himself, Joss had a pretty good idea Markus had him in a come-along hold. Her heart went out to him.

Joss raised her hand. Silverhielm and Bax headed her way.

"Ah, Ms. Chastain, so we meet again." Silverhielm took a seat across from her. "We have brought your young friend. And you, have you brought my property?"

Joss's heart hammered against her ribs. "Perhaps." She looked over to where Oskar stood with Markus next to the door. "Bring Oskar over here so that I can be sure he's all right."

"Show me the stamps," Silverhielm countered.

Bax sat down beside her. "Oskar seems to be okay."

"What do you mean, okay?" Joss demanded. "He's bleeding."

"Do you wish me to make it worse, Ms. Chastain?" Silverhielm asked gently.

Just then, the pretty girl they had seen Oskar with during their earlier visit peeked around the barrier and cried out in mixed pleasure and concern. She ran across to Oskar, jostling Markus as she put her fingers to Oskar's neck. Others came around the barrier from Kristallen. In moments, Oskar was surrounded by a barrier formed of his friends.

"Who are those people?" Silverhielm demanded, half-rising from his seat. "What are they doing here?"

"I can't imagine," Bax drawled.

Silverhielm's eyes narrowed in fury and there was a sudden, metallic click. "No one betrays me," he growled.

Joss tensed.

"You are not the only person who can call for a change of locations, my friend," Silverhielm said, jerking his head at Markus, then nodding toward the door. "We are going outside."

"Hey, what are you doing," one of Oskar's friends cried.

Silverhielm looked over to the door and in that instant, Joss shoved the table at him. The heavy wood caught him in the chest as he was rising from his chair and sent him tipping over backward. There was a deafening explosion and Bax spun away.

Joss dived over on top of Silverhielm, adding her weight to that of the table, pinning him against the floor and his chair. As he struck out at her, she jerked her head back out of his way. Where was Bax? What had happened with the shot? Silverhielm landed a punch and pain exploded through her head.

Then she heard shouts and hands were on her, pulling her away.

"No," Joss screamed desperately as they lifted her up, kicking. "Let me go. You don't understand. He's a killer."

"We know," said an urgent voice and she turned to see Rolf, surrounded by a phalanx of officers.

And behind him she saw Bax lying on the floor, a red stain spreading across his side.

24

HOSPITALS LOOKED the same no matter where you went, Joss thought as she walked down the ward. Clean, cheerful walls, purposeful doctors and nurses, ranks of rooms, ranks of beds.

And always the underlying sense of crisis and disaster, because except for childbirth, no one would be in a hospital by choice.

She waved to the ICU nurses she'd grown to know well in the previous days and ducked into Bax's room. He was asleep, his face relaxed in the way it so rarely was when he was awake. His lashes formed little fans on his cheeks; she'd never realized before how long they were.

She couldn't bear to walk away from him.

She had to.

Bax stirred, his mouth tightening slightly in pain as he awoke. Then he opened his eyes. For a moment or two, he frowned in puzzlement that cleared when he saw Joss.

"Hey," she said softly. Without thinking about it, she sat in the chair she'd grown all too used to. "How are you feeling?"

"Like I've been kicked by a mule."

"You get kicked by mules a lot?"

He smiled crookedly at her. "No, but I've got a vivid imagination." He closed his eyes briefly. "I've definitely been having some weird dreams. How long have I been in here, two or three days?"

Joss swallowed. "Try a week."

IF HE THOUGHT about it, it would make him crazy, so Bax did his best not to. All right, so he'd lost a week, a week of days blurred into nights, waking in pain, sliding back down into the sweet oblivion of medication. A week of his life and he remembered nothing of it. Or almost nothing, he corrected himself. There was one thing there, always. A hand in his, soft, strong, determined. A hand that wouldn't let him go.

"You were here," he said.

"I might have checked in on you now and again." Joss looked back at him and he saw the lines of exhaustion carved into her face. And a dark smudge under one eye that was more than lack of sleep.

Bax frowned in concern at the bruise. "How did you get hurt?"

"Silverhielm caught me a pretty good one when I was trying to pin him down." Her smile was shaky. "I didn't want him to get loose. I didn't know what he'd do to you."

"What happened? I remember noise from Oskar's friends and the table going over and that's pretty much it."

Joss slid the chair to the side of the bed with the ease of long familiarity. "You didn't miss much. When I shoved the table at Silverhielm, his gun went off, which is how you got shot. It was a good wound, or so the doctors tell me. Went through your side without hitting anything important."

"Nice to know so much of me is irrelevant."

"It's a good thing," she agreed. "Anyway, I jumped on top of Silverhielm and the table to keep him down, which is how I got pasted. Dinged up a couple of his ribs, too, I'm told," she said, grinning unrepentantly.

"Where was Markus in all of this?"

She shrugged. "Anyone's guess. Oskar's friends were too busy pushing him away and he backed out the door."

"Markus, back away from a bunch of kids?"

"Maybe he felt sorry for them." She smiled faintly. "By the time Rolf and his team showed up, he was gone."

"And Silverhielm?"

"In jail under charges of kidnapping and assault, not to mention the Swedish equivalent of grand larceny. Rolf got his search warrant. Now that he's got access to Silverhielm's records, he's expecting to put him away on stronger charges for a good, long time."

"And the stamps?"

"Got them both. The police have to hold on to the one-penny Mauritius for a while until they prosecute Silverhielm. The Blue Mauritius is back in the vault for the time being."

Bax nodded, suddenly exhausted. He fought to keep his eyes open, to focus on her face. When his lids drifted closed, she was the last thing he saw and she followed him into his dreams.

When he awoke again, he was in another bed in another ward. But one thing was the same—Joss was there.

"Awake now?"

He stirred a little bit and for the first time felt the itch of healing on his side instead of the merciless whip of pain. "Now. When is it?"

"A day later than last time."

He glanced around. "The room looks different."

"You're in a medical ward, now. No more ICU. The doctor said you've bounced back amazingly well."

He smiled wryly. "That's me, star of the class." He studied her. She looked different too. She wore her red jacket; her battered leather satchel sat in a heap on the floor by the foot of the bed. Bax felt a quick spurt of alarm. "Are you going somewhere?"

She nodded. "You're on the mend. The doctors expect you to be up and around in a week or so." Her voice was falsely bright.

"So you're going back to San Francisco?"

She glanced away. "Time to get on with life, don't you think?"

There was a time he'd have been relieved. There was a time he'd have been happy at the prospect of being on his own again.

But that time was long past.

JOSS STOOD by the bed where Bax stared up at her.

"Don't go," he said. "We've got things to talk about."

But if she didn't go now, she'd never be able to. "It's time, Bax."

"No. That night at Silverhielm's, when I saw Markus with his gun on you, I realized—"

"Don't," she said sharply. She wouldn't let herself listen, she couldn't. She knew what would happen later, after he'd gotten out of the hospital, after he'd recovered. "Until everything went to hell in a handbasket, you knew what you wanted. And when I'm no longer your bedside companion or your damsel in distress—"

"I was wrong, before."

She wanted to listen, she wanted to believe him, but she knew it was only temporary. "How can you be sure things are different?" she demanded. "How can I?"

"Trust me."

"I can't." Her eyes softened. "Right now, you're feeling like you want me to be a part of your life because you're hurt. I'm not going to take advantage of that. Take your time. Heal and get past this and then we'll see."

"I'm thinking just fine, Joss. I don't need to get out of this hospital bed to know how I feel about you."

"You need time, Bax, we both do. I've got to get my life straightened out, too. On my own. You told me once you couldn't be my salvation, remember? You were right." She smiled and tried to pretend her heart wasn't breaking.

"So that's it? You're saying goodbye?"

"I'm saying goodbye for now." She would not cry, not now, she told herself fiercely and rose. "Maybe one of these days…" Her voice caught. She leaned over and kissed him on the forehead, smoothing his hair back. "Be well, Bax."

And she made herself walk out.

"HAS IT LANDED, yet?"

Joss and Gwen stood in front of the monitor in the international arrivals hall at the San Francisco airport, checking the screen for their grandparents' flight from Sydney. Only days before, Joss had walked out of the gates from customs herself, coming home from Stockholm.

Having left everything that mattered behind.

Joss skimmed the list of world capitals until she spied their listing. And then stared helplessly at the listing for a flight from Stockholm just above it. For a moment she missed Bax so badly it was like a physical pain. If she'd been at home, she could have curled up into a ball of misery. Here, she was in public so she just stood woodenly and stared at the letters as though the sight of them would prop her up.

"Hey," Gwen said softly. "You okay?"

Joss gave a quick, empty smile. "Yeah, sure. Why wouldn't I be?"

Gwen slung an arm around Joss's shoulders and

squeezed. "I was just where you are not too long ago, remember? Don't try to hide from me."

"Ah, hell, Gwen, what am I supposed to do, keep being a basket-case every time I see anything that reminds me of him?"

"No. On the other hand, you've only been home a week. Cut yourself some slack. It's going to take longer than that, you know."

"I know," Joss agreed. It was going to take a lot longer than that.

It felt like it was going to take forever.

"Anyway, there are better things to think about," she said briskly, moving to the sliding glass doors that shuttered the hall from Customs. "Gramma and Grampa are home and we've got good news instead of bad. How great is that?"

"God, I've been dreading this moment for two and a half months, ever since Jerry stole the stamps," Gwen said. "I couldn't imagine telling Grampa about it. I can't believe we got them back."

"You can't? Since when have we set our minds to something and not done it?"

"The Chastain sisters, a force to be reckoned with?"

"Damned straight," Joss agreed. "Look, there they are!"

Their grandparents came through the doorway looking tanned and healthy and about a decade younger than when they'd left.

"Over here," Gwen said, waving to them and then running up to greet them with hugs.

"You girls are a sight for sore eyes," said Hugh Chastain, blue eyes twinkling.

"Oh, we've had the most fun, you can't imagine," said his wife, kissing Joss on the cheek. "We've got so much to tell you."

"So do we," Joss murmured. "So do we."

A NEW LIFE. She'd come back from Stockholm knowing what she wanted to do with her life. Now, she had a career to pursue. Now, she had a goal. And if hours and minutes of her new life dragged every time she thought about Bax, she had plenty to distract her. In fact, she'd packed her schedule with so many classes and practice sessions and study hours that she barely had a minute to herself.

How then, was it that she still found time to miss him?

Joss shook her head impatiently. It had been weeks. Weeks, and the hurt was still as fresh as it had been. She ought to be able to get past it. This was her new life. She shouldn't be spending most of it thinking about the old.

Gwen walked into the empty showroom. "Grampa's headed out for the night. Are you just about ready to shut down , here?"

Joss stirred. "Just about. Can you close out the register? I've got to get going, tonight. I've got an early Tae Kwon Do class."

"Are you sure you're not trying to do too much?"

"I'm fine," Joss replied quickly. "The more I take, the faster I'll get my P.I. license."

"Yeah, but it won't do you any good to have a license if you run yourself into the ground before you get your first client. Work doesn't make it go away, Joss."

"I know, but it beats Parcheesi."

Gwen rolled her eyes. "Get out of here. I'll take care of things." She glanced up at the chime of the front door. "Whoops, actually, let me check something in the back, first."

"Hurry, Gwen," Joss said over her shoulder as Gwen walked into the back. "I don't have much time."

"Do you have time to talk to me?" asked a familiar voice.

And she turned to see Bax.

For a moment, she simply stared. He stood at the counter leaning on a cane, which looked incongruously dapper with his T-shirt and jeans. He'd grown thinner, she noticed, so that the bones stood out strongly in his face.

"When did you get back?"

"About three weeks ago." He watched her closely.

"How are you feeling?"

He shrugged. "Everything seems to be working all right. I should be able to get rid of the cane, soon."

He'd want to set it aside as soon as humanly possible, she knew. He'd look at it as a challenge, a barrier to be surmounted. And he wouldn't give up until he had.

"So how have you been?" he asked now.

"Okay. I've started martial arts training and I'm taking a course in the penal code. I'm working here while I get my investigator's license."

He raised his eyebrows. "So you were serious about that."

"I told you I was," she said shortly.

"Yes, you did. I should have listened. I screwed up that night. I said a lot of things I shouldn't have." He looked down at his cane and twisted it slightly back and forth. "And I missed saying a lot more that I should have."

"You did what you needed to do."

"No, I didn't. Can we go somewhere and talk?"

"I have a class to get to."

"Where is it?"

"Up the street."

"Well, then, can I walk you there?

"You don't look like walking's the best thing for you. We can talk here for a little while, if you want." She opened the register drawer and got out the spare key for the door. "Just let me lock up."

If she took long enough with the security gates and the door, maybe she could figure out how she felt about him showing up here. She didn't want gratitude. She didn't want guilt. It was impossible to squelch hope, but it was equally impossible to forget what they'd been through.

What she was still going through every minute of every day.

"There are chairs," she told him, pulling one over for him before she walked behind the counter. Keep the distance, she thought. "So, what's on your mind?"

For a moment, he was silent, just looking at her like a man stranded in the desert looks at water. "I've been doing a lot of thinking. I spent weeks in that hospital bed after you left with nothing much to do but think. About you and me, about the baggage you keep and the baggage you throw away." He rubbed his thumb along the chrome edge of the display case. "I know I said some bad things to you that night in the hotel. It wasn't about you. It was about me trying to run away." He gave a humorless smile. "But you know how that goes. You can't run away from yourself. And you can't run away from truths." He took a breath. "I love you, Joss, and that's the truest thing I know."

"You don't," she countered, panicked because she wanted to believe him. Panicked because she didn't think her heart could survive being broken again. "You just think you do. You're confusing love with gratitude and protectiveness."

"I'm not getting anything confused. I'm really, really clear now. You've got a right to be upset with me. I blew it. Getting involved with you scared the hell out of me and my knee-jerk reaction was to bolt. But that's over with. I don't want to run from it now." He smiled slightly and raised his cane from the ground. "Even if I could."

"How can you be so sure?" she demanded. "You say it's all different, but how do I know that in a week or a month you're not going to turn around and tell me you don't want to be in a relationship, that you just want to be on your own?"

He frowned and glanced away. "The same way I know that you won't." He looked at her, then. "I'm willing to trust in us. I'm hoping you'll do the same."

"I already did that, thanks. I'm not in any hurry to go through it again." Especially when the pain was still going on.

"Look, I was wrong." He rose, pressing his hands on the edge of the counter. "I'll say it again, if you want. I was wrong. I got caught up in the past but I'm telling you, it's done. And I am going to keep telling you until you believe me. I don't care if it takes a while. I've got the time and I am not going anywhere. I'll come back here tomorrow, and the day after tomorrow and every day after that for as long as it takes." His gaze arrowed through her. "As long as it takes, Joss, and when you're through testing me, I'll still be here. Because I love you and that is not going to change."

There wasn't enough air in the room, she thought, stunned. Surely that was why her lungs wouldn't work. Surely that was why she couldn't speak, why her mind couldn't assimilate it all.

A second passed, then two, and finally Bax shrugged. "Well, you've got to get to your class." He winked at her with a mixture of humor and defiance. "I'll see you tomorrow." He started to turn away, then swung back toward her. "Of course, while I'm happy to come to the store every day we could actually do something civilized like dinner. I'd join your class but as you can see, I have issues. Anyway, I'll see you later."

"No!" Suddenly, she found her voice. "I mean yes. I mean...hell, I don't know. Oh God, Bax, do you mean it?"

His lips twitched. "I stand here and pour my heart out to you, with your sister no doubt listening, and you have to ask that?" He smiled. "Okay, for the record, I am crazy about you. I think about you every minute of every day. I want to spend the rest of my life with you, and a couple of lifetimes after that, if we can manage it. And I would be very happy, honored, even, to stand up in front of a room full of witnesses and say it all again."

And it was that easy, Joss thought dazedly as she came around the counter and he gathered her into his arms. His body was hard and warm and real against her, and it was then that the tears started. "I've missed you so much," she murmured, blinking.

He exhaled. "It made me nuts, staying away from you, but I figured I had to or you wouldn't believe me." He pressed a kiss into her hair. "And then I figured the hell with waiting. I'd find some other way to convince you."

"Have you figured that out, yet?"

"No, but I'm working on it." And then he kissed her.

If you enjoyed what you just read,
then we've got an offer you can't resist!

Take 2 bestselling love stories FREE!

Plus get a FREE surprise gift!

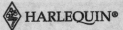

HARLEQUIN®

COMING NEXT MONTH

#201 UNZIPPED? Karen Kendall
The Man-Handlers, Bk. 2
What happens when a beautiful image consultant meets a stereotypical computer guy? Explosive sex, of course. Shannon Shane is stunned how quickly she falls for her client, Hal Underwood. As the hottie inside emerges, she just can't keep her hands to herself.

#202 SO MANY MEN... Dorie Graham
Sexual Healing, Bk. 2
Sex with Tess McClellan is the best experience Mason Davies has had. Apparently all of her old lovers think so, too, because they're everywhere. Mason would leave, except that he's addicted. He'll just have to convince her she'll always be satisfied with him!

#203 SEX & SENSIBILITY Shannon Hollis
After sensitive Tessa Nichols has a vision of a missing girl, she and former cop Griffin Knox—who falsely arrested her two years ago—work to find her. Ultimately, Tessa has to share with him every spicy, red-hot vision she has, and soon separating fantasy from reality beomes a job perk neither of them anticipated....

#204 HER BODY OF WORK Marie Donovan
Undercover DEA agent Marco Flores was used to expecting the unexpected. But he never dreamed he'd end up on the run—and posing as a model. A nude model! He'd taken the job to protect his brother, but he soon discovered there were undeniable perks. Like having his sculptress, sexy Rey Martinson, wind up as uncovered as he was...

#205 SIMPLY SEX Dawn Atkins
Who knew that guys using matchmakers were so hot? Kylie Falls didn't until she met Cole Sullivan. Too bad she's only his stand-in date. But the sparks between them beg to be explored in a sizzling, delicious fling. And they both know this is temporary...right?

#206 DARING IN THE DARK Jennifer LaBrecque
24 Hours: Blackout, Bk. 3
Simon Thackeray almost has it all—good looks, a good job and good friends. The only thing he's missing is the one woman he wants more than his next breath—the woman who, unfortunately, is engaged to his best friend. It looks hopeless—until a secret confession and a twenty-four-hour blackout give him the chance to prove he's the better man....

www.eHarlequin.com

HBCNM0805